YELLOWSTONE KELLY

GENTLEMAN & SCOUT

PETER BOWEN

A GOOD DAY TO DIE

Baldwin and Miles came out of the tent. Miles beckoned me over.

"Baldwin wants to go down and see if he can arrange a surrender," says Miles.

Before the Nez Perce kill us all, I thinks.

"Good idea, Frank," I says. "I'll walk down with you."

We got a couple of willow poles and hung white on them. When we started down we passed Haddo. He had made himself a rifle pit. Haddo grinned and nodded and shifted his quid of tobacco.

The Nez Perces hadn't fired a shot this day. The blue-coats were dug in at the maximum range of a rifle, and while we had more than enough ammunition, it wasn't likely that the Nez Perces had any to waste.

I went at a pretty brisk clip, afraid that some fool would commence to fire. One of ours did. The Nez Perces retaliated, but not at me. I passed Haddo's rifle pit.

"It was..." he yelled, and then a bullet tore into him above the heart. He somehow got his pistol out and aimed and fired, but not at the Nez Perces. At Red Mike, and Haddo hit him in the forehead, and both were dead before they hit the ground.

The shooting stopped as quick as it had begun.

YELLOWSTONE KELLY

Gentleman & Scout

A Novel
PETER BOWEN

BANTAM BOOKS
NEW YORK · TORONTO · LONDON · SYDNEY · AUCKLAND

YELLOWSTONE KELLY

*A Bantam Book / published by arrangement with
Jameson Books, Inc.*

PRINTING HISTORY

Jameson Books edition published 1987
Bantam edition / August 1990

ISBN 0-553-28597-1

Published simultaneously in the United States and Canada

PRINTED IN THE UNITED STATES OF AMERICA

RAD   0 9 8 7 6 5 4 3 2 1

FOR HUGO ECK
FRIEND, TEACHER

1

I was down to my desk in the War Office when the news came that McKinley had died, and it seemed that my old friend Teddy Four-Eyes was the new President. I'd first met Teddy some twenty years before, when he was gentleman-ranching. He was as good a feller as you are likely to meet, but then I have never been comfortable with the idea of a government run by any of my friends. I know them too well, you see. Teddy enjoyed life more than anyone I ever met. The thought of him with all these new toys—battleships and armies and such—was a mite uncomfortable.

I ain't much accustomed to riding a swivel chair. I had taken an Igorotee arrow in my thigh out in the Philippines and the wound was slow in healing. I had spent quite a few years helping to drag our red brothers off the free life on the Plains and onto reservations where they could raise alfalfa and such and learn to be as unhappy as the rest of the farmers—plagued with church, newspapers, regular baths, the whole disaster—and I had recently got back from helping to visit the same upon our little brown brothers over China way and they didn't like it any better. The Army was proving as good at massacring brown as red. Put 'em under the ground, it's good for the corn. Good for business.

There was a bar across the street, Scanlan's, so I went there for a drink. It's always the same with me when something tragic happens to a friend—death, getting married, becoming President—and I needed to be alone with myself. I put some money on the bar and had a drink or two and pecked through the ruins of the free lunch that Ollie, the owner, set out every day.

I heard a Sioux war whoop behind me and my hand went for the gun I wasn't wearing—some habits is hard to shake—and when I turned around there was Buffalo Bill Cody. I had seen the posters advertising his show and had planned to stop in that night. I had a lot of friends who were in Bill's Wild West Show, and I had known and liked Bill for thirty years. Liked him some of the time, anyway.

"Well," says Bill, "looks like Theodore is the new President."

Bill was dressed like he always was these days—fringed white doeskin coat, white pants and embroidered white shirt, a big glob of silver and turquoise at his throat, thigh-high dragoon's boots. Bill was much better known than McKinley. All of the loafers in the bar (I had business there, you see) got goggle-eyed and began to edge over to us. Bill waved them away without ever quite looking at them.

"Before you ask," I says, "I do not want to rejoin your show."

"I'm damned sorry to hear that," says Bill, "since you are the handsomest feller, Luther. You look like what every mother wants for her daughter. Had you gone on the stage instead of to our great West, you would be a wealthy and respected idol of the footlights."

"I can't help how I look," says I. Well, damn it, I do look like the dark-haired feller in the ads for elegant suits. It has caused me no end of trouble.

"Think of the money you could make," says Bill.

"I ain't parading around like a prize bull at a goddamn stock show," I says. "To hell with you."

I looked myself over in the mirror behind the bar. Well, if you want a tall, black-haired, moustachioed, modern gentleman, I'm it so far as appearances go. And that's as far as it goes.

And as for Bill's show, I'd done that for a few weeks back in '88 and I am hard put to think of anything I ever hated more. My part in the proceedings was to thunder out from stage left and haul a buxom actress name of Gertie Jordan up behind me on the horse. She wore so much whalebone she made a sound like a stick run along a picket fence when she slid up the saddle skirts. And then I was supposed to say, "Fair Maiden, do not fear, for Kelly is here with you now, and I shall gladly die to save you from these savages." Try it at the top of your lungs sometime, while you're sitting on a banister and hauling an overstuffed chair up one-handed.

Bill was a great one for what he called "veracity," which as near as I can figure means the bull is covered with fudge. Some stagehands was painted up, dash here, splash there, and they'd wave tomahawks and sort of hop up and down. Then I would ride the horse off stage right and Gertie would reveal this and that portion of her anatomy. Me, I'd look noble; it's a trade, you see. Ladies threw gloves, flowers, room keys and notes on the stage. They piled up at the stage door like hens at a feedbox. Made me nervous as hell.

This was supposed to be a re-enactment of the time I had snuck into Red Hand's camp to winkle Sally Parmenter

out of a tight spot, up near the Musselshell River. Sally
was to be the center of attraction at a gang rape as soon as
Red Hand and his chums and squaws and such were
finished skinning out her pimp, who was providing a fair
amount of noise and cover what with shrieking in agony
and begging for mercy (fine with me, you see, I knew him
pretty well and would have been happy to help, if I had
been asked polite).

Sally had a map she'd diddled out of an old drunk who
claimed he'd been one of Plummer's cutthroats and knew
where Plummer had cached his gold, down in Idaho. A
million dollars in coin, nuggets, and dust, which sort of
riveted my attention. The map was laced up somewhere
on her pulpous person, so I snuck in and cut her loose.
She commenced to caterwauling, torn between curiosity
about what was to come and Frank's piteous bubbling
wails for mercy. So I whopped her up side the head with
my Colt to get her attention and then hissed like a rabid
badger. "Shut up, or we're going to look like horse doovers
on the ends of them lances. If we're lucky." She piped
down to a snuffle and we snuck back to my horse.

The camp dogs was raising hell as we lit out, me
thinking of Frank and thanking him for such a fine performance. Red Hand's bunch was so drunk that they
couldn't have ridden Sally, much less any of their ponies.
Matter of fact, they was so drunk they was grabbing
handholds in the grass in order to pass out. (A month later
I was eating dog stew in Red Hand's lodge, and no word
about any of that, which is Indians for you. Frank was still
with us in the form of two pemmican bags and a chairback.
Waste not, want not. I never found the gold, either, come
to think of it.)

So here I was in Scanlan's thinking back, you see.
Instead of forward or even now. Memory is an unruly
thing. I looked over at Bill, who was shedding a manly
tear—about a teaspoon's worth.

"We have lost a great man," says Bill. He signaled for another whiskey.

"Who?" I asks, wondering who'd died now.

"Our President."

Thing about Bill is the simple-minded sonofabitch is exactly as the dime novels have him, although worse lately on account of how many he reads to keep up with himself. He was always that way, and a couple of times it almost cost us our hair. There we would be, in a tight spot, and Bill would get this dreamy, wet-eyed look—sort of like he'd been called and couldn't come—and go to composing a speech. I have come nigh to shooting him out of sheer exasperation oftener than I like to think of. And to this day I don't know if he was funning me or not. Play poker with him, you'll see. You'll lose.

"I must go prepare our show, and tell those who may not have heard that we have lost a great man, and we must have the proper equipage of mourning," says Bill.

"How do you spell that?" says I.

Bill ignored me. He was playing to himself in the mirror back of the bar.

"We must bear this loss like men and Americans," he went on.

"It wouldn't be seemly for us to grieve like women and Turks," I says. "How 'bout an anchovy for strength?" I guzzled about four fingers of Ollie's Old Popskull. One thing that has always fascinated me about Bill is that there is no way to insult the man. He just don't hear it.

"So many gone now," he says. "Over the Great Divide."

"Deader than smelts," I says, eating another anchovy.

"I must compose a eulogy." Bill cast his eyes upward.

"I don't know how to spell that," I says, "but it ain't a oo-logy, it's a you-logy."

"Fond friend," says Bill, laying a bead-encrusted gauntlet with a hand somewheres in it on my shoulder, "I must go now and prepare for the evening's performance. Our

President lies dead. . . ." He put his gauntlet over his heart and took off his hat. His hat was big enough to house a whole family of Eye-talian mackerelsnappers, and you know how they breed. Bill walked toward the door, head slightly bowed.

"How 'bout paying for yer drinks before I have to," I hollers. Ollie don't care if it's Buffalo Bill or Queen Victoria, drinks equals money.

Bill ignored this sordid behavior on my part and sashayed out into the traffic on E Street. Ollie made change from my money and swept away Bill's glass.

"Are you going to have it stuffed?" I says, as Ollie looked lovingly at the smears made by Bill's fingers. Ollie scowled at me and plunged the glass into the soapy water he kept near the sawed-off shotgun underneath the bartop.

I had another drink, in memory of McKinley (a bird who looked to me like a feller you wouldn't want to hold the bet money), and then I had another, and the truth of the matter is that I just felt like getting drunk. I was all of a sudden sad. You see, there was a lot of good times and free country out there before the honyockers plowed up the grass and the railroads cut the land up like so many stitches on a wounded body. I was one of the first white men to go through those dry hills between the Yellowstone and the Missouri and live to tell about it. I knew everybody that you hear about these days—Bill Cody, California Joe, Custer (a pure bastard), Jim Bridger, Shanghai Pierce, Tom Horn, Texas Jack Omohundro. And Crazy Horse, who was the best man ever I knew—I ain't even sure that he was human, and if you had known him you'd agree.

Hell, I thought, I ain't even sure that I can remember in which order some of them things happened out there. Just then one of them newfangled electric trolleys went clanking by in the street outside, making my face in the mirror dance. How'd we get to this? I thought.

"Ollie," I says, "you got a pencil? And maybe some paper?"

"You don't want to write a check, do you?" he says, suspicious-like. He took one from some English lord ten years ago, which he still has, and it rankles him yet.

"No, Ollie, I'm going to write a book." This was obviously gone-round-the-bend drunk talk, like Ollie was used to and comfortable with, so he rummaged around in a couple of drawers and found me some foolscap and old bills with the backs hardly used and a stub of a pencil. I resolved that tomorrow I would go to a stationer's and get all properly equipped for the writer's trade. Well, I'd been a buffalo hunter and a wolfer and a scout for the army and a dude wrangler and I knew that the proper tools is half of the job. I was even a Catholic bishop once—it's a long story, I'll tell you some time.

"He's going to write a book," Ollie says to a few gents holding down the other end of the bar.

I got some amazed looks. First, Buffalo Bill Cody, and now someone who had said he was going to write a book. The day looked brighter. Maybe a geek would wander in and bite off a few chicken heads if their luck held.

"Yer gonna write a book," says one. Guffaws.

I retired to a table with a bottle of Sinner's Cider and my foolscap and pencil. I put the bottle in front of me and the glass over to the right and then I put the paper on the table between my elbows. I whittled a point on the pencil with my pocketknife. I bit my lower lip and squinted at the paper, the same squint I use looking for tracks on broken ground. I stared at the paper and it stared at me. I remember Charley Russell, the painter, telling me he always began two or three canvases the night before, when he was blind drunk. He had awakened one morning to find an empty canvas on his easel and the sight haunted him ever after.

Maybe I'll get one of them silk-lined capes, I says to

myself. Oscar Wilde had been wearing one when I got
him out of Salt Lake City one step ahead of a lynch mob.
Oscar was in jail these days for buggery, so I heard. There
seemed to be hazards in the writer's trade.

I was staring at the paper so hard I didn't notice right off
that the bar had got real quiet. When I looked up, there
was an elegant gent standing at the bar. He had on a
well-cut suit, spats and calfskin shoes, a diamond stickpin
in the silk cravat at his throat, and a big blue stone on the
end of his ebony cane.

He was also a nigger, and in Washington, D.C., in 1901,
niggers didn't come into bars on E Street, unless it was
after closing to clean up.

Ollie smiled nasty as a weasel at a crippled bird and
says, "What will it be?"

"I would like a gin," says the nigger. He had a deep
voice and a northern accent.

Ollie polished a glass before setting it on the bar. He
poured the gin with great and exaggerated flourishes. He
slid the gin in front of the nigger.

"That will be fifty dollars," Ollie says. He had his hand
beneath the bartop, where the sawed-off shotgun was.

The loafers guffawed and elbowed each other.

The nigger nodded and reached into the inside pocket
of his coat. He took out a wallet and opened it. He peeled
five one-hundred-dollar goldbacks from the wad he had
and dropped them onto the bar.

"I'll take ten of them," he says.

I could see his face now. It was Wilson Parnell, as fine a
singer as ever I heard. He was headlining down at the
Orpheum, and the paper said he was being paid three
thousand dollars a week.

2

In the early fall of '77 I was doing a bit of loafing up on the Big Bend of the Missouri, looking for likely spots to kill wolves in the winter. I was supposed to be scouting for hostile Indians. I had spent over a year guiding the U.S. Army to camps where they then slaughtered as many Indians as they could, and burnt the lodges and the dried meat and berries. Thirteen babies had frozen to death in Crazy Horse's camp alone. The Plains tribes were done for—Sitting Bull was up in Canada, Crazy Horse was on a reservation. I had spent a lot of time either chasing after Crazy Horse or running from him. For some reason the news of his surrender gave me pain, as though I had lost a dear friend.

The then Colonel Nelson Miles had given me orders to find the redskins, which I was being quite careful not to do. Oh, they were somewhere out there, all right, but they were so much more mobile than the United States Army it made no sense to do anything until the winter pinned the Indians in camp. Then the army could take advantage of its superior supply and firepower. I'd bird-dogged for the Fifth Cavalry—I'd point and they would do the dirty work. I was sick of it, so I made sure that I avoided hostile redskins, whiteskins, brownskins, and them buggers with polka dots. Me, I fight only when there's no chance to run. Still have my hair. Luther Kelly, scout of the Yellowstone, wolfing on government pay.

A prime wolf pelt was bringing five dollars. Two winters before, I had found as many as twenty big loafer wolves around a single bait. We used strychnine, three-quarters of an ounce to a cow buffalo. Wolves are particular eaters, they won't touch tough bull meat unless they're starving.

We'd find dead eagles and crows and ravens and magpies, too. There would be an occasional skunk or badger. The scavengers would eat what was left of the bait, or rip open the wolves' bellies and eat the poisoned meat in their stomachs. Then they would die, too. That strychnine, it just never quits.

The pelts wouldn't be prime for another five months. I had been all over this country, of course, but there are thousands of little draws and streams that cut down to the Missouri through the hills, and I couldn't look at one without I wanted to know what was up it. These little streams gnaw at the hills like worms. Sometimes a stream will chew right through a ridge and draw the water from another little stream, capturing it, sort of, and then the part below where the other stream got captured becomes a dry draw, down to the river.

The dry draws are good places to camp, they still have some buried water and the shrubs and trees will reach down to the moisture below. The cover is tangled enough that no one can sneak through it without making a hell of a racket. How long you live out there depends on how good you are at hiding. Many times I have holed up during the day and traveled only at night.

It was more than a year since George Custer had managed to get himself killed (he was not only stupid, he was real aggressive, a bad combination) along with two hundred and twenty-seven other men at the massacre on the river the Indians call the Greasy Grass. A few friends of mine died there—Mitch Bouyer and Lonesome Charley Reynolds and Myles Keough. Rain-in-the-Face had cut out Tom Custer's heart and eaten it (bon appetit to old Rain, says I; Tom was an even viler specimen than his better-known older brother). George had tried to borrow me for a bit from Miles. I told Miles I wouldn't go with that idiot to see a vaudeville show, much less scout for him.

The battle of the Little Big Horn was high tide for the Horse Indians. The army crushed them the following winter—the tribes helped out by quarreling bitterly among themselves. Crazy Horse was the only one who could lead all of them. But then, he always was more than a man. The news of his death meant to me that for the Horse Indians, it was all over.

I had bought supplies at Fort Buford, where the Yellowstone meets the Missouri, and had then gone slowly up the Big Muddy. Any hostile bands would be heading for winter camps on the south bank of the Yellowstone, where there was saltweed for their horses. I had plenty of staples to last me until late spring. I had planned to loaf and hunt wolves and dilly-dally, and see Miles in April, when it was too muddy to do anything unhealthy, like picking fights with Horse Indians.

There had been some more bad news over in Idaho. The Nez Perces had killed a dozen or so settlers and then fled. General Howard pursued them, and Colonel Gibbon had fought a pitched battle with them over in the Big Hole. I supposed the same thing had happened that always happens. The government made a treaty with the Indians, and then land-hungry whites poured in, violated the treaty, killed some of the Indians (not even human, you know), and then the Indians got fed up and made paint and then made war. The rumor of gold was worst of all. Custer had found gold in the Black Hills, the holy Pa Sapa of the Sioux, and the army hadn't enough men to stop the prospectors from pouring in. Someday the Indians would be pacified, all right: dead, every last one of them.

The Nez Perces was lost somewhere in a million square miles out there. Miles was playing checkers with Baldwin at Fort Buford, and Kelly was seldom seen and meant to keep it that way. Kelly was going to meet up with Buffalo Horn, my Bannock partner, and make a few thousand easy peaceful dollars off the wolves.

When things start to go wrong, it's always some little goddamn pissyass thing, which when you look back on it was insignificant at the time. In this case, it was a willow thicket. I noticed that them willows was flailing around more than they should have in the light wind. Then they began to thrash about like a broom in the hands of a madwoman. I caught the rank scent of bear. I'd come up on a river-bottom grizzly, the worst kind of bear—so pale that he was almost white—and I'd done it from downwind.

My rifle was in my right hand, across my saddle. I whipped it up just as the bear stood up, and shot him high in the forehead. The bullet just plowed a furrow and whined off. That damn bear had a skull thicker than a Baptist's. The bear let out a beller, and my horse decided he was Pegasus. The pack mules did a fast one-hundred-and-eighty-degree turn and leapfrogged each other till they was over the hills and gone. My horse went about fifteen feet straight up, and was gone like a puff of smoke. I sailed through the air and landed in a tangle of wild roses and moonseed vines. Big hornets' nest in there, too. I couldn't remember when I'd been so happy.

I levitated sideways about thirty feet and bounded up a big old cottonwood tree, leaving most of my fingernails in the bark. I sat on a limb about twenty feet off the ground and tried to catch my breath. The hornets had mostly gone after the horse, so I'd been stung only ten times or so. The bear was thrashing around in the bushes, bellowing in rage and pain, throwing around logs thirty feet long and three feet through like they was so much kindling, and sniffing the air for my scent. He soon had it, and found the spot where I had gone up the tree. The bear then began to tear the tree down. It was a big cottonwood, more than six feet through at the base. The bear was roaring and ripping at a rate I figured would have the tree down in half an hour or so. He was single-minded in his efforts. I still had my pistol, and I shot him a few more times. The bullets didn't bother him any more than the hornets had, which is to say not at all.

Kayrist, Kelly, I says to myself, why the hell didn't you become a dentist or something?

Some scout. The tree was shaking like a shot-tower in an earthquake. I run through all of the cuss words I knew in English, Sioux, Cheyenne, and Blackfeet, and was starting on Gros Ventre when there was a loud boom off to my left and the bear slammed into the tree so hard the trunk quivered like an arrow shot into an oak board. The grizzly screamed once, a high-pitched wail like a terrified woman's. The scream trailed off into a soft bubbling moan as the bear slumped to the ground, dead. The shot had come from a blackpowder gun, a big one that left a great filthy cloud of smoke.

My savior emerged from the sulfurous mist. I looked down upon a living legend, one Liver-Eating Jack Johnson, to be precise. He was dressed like a mountain man of fifty years before. Buckskins and red flannel leggins, buffalo horn and wolf-hair hat, a Green River knife the size of a plow in a quilled sheath, and a Hawken 58 caliber cap-and-ball rifle with a couple hundredweight of brass tacks in the stock.

"Wall," says Jack, "effen it ain't the great Yallerstone Kelly, paused up in a tree. You stay there, chile, like Lewis an' Clark, to jerk yer meat?"

"Waugh WAUGH WAUGH WAUGH." Jack had a laugh sounded like a combination of a whale blowing and a scrap-iron wagon turning over in a tight alley.

"Much obliged," says I, showing the impeccable manners of one who has just been saved and will never be allowed to forget it. "As a matter of fact, I was just preparing to put my knife between my teeth and jump down and fight fair when you done spoiled my afternoon's exercise. Do you know how long it took me to find a bear the right size?"

Jack was near six foot eight, and had the bashfulness that you associate with giants around other people, especially women. He was hard to provoke, but I had once seen him crack the skulls so hard together of two drunk and quarrelsome keelboatmen everybody in the barroom was spattered with brains.

"I been down to the south," he says.

Time I was down the tree he had reloaded his rifle and was up on a deadfall looking in all four directions at once. That was why he was still alive.

"You still scoutin' for Miles?" he asked. He squinted at the hills across the river.

"I will be, soon as I can catch my horse," I says. "Did you see which way he went?"

"He come lookin' to me fer portection," says Jack, in his barbarous plug-a-plew mountain man dialect. "I tied him to a bush over yonder an' told him not to worry none. Yore mules got lonesome an' are comin' back directly." Jack and Jim Bridger were the two scouts I knew who could look through the hills and trees as though the land and all that lived up on it were as transparent as window glass. They could smell enemies miles away. Eerie men, both of them, half in the other world.

"I got baccy and trade rum," I says, standing spread-eagle on account of the shit and piss in my pants. "I got to go get cleaned up."

Jack waited to fire his parting insult until I had waddled off twenty feet or so.

"By god," he says, "I was full of the perplex for a minnit thar. Now I sees it. You was able to outrun that bar 'cause you had the advantage of runnin' on dry ground, while that pore animal was slippin' and fallin' on that slick trail you done left."

"Waugh WAUGH WAUGH WAUGH."

We made camp and built a quick fire of dead aspen with the bark peeled off. It don't smoke. We never lit fires at night, unless we were waiting for company or in a group so big that the Indians would leave us alone.

Jack had a haunch of antelope and some fat backribs of buffalo—the marrow was as sweet as butter. He drank long draughts of the bottle of trade rum I gave him, and the second time that I refused he said, "You gone with the temperance? Come to think of it, I ain't never seen you drink except in a town."

I sighed. Well, he had saved my life.

"I never drink out here because when I drink a few days straight I have an attack of gout."

"Gout?" says Jack, squinting one black eye at me through the gray shag of eyebrow—he only had one, and it went across his face in a straight and bushy line. I believe small creatures lived in it.

"Ever had it?" I asks, wondering just how the story was going to make the rounds after Jack had had time to ponder and embellish it.

"No, can't say as I have," says Jack. "Had an uncle to

home that had it. He done shot off his big toe one time when he was hurtin' by it."

"Well, that's why I don't drink out here."

"Nezzz Percies crossed up to Cow Island four days ago," he said. "Got a lot of ponies, more than a thousand, and their women and children and old folks. Gibbon caught up to them in the Big Hole, and they fought him to a standstill, even captured one of his cannons. Then they made away, went through Colter's Hell. They're tryin' to make it to Sitting Bull up in Canada. Guess they ain't heard the news, Sitting Bull is turning everyone back, even some Minneconjous."

"Shit," I says, "I'll have to go back and tell Miles."

"Naw," says Jack, "I run onto Buffalo Horn three days ago and he hightailed it for Fort Buford. Miles likely will put all of the baggage on the *Far West* and run the pony soldiers and the cavvy hard till he cuts Nezzz Percies sign."

It was maybe two hours till sundown. It was pleasant, there by the campfire. The early frosts had killed the mosquitoes, and the air smelled crisp and new (so long as Jack was downwind).

"I'm going to go get those claws and teeth and one of the paws," I says. "Do you want them?" The claws was worth a hundred dollars; European collectors favored them, why I can't say. There was a small and thriving industry over Seattle way—carving fake grizzly claws and teeth out of whale teeth.

"Naw," says Jack. I knew he wouldn't. His time with the Arapahoes had made him some Indian in his way of thinking, and the grizzly was his medicine. The Arapahoes called Jack Bear-With-Man's-Face, and come to think of it I have seen quite a few bears would dust Jack right off in a beauty contest.

I cut out the claws and teeth and sawed off one of the paws. The bear would go at least twelve hundred pounds easy, I noticed. When I got back to camp the light was fading and the wind had shifted to the east, like it always does for a little time just before sunset and just after dawn.

"Luther," says Jack, sniffing the wind, "we got company comin'. Horse soldiers."

I scurried up the hill behind us and sure enough I could see half a dozen troopers riding ragged and exposed. I cussed and took out my long glasses and tried to see if there was anything coming on behind them. The Indians had been defeated but they damn sure weren't all down yet—matter of fact, I am more concerned about meeting Red Hand when he ain't blind drunk than I am about meeting that pissant Geronimo on his best day. Six troopers wouldn't even whet Red Hand's appetite over-much.

"I am going to try to keep them from getting killed," I says, tossing the saddle on my horse, "and us, too. God damn it, Jack, I am sorry."

I was, too. I was sure that Miles had sent them to look for me. Buffalo Horn was likely following them—probably in front of them, but tracking them all the same. I wouldn't put it past that Bannock son-of-a-bitch to recommend that they ride the ridges, in order to sooner attract my attention. I let my pony stretch out and took the straightest way—if they had been seen it wouldn't matter anyway.

I come up over the top of the hill and saw them coming down the next slope, a steep one. They was all leaned as far back as they could and their stirrups was raised halfway to the horses' heads and two of them had grabbed their horses' tails for support.

My sudden appearance startled them, and one trooper fell off his mount scrabbling for his Spencer carbine with both hands. Bright fellow.

"GOD DAMN YOU IDIOT BASTARDS," I yelled, while my horse twirled in a tight circle in front of them. The leader was a pimply Lieutenant, looked all of four-

teen. "IF YOU BRING ANY GOD DAMN INDIANS
DOWN ON US, I'LL KILL YOU MYSELF." I went on in
that vein for some time, though of course it was Buffalo
Horn I would have liked to have seen. I'd have shot that
bastard instanter.

When I had run out of breath and was occupying myself
just being a deep purple shade of apoplexy, the Lieutenant
managed to squeak out a few groveling words.

"Apologies, sir," he stammered, his voice jumping from
low to high like a goddamn ocarina. "Colonel Miles has
sent several patrols to find you. He's coming upriver on
the *Far West*. The Nez Perces have crossed at Cow Island,
sir."

"How far downstream is Miles?" I said. "It's that way, in
case you've forgotten." I pointed.

"He should be here about midday tomorrow, sir. There
are woodcutting parties riding ahead." The youngster's
face was white and drawn, his horse was salted white at
the withers and damn near ready to fall over.

"You come with me," I says. "Single file and no talking.
Check your harness, I don't want to sound like a god damn
string of sleighbells." They followed me to the camp,
starting at every owlhoot and beaver fart, and they all near
died of fright when a loon screamed from a nearby slough.

Jack was not in camp. He'd piled the claws atop the paw
which he'd stuck on top of a beaver-chewed stump. My
pony whinnied at the smell. I swung down and gentled
him. I always ride geldings. Mares come in heat and
stallions can smell them miles off—more than one fool has
died not thinking that the Indians know that too.

"My card and compliments to Colonel Miles," I says,
handing the stripling the paw. I had sent a bear's paw to
Miles when we had first met, with my signature on the
great pad. He was most taken with my little joke.

The kid looked at the paw—it was ten inches wide and

sixteen inches long—and he croaked, "Is this a grizzly, sir?"

"A very young and undersized bear in extremely poor health," I says, "and not wanting to waste powder or attract Indians with gunfire I rassled him to a frazzle and then stabbed him to death."

"Waugh WAUGH WAUGH WAUGH." The soldiers all went for their arms and their horses reacted to their fright by bucking and such. None of them was over twenty. One lame Nez Perce squaw could've beat them all to death with a gourd.

"Wh . . . Wha . . . What was tha . . . ?" the Lieutenant asks, trying to stay on his horse. He'd grabbed his pistol the wrong way round and was apparently going to beat his enemies to death with the hammer.

"A bird," I says. "A Big-Assed Rocky Mountain Bull Buffalo Bald-Headed Peckerwood. A bird of foul habits and low character."

"Waugh WAUGH WAUGH WAUGH."

"I can't believe that's a bird, sir," the Lieutenant says, exhibiting his first sign of sense.

"The Big-Assed Rocky Mountain Bull Buffalo Bald-Headed Peckerwood is so rare that hopefully it will soon be extinct. It shits exclusively on mountaintops, which is why they are white even in the summertime out here."

"Waugh WAUGH WAUGH WAUGH."

I was amusing myself watching six pairs of human eyes and six pairs of horse eyes go white around the edges.

"Liver," I hollers, "they don't think you're no bird."

Jack stepped out of the bushes. There was still plenty of light. Jack had gone to the grizzly and dug the liver out. The damn thing must have weighed fifty pounds. So there stands Jack, liver in hand, tearing out chunks with his teeth, and shaking the mess like a terrier does a rat. I have seen more prepossessing sights myself.

"BAR LIVER'S GOOD GRUB," says Jack, loud enough

for Miles to hear him over the steam engines thirty miles downriver. "WHEN I AIN'T GOT INJUN LIVER I LIKES BAR LIVER JUST FINE."

Jack delivered himself of a belch sounded like a dyspeptic volcano, and by the by threw off a dense and heavy dark red cloud of spray.

"I'll give Colonel Miles your message, sir," the kid says, clutching his horse's mane, his voice a screech. "Men, follow me!" The troopers had left some time ago.

God, I thought, this is mild behavior on Jack's part. I saw him eat a rattlesnake once, on a bet. He bit the snake's head off and spat it into the fire, and then swallowed everything up to the rattles and then bit them off and handed them to California Joe, who forked over two hundred in gold, or about ten bucks per rattle. Then Joe went off to the bushes to puke (along with most everybody else) and Jack had himself another quart sip of trade whiskey and wondered aloud about where could we all have gone to. And then what the hell was for dessert. A Gila Monster would go down nice for dessert, he said.

Once Jack had gotten caught by the Blackfeet, and some lucky brave managed to crown Jack with a big rock, and when Jack woke up he was trussed up like a baking duck. He was under the guard of their best warrior, and the rest of the party was dancing around so as to work themselves up into a first-rate torturing mood. Jack bit through the rawhide thongs they had tied him with—he said he'd paid a dentist to file two of his teeth for just such emergencies— and when he had his hands free he slid the handleless knife he always carried in his leggins out and slyly undid his feet. Then he whopped his guard, and sawed off the guard's right leg at the hip.

With his travelin' vittles slung over his shoulder, Jack took off in minus-twenty-degree weather and hoofed it all the way to Lisa's post on the Tongue River.

"And how was that?" I asks.

"How was what?"

"The Injun leg."

Jack spat into the fire and took a long think.

"Wall," he says, "it was kind of stringly, like an old bull buffalo. But if you should run onto any Blackfeet you tell them that I enjoyed it hugely. Yessir, hugely.

"Waugh WAUGH WAUGH WAUGH."

3

I heard Jack slip off in the night; he moved as silent as smoke for all of his size. Maybe, I thought, he's et somebody's liver he shouldn't of, and doesn't want to see a lot of soldiers right now. They was the only law in the Territory, you see, and military justice is a quick and crude thing the world over.

Miles's Crows was the first to appear, on the north bank of the Missouri—*Minnishushu* in Lakota; I have always thought it spoke prettier than my own native tongue—and they was moving fast. I saw several that I knew by their paint and feathers, and a chief I had often dined with— Old Bull Calf. I have always liked the Indians for what they are—I like their religion and I like the way they treat their children, too. They don't think or act like whites, which is all that most folks judge them by.

They was looking to cut Nez Perce sign, and would before long wheel north by northwest. They wouldn't be asked to fight, just to steal the pony herd and keep the Nez Perces nervous and stirred up.

I figured on just waiting for Miles to show up.

If I rode downriver it would be only to ride upriver again. As soon as the band of Crows was out of sight (I trust everybody, see), I swum my horse and the mules over to the north bank and spread my clothes out on the bushes to dry.

The Nez Perces was probably trying to join Sitting Bull up in Canada—I guessed that they hadn't heard or didn't believe that old medicine man was driving Cheyennes and Gros Ventres back across the border. There was about sixteen Mounties between Ottawa and Lake Louise, and Sitting Bull was quite happy with that arrangement and didn't want to make his new friends nervous, or at least no jumpier than they already was. Sitting Bull was a deep man. I have felt sorry for him, for he saw more than he wanted to.

I remember that day as the last good one of the year. The sun was warm, and the last of the bees was taking advantage of it to make a final round of the wild primroses. The white man's flies, the Indians called the honeybees. If an Indian saw a white man's fly then he knew it wouldn't be long until he was crowded out. Not for nothing that the Mormons use that bee as their symbol.

It was so relaxed and quiet, just the popple leaves rattling—the bright crimson aspens which, some say, shake forever because they were the wood used to make the cross upon which the Romans nailed Jesus. Utter rot, that. I have never seen an aspen more than six or eight inches in diameter. I fell asleep in the sun on a buffalo robe. The dark hair gathered the heat.

My horse woke me, whinnying at the approaching cavalry's mounts. I dressed and walked up a deadfall till I was ten feet or so above the ground. Pretty quick I could make out the guidons and pennants of the Fifth Cavalry, pickets and flankers riding their horses shoulder deep through the yellow buffalo grass.

I waved my hat—I wear a big Monarch of the Plains Stetson, white underneath, the way it comes out of the box, and smoked brownish-gray on top. One of the flankers caught my signal and raised his yellow-gauntleted hand in greeting.

If you have never heard a horse troop, it is a stirring thing. First a thick sound far off, like a porridge of thunder too many miles away to hear, but you can feel it. Then the thunder breaks into hoofbeats, and the jingle of tack appears, and finally you hear a distinct one-two beat, for the horses are all leading with their left sides.

The cottonwood log I was standing on began to vibrate like a drum. The troopers came into full view, their horses kicking up dust and chaff, and if you put your ear to the ground you could hear the Fifth up in Canada. Sitting Bull was hearing it, I was sure of that.

All of them hours at horse drill was showing. The troopers swept the gullies and then converged on a big meadow. Sentries dismounted on the tops of hills and began to glass the country. One rider came straight for me—a Captain name of Mitchell. He was as weathered as an old stump, though he couldn't have been more than thirty. He'd spent four years chasing the Apaches, and that will age a man faster than anything I know.

Mitchell stopped his big bay horse about ten feet from me and slid off him smooth as a stream of water.

"Mr. Kelly, sir," he said, extending his hand, "the Colonel's compliments and mine own." Mitchell rarely spoke, and he had a twinkle in his eye all of the time, as though he had a joke of his own devise that included everyone he met.

"You've heard the news, of course," I said. "Joseph's three days ahead."

"We'll ride on a three horse to a trooper remount if need be."

"I saw your allies go by eight hours ago," I said. "I think if Miles wants to catch Joseph, you'd best head northwest now."

"The *Far West* isn't far behind," Mitchell said. "We can leave at first light. Do you have any suggestions as to placement of sentries?" He had a soft trace of Tidewater Virginia in his speech.

I mentioned a couple of spots. Mitchell remounted and rode off. The troopers were felling trees and dragging them off to form breastworks. These were good soldiers, no mistake.

By the time the troopers had finished with their corral, I could hear the thump of the *Far West*'s engines. Grant Marsh was at the wheel, he who had picked up the wounded from the Reno-Benteen fight on the bluffs west of where Custer had got his, and set a record for speed to Fort Buford. I had once seen Marsh throw a tinhorn gambler, holding him by the throat and crotch, into the paddle wheel. There were no charges filed.

Marsh had to pick his way carefully through the channel—there was a lot of big cottonwoods which had been uprooted and then buried up to their tops in the mud and sand, leaving the rootball to flail like a giant's club just below the surface. They were called sawyers and were the most fearsome hazard on the river. Later there would be big steamboats with winches—they called them Uncle Sam's toothpullers—to haul out the sawyers, but for now it was just Grant Marsh's uncanny reading of the water keeping the boat safe.

The steamboat anchored in a good-sized eddy, and the crew poured down the gangplank and began to cut wood for the boilers—the soldiers had sawed quite a bit. They would cut twice what the boat could hold, and hope that the Indians wouldn't set fire to the stacked wood.

A hostler—couldn't have been fourteen, the age at which I joined the Union Army—came for my animals. He saluted me and said, "With the Colonel's compliments, sir, and he would like to see you right away."

I stomped up the gangplank, hearing the hollow thump of my bootheels on sawboards—an unfamiliar sound. I crouched and had my pistol in hand in an instant. The sentry at the gangport looked at me quizzically.

"Out here you learn to listen for sounds what shouldn't ought to be if you want to keep your hair," I says, half embarrassed, or at least enough to make an excuse for my behavior.

"Jaysus, Kelly," Baldwin's big voice boomed. "Are you ready for the asylum yet?"

The first time I met Baldwin I was playing the fool, and I volunteered to take a message through the country to Fort Fetterman. I was acting like a halfwit—for the practice, you know—and when Baldwin asked me what I would do if captured, I said I would act the madman, since the Indians are superstitious about madmen and never harm one. I got to enjoying it, and Baldwin ever after would remind me of our first meeting.

Frank was the second in command, and as good a soldier and man as any. We got drunk one night in St. Louis and with that peculiar intensity that whiskey gives, he had fixed me with his Black Irish eye and said, "Jaysus, Kelly, it's not heroes I want to be commanding, it's run-of-the-mill cowards with their backs to the wall. I never met a hero who had a hat size bigger than five and one-eighth."

"Hello, Frank," I says, "and good evening to you."

"You're just in time for the wrestling match, me against him," says Baldwin. "Now wouldn't the papers have fun with this?"

Christ in pantaloons, I thinks. It ain't enough he has to send his troopers out to get their heads blown off, they get to spend their free time playing football and doing rope pulls and three-legged races and tossing horseshoes. Miles was strange, no doubt.

"Wrestling match," I says. "How perfectly grateful I am to have such an entertainment. Might I wager on the outcome?"

"Of course."

"Well, I'll take Miles. Or I could bribe you to break his goddamned neck."

Baldwin laughed and jerked a thumb toward the rear of the boat, where Miles had his office. He also carried a Turkey carpet with him on campaign and a folding India-rubber bathtub.

"The commandin' officer and me are wrestling for the privilege of the double bed atop the wheelhouse, so the victor can freeze his ass off in the midnight air. Well, my mother used to say, 'What's the use in being Irish if you can't be thick?'"

There was a wrestling ring set up on the stern deck, and even a couple of junior officers with buckets and towels trying to look like managers. Miles was preening his muscles—they was about half flab now, but he must have been strong when he was younger. Miles had a cast eye, one just a bit off center. It was unnerving to have him stare at you. I thought he must have got most of his promotions that way. The most memorable in a field of bad candidates.

"Ho, Luther," says Miles, all jolly, "another of your calling cards, eh? I think this one is even bigger than the first one you sent!"

He extended his hand and we shook paws, and when he let go to turn and flex his muscles some more I looked at the sheen on my palm and realized that he had oiled himself.

It was a fair match, as to size. Baldwin could have easily been the victor, but he was, of course, too smart for that.

Rank was hard to come by these days—there were men serving out here as captains who had been generals in the Civil War. There weren't any great slaughters to clear the field of an oversupply of eligible candidates. The Indians had never heard of frontal assaults, which leads to rapid promotions.

I left them straining and grunting and wandered off to the riverside rail. Someone offered me a flask, which I refused. The water was low and pretty clear. I watched the river go by and listened with half an ear to the grunts and thuds. A fingernail moon came up and the river began to steam as the night air cooled.

A bullboat was passing us by. I almost sounded the alarm, and then a voice came straggling over the river, over its low roaring sounds of stones and sand and trees and carcasses rasping toward the Gulf of Mexico.

"Nezzz Percies crossed at Cow Island four days ago," a reed-thin voice wafted across the foggy river.

"We know," I hollered. "Where you from, where you headed?"

The bullboat was spinning, I got only one word out of the sentence that followed. It was enough.

"................cholera......"

I shuddered.

Hands were clapping behind me, so the match must be over. I walked back to the crowd on the afterdeck. Backs were being slapped and money was changing hands.

Baldwin had won. It gave me a puzzlement, and then I remembered that as crazy and devious as Miles was, he knew better than to surround himself with arse-crawling sycophants. There is nothing so discouraging as written requests for written instructions in the middle of a battle. Miles was a lot more afraid of Howard stealing his newspaper headlines than he was of the Nez Perces, but he was smart enough to know he needed men of judgment.

Besides, he could always screw his subordinates out of their fair share of the glory later.

Miles beckoned to me, and walked over to where he was toweling himself off.

"How far behind do you reckon we are?" he says.

"If you force every ounce out of your men and horses, maybe a day and a half, maybe two," I says. "They are pretty well encumbered with everything they own that's portable and they've got their children and old folks, too."

"We leave at first light!" Miles shouted. "One hundred rounds per man, one remount, one hundred and fifty rounds on the pack mules. Bacon and hardtack only."

"I suggest you leave now and find out exactly where they are, Kelly," he smiled. "After all, that's what Uncle Sam pays you for."

Like I said, he wasn't all that dumb.

4

I settled my pony into his ground-eating lope, and we drifted up the trail under the faint starlight. He was a damn good horse, and once he got which direction he was supposed to go in, I could sleep in the saddle, he was so surefooted.

We come to Cow Island just at dawn. I glassed the Island and both sides of the ford from a hiding post in a clump of chokeberry bushes. There wasn't any activity, and I hadn't expected any. There on the north bank was a sight I goggled at for a full minute. A boiler, gleaming with brass and German silver, smack in the middle of an Indian uprising. It had been block-and-tackled up the bank from a sunken wreck. The great muddy swath where there had been roller logs was as visible as a cut on your face.

I could see the Nez Perces' trail, too, winding up the draw and out onto the high tablelands to the north. So they was gone, like I thought. Even the rearguard would be at least two days' travel ahead. I rode cautiously up to where they had made camp. It had rained here and the ashes from the cooking fires touched sharply in the nose. I knew that they had come up through the Judith Basin, and I looked for the red grass seeds in the horse turds—the seeds are from a grass which grows there and not much of any place else. They were there. The Nez Perces' trail was two hundred feet wide, overlaid with the prints of the Crow ponies.

I started up the trail, and then I saw some cache turves stacked to one side of the trail. The Crows had opened the caches, which had been dug by the Nez Perces.

You know what was in them? Gold pans. Hundreds of gold pans, many kegs of nails in another, kitchen crockery in another, all piled up by the salvage crew who run off when the Nez Perces came.

It was a real head scratcher. Here's this bunch of folks, who have already run some seventeen hundred miles, soldiers behind them, and God knows what coming in from their flanks, having fought several pitched battles, and within a hundred and fifty miles of safety, they spend a day caching goods they don't need and can't possibly use. An Indian got about as much use for a nail as I do for a bustle. It was as though they knew that they weren't to make it, and dallied so it wouldn't be worse than it was.

All of the time that I had been poking about I had been scanning the ridges. A scout, if he is any good, looks like a feeding chicken—peck down and stare up. Peck and look, peck and look—about four pecks and three looks into my routine I saw a rider dash between two huge rocks two miles away. I hightailed it to a good spot and rein-hobbled my horse and saw to it that my gun had one in the chamber and a full deck in the magazine.

Pretty soon he come trotting down the trail, waving like a Mick politician on St. Paddy's Day, all smiles and hoots. He came right for me, because if he'd been in my boots, that's where he would be.

"Pip, pip, old man," Buffalo Horn hooted. "Jolly good, don'tcher know. Pass the port. Pass the girl. Oh, what rotters are we. Sun never sets."

"I think I am going to kill you," I snarls.

"Tut, tut, old man, port out and starboard home. By god that's the biggest bloody moose I've seen since last I dined at Crowell's. D'you have the time or at least a paper? Pip, pip, old fellow, we shall never make it at these rates. The niggers start at Calais. Beastly hot, ain't it?"

Buffalo Horn had spent a portion of this season guiding dudes from the Sceptered Isle and he was quite bonkers (to use a term) and homicidal, too. Texas Jack Omohundro had recruited him—down under that copper skin and the outlandish garments beat the heart of a greedy, avaricious little bastard.

I stood up and whistled for my horse. Buffalo Horn sat on his mount and grinned like a shit-eating dog. He was a Bannock, from across the Rockies. He wore the Bannock hat, a circular arrangement of otter fur with buffalo horn tips for decoration.

"Good meat," says Buffalo Horn, holding up a mesh bag full of tins.

We ate anchovies, liver paté, canned tomatoes and peaches, and had evaporated milk for our coffee.

5

Buffalo Horn and me took off after a few hours sleep, following the Nez Perces' trail. It went as straight as the country would allow—north. We come upon a grave that they had made. A small one. A child must have died. I couldn't help but think that this was a rotten war, and then I couldn't think of a good war. I had nothing against the Nez Perces.

At dawn we found the tracks of Miles's Crow scouts. They had cut across and were up ahead, harassing the fleeing Nez Perces. They had strict orders not to engage the Nez Perces, which orders would probably hold about the same amount of time your orders do when you tell your dog to stay the hell off the couch. As long as Miles's eye was on 'em he could expect to be obeyed.

We had come maybe forty miles by noon. We stopped to let our ponies water and cool themselves and chew a bit of the sweet buffalo grass. The wind quartered for a moment, and we smelled the sweet fishy smell of death.

There were three bodies beside the trail, tumbled off into a little wash. They were Crows, and each of them had been killed by a shot to the head. Most Horse Indians can't shoot for sour owlshit—it's the boom that matters— while most Corn Indians are pretty good with a rifle. But the Corn Indians don't fight much, and the Horse Indians do. I suppose the Corn Indians are good shots because they have to trim back the gopher population.

"Wal," I says, pointing to the three bloated corpses in the bed of the wash, "looks like them Nez Perces can shoot, anyway."

Buffalo Horn laughed. We both heard the horses at the same moment and were both behind the same log an eyeblink later. We was scanning the ground and ready to toss off a shot at the first topknot to show itself.

Someone halloed. The party clattered up the wash bed, the horseshoes clanging on the stones.

"Shit," I said. It was the word come first to mind. There was this young soldier, and behind him the man I hated most in all of the world. You know someone who does something that you do and twists it and makes it a vile thing? Something that you do that you love?

Red Mike was about the vilest critter I had ever met, and Miles, the bastard, had sent him along after me. Clever fellow, our Colonel. Send two men who hate each other's guts to do the same job and they will likely bust ass to prove each other a worse case. And if one should come back with some tale of woe befallen the other, there is always the entertainment of a good court martial and hanging.

I smiled nice and thought, by god, I am going to figure out a way to kill you, you bastard.

"Howdy, Kelly," says Red Mike, grinning and showing his big gapped teeth. "What a sartain pleasure to work with you once again."

Mike was such a gentleman he preferred to scalp squaws'

lower pelts, if you gather what I mean. It's hard to think of company that would find that polite conversation, but there you are.

The soldier rode his mount between us and reached a hand down.

"Pleased to meet you," he says, his eyes never leaving the ridges. "Name's Haddo. Corporal, Fifth Cavalry."

He was an open-faced young feller in his middle thirties, trim and small, and as graceful as a cat. He slid from his saddle and loosened the cinches, took off the saddle and the sweaty blanket. The horse rippled its hide, glad to be free of the hot load on its back. Haddo tore a clump of grass from the earth and began to rub his horse down. The pony closed his eyes halfway and stood stock still, except for an occasional flick of his tail to disturb the flies.

"Which way you figure them Nezzz Percies gone?" says Red Mike. His horse was bloody on his flanks from Mike's spurs, and his lips were torn from the war bit Mike had put on him. What I liked least about Mike was that he was a fool. That horse could mean the difference that would save Mike his life, and here he was, through simple cruelty, wrecking the animal that might save his hair. Just for the joy of causing the horse misery. Stupid bastard.

"Straight up in the goddamn air," I says, "and if you care to follow me I will do my best to see you get your filthy stupid ass shot off."

I took off on that cheery note, hoping Red Mike's horse would founder and I'd be rid of the sonofabitch. He was dumb enough he might have followed, but I'd forgotten Haddo. The soldier just waved and walked his horse around, and when Mike began to curse at him and make gestures toward Buffalo Horn and me, Haddo just laughed and went on walking his horse in a circle, his white teeth bright against the dark beard on his face. It was a killer's smile that said, "Not now. Now is not the time. Later."

I looked back from the crest of the hills, and I could see

the two of them below, Haddo still walking his horse in a circle, Red Mike waving his fists, while his horse was beginning to show that droop at the haunches that is the sign of being windblown. They would follow later, god dammit.

Buffalo Horn and me made a dry camp just north of the Cow Creek Divide, and were well on our way before daybreak. It was only about twenty miles to the Bear Paws, a small range of mountains dropped out in the high prairie, I think by mistake.

Me and Buffalo Horn split up at dawn. I went east, looking for a good look-see place, and came atop a butte by a back trail. I looked through my binoculars and spied the Nez Perce camp. I could see men digging trenches and breastworks in a businesslike manner. This was going to be bloody work. They had corraled their pony herd in a shallow depression. The herd seemed smaller than I had calculated, so the Crows had stolen many horses. I went down the trail and rode off to find Miles. It took me until ten in the evening. He had driven his troopers himself, and the infantry was forced-marching all through the night.

Miles heard my report and pulled at his moustache. The Nez Perces had cut up Gibbon and his men in the Big Hole. They were the most soldierly Indians ever.

"I'll be going," I said to Miles. And I rode back the way I had come.

6

The dawn spread like a gray stain, washing over me and reaching toward the sun that had been glittering on the fresh snow atop the Bear Paw peaks. When the light met the stain I saw some movement at the foot of the mountains, where the Nez Perces were. They were still digging trenches, and if Miles decided on a frontal assault—which he probably would, since his big fear was Terry showing up, and pulling his rank—a lot of soldiers was going to die for nothing.

Canada was only thirty miles away. I watched men and women and children move the bitter earth. There were occasional puffs of smoke from the rifles as the Crows and the Nez Perces pestered each other over the horses. They were mostly Appaloosas, which the Nez Perces invented.

Miles wouldn't be long, so I got a little sleep. My horse was trained to make a noise if he heard anything, and when he snorted I came awake, Colt in hand. It was Buffalo Horn. We had been saying for some years that,

heh-heh-heh, we might one of us kill the other by mistake
and how awful that would be. Both of us knew better—for
one thing we worked as partners, which is a rare thing in
the scouting trade. We was both too old to waste time
training some young pup—hell, I was already twenty-six
and Buffalo Horn had been birthed or found under a wet
rock nearly thirty years ago. He was ever reminding me
that he was ancient and full of the ague.

Miles would be along sometime today, I figured, and
when he came he would have at least two light mountain
howitzers. If he was smart, he would just keep lobbing
shells over at the Nez Perces until they gave up from lack
of sleep or boredom. Then I remembered that General
Howard was likely near. If I wasn't required as a scout—
which legally I wasn't—to participate in a frontal assault
against well fortified marksmen, I would consider offering
advice or tearing bandages or something.

"Horn," I says, "we have a problem. Or rather, I do.
Miles ain't seen you but a couple of times. Me, I'm
thinking we should reconnoiter over yonder, and bravely
blockade the route the Nez Perces will take when they
retire to Canada."

Horn looked at me, and me, I looked at him, and we
headed on a breakneck speed (a-circle so as not to overly
amuse some Nez Perce marksman) to find some place to
lie low so as we could thunder bravely back and offer our
gallant aid—alas, a moment too late—and not get our
arses shot off.

We selected a spot with fine cover well away from any
path that might interest anyone, and I carefully put the
sun covers on my binoculars, and then we ate and drank as
much as we could hold knowing mealtime was likely to be
irregular here for a few whiles.

Along about two in the afternoon we saw Miles at the
head of his column gallop up to the Nez Perce trenchworks,
and when he saw them he flung up his arm to halt the

column. I knew he was bawling orders and I watched the troopers form ranks right and left, drop their dunnage, and check their sidearms.

"I bet you ten plews that they get fifteen," says Buffalo Horn. Indians got the same vices as us, but less practice.

"Ten on twenty," I says. "Middles split the difference."

What that means is I was betting on eighteen and above, and Horn on seventeen and below. I was watching Miles with the glasses, hoping to see a few newspaper reports riding near him so he could perish nobly—heroically— but no. Not a civilian in sight.

Miles and his staff found a nice seat and the troopers started out. They was maybe three hundred yards from the Nez Perces when they started, and the Nez Perces didn't open fire until the troopers was halfway there. One man made it to the seventy-yard mark before pitching into the dust. The charge had degenerated and like all them close encounters the dust was obscuring everything.

Me and Horn sat up there waiting for the breeze to clear the dust and reveal the daily bag. We had a nice sociable chaw of Burley tobacco and reminisced about this and that and the breeze cleaned the dust away, and I counted eighteen blue forms on the ground and one horse. Horn rattled off an impressive string of Bannock cuss words and stopped midway through the last one.

"One man is crawling away," he said.

"B . . . gimme those," I snarled. I followed his pointing finger and sure enough one man was crawling at a right sprightly pace.

I watched as the trooper elbowed his way to some boulders which kept him out of sight until he was too far away from the Nez Perces for them to spot him.

We lathered our horses up some and swept up looking disappointed as could be that we were too late to get killed because of some god damned officer's vision of another glob of gold on his rank patches. I figure it's a man thrown away, in any rank over major, for each and every little gold thread.

Miles was bellowing orders and his staff was bellowing orders—the senior staff sounded like a bunch of Delmonico's waiters screaming at the kitchen help when the stock market has a good day. Pretty soon the sergeants got everything under control. The troopers off-mounted, and many of them couldn't stand and sat down hard on the ground. A lot of them were crying. A lot of them had lost weapons. Oh, Kelly, I thinks, this is going to be just a great and entertaining evening, with our troopers out there trying to bring in wounded, and the Nez Perces out there trying to get weapons.

Miles saved me from outright mutiny by bellowing, "Kelly, go find those damn artillerymen!" Three of the four available directions to go were highly desirable, the fourth not. Back to find his overgrowed popguns was a desirable compass heading, so I took off at a fast clip, before Miles got enough sense back to think of the fact that any green trooper could have done the same.

I thought of the carefully cached goods back at Cow Island, and then it struck me why the Nez Perces had built a fort.

They must believe that they are in Canada, I said to myself. Oh god, those poor folks.

I found the artillerymen flogging the fieldpiece teams and caissons of ammunition moving at a satisfyingly slow pace sufficient distance from that imbecile mess up there to ensure that they would arrive after dark. I aimed to please.

"I've been sent to guide you," I said to Lieutenant Keegan—a good man, and no fool.

"Jaysus, Kelly," he laughed, "it looks like a herd of buffalo a million strong came through here."

"No it don't, Keegan," I says. "A buffalo trail goes zig-zag like. Their eyes is set on the sides of their heads and they can't see front ahead straight at all. So they amble a hundred yards, turn, amble sixty, so forth and so on."

"How bad was it?" says Keegan.

"Pretty bad. Seventeen down—don't know who's dead and who's just wounded light enough to make it."

Keegan looked straight ahead.

We come to the main camp an hour after dark.

The lamp was lit in Miles's tent, so I stopped in. Haddo and Red Mike were there. Mike looked like a rabbit when it first sights a weasel close enough to strike. It seemed that Red Mike's horse had foundered, and Haddo had to shoot it. Haddo's horse was too tired to carry them both, so they put Red Mike's saddle and tack on top of Haddo's and were walking.

They heard a horse whicker, and riding down the trail toward them was a very old Indian woman on a very old horse. Red Mike shot her before Haddo could think he might do any such thing. Haddo was shaking with rage.

"Fortunately, she was apparently and patently alone."

"Haddo," said Miles, "forget it. You," he said to Red Mike, "if you ever do such a thing again I will hang you so help me god. Both of you get out."

"Anything for me to do?" I says, putting in a tired whine indicative of exhaustion and yeoman service. Miles shook his head.

7

I awoke to the sound of the cannon. Miles was always mentioning that Napoleon had called artillery "the thunder and lightning of campaigns." Miles talked like that a lot. One newspaperman and he'd order an arms blanche charge. I am not very pleasant when I am awakened by such noises. If they don't run out of ammunition by tonight, I thinks, I'm going to spike the god damn things.

I breakfasted on pemmican I had pounded up in the summer—buffalo meat and berries pulverized together, and then hot buffalo fat poured into the little leather bags called parfleches. You can winter on nothing but that and live fine. The slop the Army gets is salt pork and hardtack. So everybody but the officers has dysentery all the damn time—they can afford to buy canned rations and such. You can tell a trooper who's been out on the chase for three days or more. Worst of it is, the Cavalry gets boils on their butts and other infections which present serious distractions in what can be a very dangerous living, especially if you need all of your concentration. Take Indian fighting, say.

Miles was in his tent, slumped on the map table, a little pile of drool glistening at his open mouth. Major Baldwin, victor in the wrestling match of two nights ago, had been up all night crawling around, trying to get the wounded troopers back, carrying a knife in his teeth and his revolver in his hands. His uniform was gone half off him and his knees and elbows was scratched and full of thorns and dirt.

"Where is Howard?" Miles said suddenly, though he was still asleep. It made a purty sight, the two of them, one damn near dead from risking his life to save his troopers, and the other worrying in his sleep about some superior officer coming to steal his glory.

"Frank," I whispered, "come on, go see the surgeon."

"He's working on my men," he said.

"I got a medicine kit, Frank," and I gestured him to follow. He got up, his face twisting in pain before he forced a smile.

I scrubbed his wounds out. The dirt would poison his blood soon. He never flinched, though I used a stiff bristle scrub brush and yellowcake soap. I salved all of the lacerated skin and bandaged him. The white bandages made him look like a clown in the circus.

"Thanks, Kelly," he said. He struggled to his feet and headed toward Miles's tent.

Shots popped off over the hill as the pickets fired at the Nez Perces. The Nez Perces didn't fire back. (I later found out that the women and children spent the night digging bullets we had fired out of the earthen walls. Someone had found a way to reload some of their spent brass.)

Baldwin and Miles came out of the tent. Miles beckoned me over.

"Baldwin wants to go down and see if he can arrange a surrender," says Miles.

Before the Nez Perce kill us all, I thinks.

"Good idea, Frank," I says. "I'll walk down with you."

We got a couple of willow poles and hung white on them. When we started down we passed Haddo. He had made himself a rifle pit. Haddo grinned and nodded and shifted his quid of tobacco.

The Nez Perces still hadn't fired a shot this day. The bluecoats was dug in at the maximum range of a rifle, and while we had more than enough ammunition, it wasn't likely that the Nez Perces had any to waste. When there was a flash of a head down there in the Nez Perce trenches, our troopers fired a ragged volley—and for every thousand shots, a few must strike home, just out of the law of averages.

"I need to talk to Joseph," Baldwin bellered.

Silence. We walked on another fifty feet, and Frank bellered again. This time a head popped up.

"May I come down?" says Frank.

"Only you." Muffled, good English.

"Luck, Frank," I says.

"Thanks, Luther."

I turned round and he walked on. I went at a pretty brisk clip, afraid that some fool would commence to fire. One of ours did. The Nez Perces retaliated, but not at me. I passed Haddo's rifle pit.

"It was . . ." he yelled, and then a bullet tore into him above the heart. He somehow got his pistol out and aimed and fired, but not at the Nez Perces. At Red Mike, and Haddo hit him in the forehead, and both were dead before they hit the ground.

The shooting stopped as quick as it had begun.

8

Baldwin didn't come back, but on the other hand the Nez Perce didn't stick up his head atop a pole. It was my guess that all of the wounds the Indians had suffered were accidental. Hour dragged on hour. The Nez Perces hoped that Sitting Bull would come riding down out of Canada or that if they waited.... Well, these thoughts was going through my mind.

The weather turned cold and miserable—rain clouds bunched up on the western horizon, and soon a fine chilly drizzle was added to the delights of the day.

The troopers had poor protection against the elements at best. Their blue battle serge was soon wet right through. Nobody did anything, 'cept Miles, who went back to his tent and brooded on the dreadful threat of Howard showing up and pulling rank on him—or the even more dreadful threat of Terry, who was senior to Miles. I sat by his warm stove and watched the man and listened to him mutter. There was something he could have done that would have been useful. He could have detailed a few troopers to make hot coffee on top of his goddamn stove and got at least that to his troopers.

There I sat, thinking this uncharitable thought of him when we heard wagons to our rear.

Miles stood bolt upright, banging his head on the kerosene lamp over the map table.

"Oh god!" he said. "The worst is happening! Howard!"

He rushed outside, clapping his hat on backwards. I followed. It was just the supply wagons that had been struggling along after us. The teamsters was cussing—god, they can cuss so good. Miles hadn't even left an escort for them. I thought at first that if I was in their boots I'd have dumped out the goods, and then I suddenly remembered that these teamsters was bringing up supplies for their friends. I did bet that the cases of delicacies and wine and such for the officers had been mislaid, likely at the first evening camp. (I was right.)

A half hour before sundown there was a shout. Baldwin was coming back up. He wasn't hurrying none.

All of the officers were in a crowd at the top of the little incline. All of the officers but Miles, who was no doubt in his command tent making plans to wheel his force one hundred and eighty degrees and make a devastating and prolonged defense against the enemy closing in on his rear. Howard would be hurled back with heavy casualties and . . . Baldwin shook his head at them and they walked dejectedly back to their posts.

I crossed paths with him about twenty yards from Miles's tent. Baldwin stopped.

"They won't surrender. So far we have killed two small girls and blown the lower jaw off a twelve-year-old boy. He is dying quite slowly."

Baldwin was in that dangerous state of pain and exhaustion where he might snap. The eyes were all hollow and the focus of 'em was half a mile ahead. I slapped him. He touched his cheek thoughtfully, as though I had caressed it. His voice was a steady monotone of nonsense.

"Baldwin," I says, "he's in there worryin' over where Howard and Terry are. Pull yourself together, man, or you will kill him."

Baldwin turned his face slowly to me, and I had the sensation he was seeing me for the first time. He nodded.

"Thank you," he said. His voice had some bend to it now. That's the time I saved Miles's life, for sure.

The drovers and sutlers and the cooks who had been fighting and all for days, was setting up tents and gathering wood. Half the troops at a time were rotated into details to set up their Sibley tents. (Look like those pavilions the knights used. Weighed a ton and were real bastards to set up and badly designed for smoke—soldiers was always being asphyxiated in those tents.) But bit by bit the command got dry and fed and some sleep. There was sentries posted all night, of course. I went to a place upwind to sleep—the camp smelled like a cross between a slaughterhouse lime pit and a tannery.

I went to sleep, the rain pattering on my hat and the oilcloth blanket cover. There wasn't a thing that I could do, and surely not the thing I would have liked doing most.

9

At first light individual soldiers began firing at the rifle ports the Nez Perce had cut in their breastworks. It was steady, aimed fire, and a couple of times I saw a Nez Perce warrior jerk upright from the shock of the bullet. There were many more I couldn't see, of course. The faulty tactics of the day before had been corrected.

The artillery was firing at the breastworks, first a few rounds of solid shot, then some shrapnel which exploded on impact, sending lethal metal every which way. (Been invented by a German, wouldn't you know.)

One stupendously fortunate round of shrapnel silenced a whole trench. The battle was won, and the Indians must have known it, but there were no white flags.

About eleven, there was another disturbance to our rear. Here came the dread Howard. Miles was all oil and smiles. Howard's troopers had ridden well over fifteen hundred miles. If there was any of them longing for a fight, I didn't see none. Fifteen hundred miles of hard trail on a belly which only got some jerky, hardtack, and bad water wears a man down. I heard one of the soldiers say that if the Montana dust wasn't so nutritious they'd be shadows ridin' after souls escaped from Hell.

Miles waved me over—he didn't want his senior aides anywhere near Howard whilst he was describing his heavy casualties and never mentioning how he come by seven-eighths of them.

Miles gave a glowing report of me—knowing Whipple, the youngster Liver-Eating Johnson had scared so, could have found this batch of Indians and even the pitifully young Lieutenant would have had the goddamn mother-wit to do what was being done today.

"Yeah, they sure had it done for them," I says. "This bad chunk of terrain, caught us enfilade. Lucky to get off so lightly." I nodded and walked away. There was some silence, and then I heard Howard ask a question which Miles laughingly endorsed. I'd tried to warn Howard, and if he was too dumb to see it, to hell with him. I was purely disgusted with just about everything in blue 'cept for Baldwin. The man was wounded and hadn't slept in ninety hours, but there he was at his post.

The Fifth Cavalry troopers were lined about, and soon the sheer volume of bullets and the cannons broke the Nez Perce defense. They waved a white flag, and Chief Joseph climbed out. All of the fire had stopped. Baldwin went to Miles, who broke off and waved gaily at Howard. Howard was a gentleman, and in his gentlemanly way he had adjudged Miles as the man who deserved to take the surrender.

Miles was walking pompously down the hill, Baldwin and me ten feet behind the hero of the hour. We were maybe a hundred yards from Joseph when the footfalls behind us caught my ear. I started, and looked back. There were soldiers, a lot of soldiers, most of them following us.

Joseph had the greatest presence of any man I have ever seen 'cept Crazy Horse, and the two were of different orders. Crazy Horse was a god-callen hero and victim for his people. Joseph was the man of justice, man of burden, and he radiated the good that was anyman and everyman since our most remote ancestors slimed out of the sea. He pulled us to him—not all but most. The young troopers and gravel-eating sergeants and the officers, we all walked down the hill toward him, and then he raised his right hand and said, "From where the sun now stands we will fight no more forever." There were no dry eyes. We weren't bawling, exactly, just lightly weeping.

Joseph reached down deep into Miles and troubled something he had never known was there, and years later I was to witness Miles do an extraordinary thing—his soul took a long time—he was to help Joseph when he could, and get him back to his Valley of the Winding Waters.

The Indians shuffled out, weary, heartbroken, and the troopers started them on their Long Sorrow Journey.

Miles sent two dispatches to Terry, and whoever carried them must have earned himself a pretty reward from Colonel Nelson Miles. The one on top, which they both signed, said pretty much what had actually happened, with the usual lying, mis-mention and so forth. The military does not run on brains. They both signed the bottom of the second dispatch, too, a mere copy, Miles told Howard. It blamed the losses Miles incurred on Howard. The dispatch was given to the newspapers and the damage was done. The Army furtively held hearings and then, as it usually does, tried to hush it up. Material they got to work with, they get lots of practice.

Howard was destroyed. He retired and soon died, cut to the quick that a brother officer to whom he had been not just fair, but gentlemanly, had done him so.

I didn't go to the hearings, but Baldwin sent me a long letter. I couldn't have stood the hearings.

I will never forget and it will be the thing in my mind the moment that I die, looking backward up the hill, and seeing eight hundred men standing haphazardly where they had wandered, weapons on the ground, a moment a few seconds long in which I can see each face of Everyman and Anyman there.

10

The wolf pelts wouldn't be prime for another two months, and after my adventures with Colonel Miles I felt I didn't need to be wandering around alone or with my cutthroat chum, Buffalo Horn, who agreed to meet me in mid-January (1878) at the mouth of the Big Horn River, which means actually that the first one there will leave some sign in our own personal code and the next will follow him to the real rendezvous. First rule of staying alive out here is, don't leave at first light—any hostile kid knows by the time he's eight how many lights-of-day it is from any for in any direction. The second is, don't read any of them fool books purports to tell you how do you get on. If they knew they'd be out here making a thousand dollars a month, instead of busting pencils back where everybody is.

I decided to go home, at a leisurely pace, spend maybe forty-eight hours or so, and get back to the rendezvous at a leisurely pace.

I grew up near Oneida, New York, eldest son of a physician and a suffragette. Catholic, too. There were eight of us Kellys. Stand in line, we made a graph of when Ma and Pa joined forces, so to speak. Once a year, on or about the third of March if you diddled with the arithmetic. I like 'em all well enough but they'd all stayed there by Oneida and turned into lawyers and merchants and such. (In the Mexican Revolution when I was advising Pancho Villa, we happened to be in Sinaloa Province, and Pancho got a bit drunk, and Rodolfo Fierro said that he wanted to hang every lawyer in the Province. "So go hang them, my friend," says Pancho, "I don't like your face so long." Fierro hanged over three hundred. I went along. I have had some satisfactory times.)

So I rode back to Fort Buford, got on a steam packet with a load of hides. I spent three days leaning off the prow. I looked like a goddamn figurehead and had to have my neck crunched back down by a chiropract. God, them hides stank.

Took the train to Chicago via Minneapolis—and in Minneapolis I found a book written about me by a feller named James Blair. I was still in my leather and leggins and moccasins and hat, and every time I'd hoot with laughter the folks in the coach would all turn round and stare. Fortunately, the picture on the engraved cover (I was at least nine feet tall, if you scale me with the grizzly bear I was beating the bejesus out of with my bare knuckles) didn't resemble me in the slightest.

It don't take much to amuse me. I started picking my teeth with my Halsey drop-point skinning knife and bellering fer whiskey at regular intervals all the way to Chicago. I took rooms in the Black Hawk, best in town, ordered new suits and a case of champagne, and piled my greasy, bloody duds on the cashmere rug and tried to use up all of the hot water in the tank. It had been two years since I had been doing what I was doing—soaking in hot water and feeling relaxed. Out there, it is best you don't relax.

I re-ragged and practiced looking dauntless in a suit and derby hat in the mirror. Shaved and all, I felt about twenty pounds lighter and not myself at all. The ride down in the elevator was nervous-making, and it dawned on me why as I stepped inside the lobby. First time in a long time I hadn't at least one and usually more weapons on me. I asked directions to the nearest gun store and bought a double-barreled derringer. Looked like a kid's toy to me, but with it in one of my waistcoat pockets I felt a mite safer.

Chicago was busting with folks and the babble in the streets was only about half in English. Since the big fire they were building new buildings "fireproof" of brick and stone. The slaughterhouses were working round the clock, produce and such headed east, implements and such headed west. Cows escaped the yards and ran through the streets. I got back inside the hotel, and marveled at the quiet. I remembered the quiet on Roger's Pass at sixty below zero. My heart sloshing was all I could hear that night, and a faint whine I don't know the meaning of.

I strode across the lobby toward the bar—I had in mind a strong drink. I never drink out in the Big Empty—for one, it spoils my eyes, for two, each time I start in I get a hell of an attack of gout in my right big toe. The thought of trying to escape from a Blackfeet war party whilst hopping on one foot don't appeal to me worth a damn.

The bar was hid behind two enormous gilt doors covered with brown leather. I thought I would have to heave hard, but they swung open easy as a garden gate. (A fact I tucked away should I happen to take on too much Old Tanglefoot and have to proceed to my room in a series of leaps and catches. Leaps of about six inches at forty-five degrees.)

The bar must have been about fifty feet long. There

were six bartenders, every one of them slinging grog like the sealing fleet was in port. Fortunes was being made in hogs and cattle, land and railroads, grains, spirits, and what have you. The little fish did most of their business in either this bar or the one up by the Stockyards named McRory's. Some was to rise to wealth and prominence, and most was to end on their uppers and nothin' but a list of lost chances to tell to a dwindling number of ears.

The smell of the place was unwashed men, cheap cologne, cigar smoke, stale booze, and avarice. I'd been a few years away, you see, and an Indian lodge has a stink too (less the avarice), which I was more or less used to. This atmosphere rocked me back on my heels.

The drinks was high-priced—a dime for most, the fancy imports as much as a quarter. There was a couple huge sideboards full of finger food—pickled buffalo tongues (some men were holding a whole tongue in the left hand and munching away like the damn thing was an oddball apple), cheese, crackers, pickles. You could get what you wanted for food and pile it on an enamel plate and head for the perimeter. I was headed there when I got a chewed end of pickled tongue in the eye from a gent who was guffawing. Tobacco-soaked, spit-covered, salty, vinegary, greasy buffalo tongue. It is nothing I would recommend to you for a poultice if you got a sore eye. Wounded, I staggered to the rail and asked for water.

"Water?" says the barkeep, looking amazed.

"For my eye," I says, taking my hand off it. It caused him to start. He scuttled off and brung me a glass.

"I'll have an Irish," I says, putting a gold five-dollar piece on the counter.

He nodded and poured me a stiff one. My eye had gone from burning to just throbbing.

I was taking the first sip from my Jameson's when someone slapped me so hard in the back that the rest of the whiskey went down the front of my new suit.

"Kelly, by god," booms a voice could only belong to Texas Jack Omohundro. Still with his hair and lookin' like a man new to the pimping trade. "God damn, man, it's good to see you. Why, the papers is full of your heroic exploits in running down them renegade Nez Perce."

Something in my eyes stopped him. He nodded and said, "I suppose it was about like it usually is."

I nodded. He put up his big, square hand and squeezed my shoulder. "You want a drink," says Texas Jack, "or do you want to just suck on your suit a while?"

I laughed, and it was all right. Texas Jack had helped track down Quanah Parker and his Staked Plains Comanches, and Quanah such a close friend he fired an arrow into the soldiers' camp for Jack, which said, "I understand, but even brothers must sometimes kill each other." None of us—Cody, Jack, Tom Horn, Grouard, the others—liked it. We also knew that there was no help for it, and the only choice the Indians had was between capitulation and extermination.

We bear-hugged each other. I really was glad to see him—he was one of the funniest men that ever I knew.

There was a rabbity little man crouched in Jack's considerable shadow, and he was looking from Jack's face to mine and then at a foolscap notebook held in one tiny pink hand. Jack sort of choked and said, "This is Yellowstone Kelly here. Luther, this is George Hanks of the *Hartford Roden* . . . I mean *Courant*."

I smiled and stuck out my hand. I like newspaper reporters about as well as I like bedbugs, but I couldn't hardly be rude to him if Jack wasn't.

"You're Yellowstone Kelly," Hanks squeaks. "Our readers would like to know about your thoughts on the Nez Perce War."

"Let's get a table," says Jack. He got a couple bottles of Jameson's and we looked about. Everything seemed to be taken.

"Hold this," says Jack, handing me one of the bottles. He slid his Bowie knife out, and tossed it underhanded, high in the seegar smoke above. There was a solid thunggggg. Jack walked toward the thung. There was four petrified gents staring at the Bowie, which was still quivering while being stuck three inches into the walnut table top.

"Jesus Christ and all his children," booms Jack. "Feller can't leave his table five goddamn minutes 'fore some fools come along and take it. Damn." Jack had by now produced a pistol with a bore like the tunnel John Henry must have died in. The seats were suddenly empty. Jack swept the glasses onto the floor and placed one bottle in the middle.

"I'll get some glasses!" squeaked the Hartford Rodent, scuttling through the crowd. Well, he'd had a lifetime of practice, sure enough.

"Didn't mean to . . . ," Jack began.

I waved and shrugged. "You still wrangling the titled and untitled and just plain rich folks like we'd like to be around the Great American West?" I says.

"Yup. Sight easier dollar than shootin' buffalo. Sight easier dollar than wolfin', too, and the pack's big enough so the few little bands of Injuns left leave us alone. Some of them titled women don't think the trip's complete without havin' the guide poke 'em till they scream. It ain't all bad."

"Here," said the Hartford Rodent, placing three tumblers on the table. He resumed his notebook and tried to straighten his pince-nez.

"Now, Mr. Kelly, could we have some of your comments upon the recent desperate and gallant attempt by our Army, ably led by you and Colonel Miles, to capture these savage fugitives?"

"Sure," I says, filling his glass to the brim with Irish, "just as soon as you get that down."

The Rodent gulped air and then he gulped Jameson's, and the five ounces went down as smooth as water.

The Rodent coughed. "Well?"

"Colonel Nelson Miles is a farina-faced glob of puke who would be better suited as a pickpocket or senator, both being about the same in the morals department."

"Sir?" said the Rodent.

"Colonel Nelson Miles would make a fine senator," I says again, filling him to the brim. "Drink that, and then the next question."

I had drug the little two-shot derringer out of my waistcoat pocket and was sort of idly pointing it between Rodent's eyes. The Rodent slid another five ounces of Irish down his wee throat. Sufficient unto the day.

"Now about the last desperate battle," said the Rodent, "in which so many of our gallant men lost their lives . . . tell me, sir, what part did you play in it?"

"I was atop a nearby hill. I saw Colonel Nelson Miles needlessly sacrifice twenty-two soldiers because he was afraid the glory he so wanted would be snatched away from him by General Howard or General Terry. Like I said, the farina-faced glob of puke would make a great senator."

The combination of the Irish whiskey and my venom done overcome the Rodent. He glanced at his notes, and then at me, and his eyes looked puzzled, and he slid beneath the table as easy as mud flows down a hill. He didn't even make a teeny thud.

Jack looked at me, twinkling.

"C'mon, Luther," he says. "A friend of yours asked if I should see you to bring you on over. There's a great little old gooseberry farm a couple blocks from here. I don't think poor Hanks will be noticed until they sweep the floor."

We left the foggy bar and rising voices and crossed the lobby, with the soft pile carpet—dark brown, so as not to show the tobacco stains of them that doesn't care where or what they spit on.

"What day is this?" I says. "Day of the week, I mean."

"Friday. Don't make much difference out there, does it. How hot or how cold, dry, rain, or snow, how long's the fur on the worthy peltries. But not the day of the week. I'm gonna miss it," Jack said. He was beginning to weave a little—he was one of those men who can be holding a half bottle or four full ones and he goes right on doing whatever with nary a sign that he's drunk. Sometimes he can't remember what happened the night before—how he got them teeth-shaped cuts on his knuckles or what the name of the chippy he was sleepin' with might be.

We walked four or five blocks and made a couple turns and come up to a big five-story house looked like a wedding cake I once saw, only this was black and brown with a red tile roof. We walked up and Jack knocked on the door. There was gaslight ablaze in the porte-cochere and a little light come out from behind the curtains.

A peephole slid open and I saw an eye that was dark brown and the white part was a deep tan. The peephole slid shut. The door opened and we went in. A chippy took our hats and coats. The eyeball at the door was one of a pair owned by a nigger who was seven feet easy, any measurement you want to take—height, width, and I figured depth, too. But when he turned a bit to pat down Jack I saw he was a mere three feet through.

"Evening, Tusco," says Jack. The blackamoor rewarded the greeting with a rumble sounded like a bad stampede a ways off. He patted me next, and removed my derringer and gave it to the chippy with our coats.

We walked through some gilt doors standing open to our right and saw a good two dozen chippies and three or four men sitting on stuffed chairs, drinking champagne or whiskey and running their eyes over the chippies, who were looking either bored or coy.

"Rumor has it," says Jack, jerking a thumb in the direction of the monster nigger, "that he once broke up a fight between two sports here by eatin' 'em—sports, clothes, hats, boots, hardware, and armament and argument. I'd not like to get into a scrap with him myself."

"I'd druther trade punches with a mad she-grizzly," I says, "though, to be humane about it, Tusco probably wouldn't take near so long."

I had just got the words out when here come Sally Parmenter bearing down on us. She was dressed in a frilled and flounced dress, and her bodice was framed and upheld what was for my money the most splendid tits in Creation. Oh, I'd about half-guessed where we were going—for one thing she's the only whore in the world ever owed me anything.

"Luther, Jack." She swept us both close to her considerable breasts and showered us with kisses and ear-nibbles and the like. Then she threw back her head and laughed.

"Come with me," she says, taking one each of our hands. We take an open-front elevator up to the fourth floor, and Sally shoved Jack through the door on the right and me through the door on the left.

"Must go tend my garden," she laughs and pulls the doors shut, one-thunk, two-thunk.

It was dim in the room, after the bright gold gaslight, and it took a half minute for my eyes to adjust to the lesser light. A soft hand grabbed mine and I looked at the girl. She led me to a chair and pulled off my boots and unknotted my tie. She seemed to emerge from a mist, so filmy was the shift she was wearing. She sat in my lap and kissed me, and then she laced her fingers behind my neck and leaned back. An Irish redhead, with the cinnamon-speckled skin and the green eyes. I told her to get up, and I took off my clothes, and when I stood up she let the shift fall. She was beautiful, slim, full-breasted. I dragged her to the floor and punched her right then, for I'd not had a white woman since I could remember. We ended up on a bearskin rug, and I shot off like a roman candle.

"You've not had any for a bit, then?" she said, and laughed. She pulled me up and put me on the bed and then walked to the other side and got in. There was champagne and brandy and such in the headboard.

"I'll have brandy with champagne in it," I said. She mixed them in a tulip glass and gave it to me. I must have fallen asleep, for the last thing I remember was her hair brushing across my belly.

11

I woke up a couple of times and the chippy made me drink more champagne, and then we went at it again till I could feel the last of the kinks go out of my parts and body and mind. I slept deep, which I had forgotten how to do, and it wasn't till after noon the next day that I woke up. Sally was in bed with me, doing her have-you-ever-seen-a-snake-swallow-an-egg routine, which is better than any you've ever had, I can assure you.

"You like it out there, don't you, Luther," she said softly, and smiling. She was a good friend to me, and me to her. It didn't matter to either of us, come to think of it, what it was we were doing—we was friends and I have never had another woman friend. Well, she saved my head a few years later, though it cost her a lot of the money she'd saved to be old on. She was afraid of being old and alone and poor and nothing else. I'll tell you another time.

It was too early for any trade in the place, and Sally and

me breakfasted downstairs in a huge dining room—hell, dining hall, walls all covered with them whorehouse paintings of naked women painted by some feller who had heard of a naked woman but never seen one. It was a good breakfast, and I stuck to coffee. There was a red velvet swing coming down from a brass ringbolt in the ceiling, and when I looked at it and laughed, Sally laughed too, and said a good deal of Chicago's political business was transacted here and having a naked chippy swinging overhead was thought to oil the wheels of democracy. Seems like a good idea, don't it?

"I have one customer, very, very rich, who pays to lie in the center of the table, naked as a jaybird, and have one of my high-yellers piss on him. Politician, wouldn't you know it." She laughed, and when Sally laughed the crystal went ting.

"Remember when you saved me from Red Hand?" she says. "And then you were so mad when the map told you where to dig and the river had changed?"

"Map could've been wrong."

"Tell me about the Bear Paw fight."

I did, and I told her about the soldiers following us down the hill to be closer to Chief Joseph.

"Where are they now?" she asked.

"Indian territory. They were promised that they could return to their lands and be ruled by the laws of the country. Instead, they are in a desolate place, which no one has a use for. When a use has been found, they'll be shoved out of there."

Sally had taken to smoking those little seegars the upper-class Mexican women smoke—crooked and black and thin. I had one and it was good, smooth and rich.

The toast was getting cold and we sat at right angles to each other, at one corner of the slab made of four full-growed mahogany trees.

"Luther," Sally said, stubbing her cigar out in the yolk of an unwanted poached egg, "Luther, what are you going to do?"

"Do?" I says. "I'll do what I have always done. Go where folks is scarce and look for gold or furs or gems."

"Luther," says Sally, "you go for the sake of goin'. Here."

She poured me a tulip glass full of what looked like the juice of oranges. I drank it. That is what it was, along with a lot of champagne. Sal called it a mimosa.

We got to talking politics and then we got to talking whether the Oregon Trail could have been at all if it weren't for the Erie Canal. We talked until late afternoon, and Sal excused herself to prepare for Saturday night— busiest of the week, last good sinnin' day before you repent with fur on your tongue and a stomach just dicey enough to keep you countin' the words of the sermon.

I went for a walk back to my hotel. Sal had offered me a cab to the train station in the mornin', and I saw no point in trying to get drunk with the greasy lot of speculators in the hotel bar. Truth of it is, I don't like folks much and I never have. I went up to my room and paid my bill and packed my two Gladstones. I looked out on the city, building after building, most in the construction stage, pigs rooting in the streets, gangs of orphan kids who live like rats in the cellars and tunnels, houses so damn big you'd never find all of the rooms. It depressed me, it was too much and too fast.

I carried my bags back to Sally's brothel. Tusco must have been at a window, for I was just setting the bags down when the door swung open. I stepped inside and Tusco shut the door. He plucked the bags from my hands and escorted me to a different room. This one was on the fifth floor, and was painted in cream and pale blue, had a canopied bed, and a lot of flimsy-lookin' furniture it must have taken a lot of Frog years to whittle out. The view from the window went out up Michigan Avenue, with the fancy carriages and the starving kids and the drunkards in the doors and hedges. I drew the drapes.

There was a decanter and two glasses on the little table by the bed. I had a dram—old and well-cured brandy—and I took off my boots and lit a seegar and stared at the cream and gilt ceiling.

There was a tap at the door. I grunted and Sally slipped in. She was about half dressed for her evening. She took off her half and I took off my whole and we screwed in every position we could think of, some so absurd that we would laugh and fall flat on our backs.

She put herself up on one elbow and smiled at me.

"Luther, don't let us say goodbye. I'll see you the next time. Your dinner will be brought, you can have your pick of the girls, there's gambling on the third floor, and if you go out the back way to the carriage house, there will be cockfighting on the second floor."

"The next time may be tonight, Sal."

"To hell with you, Luther Kelly," she said, and flounced off.

Jack joined me for dinner, and after the first couple of whiskeys his appetite and his eyes got a little luster. We was served by two chippies didn't have enough on to wad a shotgun with. Neither Jack nor me is interested in parties of more than two, so he hauled his one off to his room and I shook my head. The girl frowned and then shrugged and left the room, dragging the dinner cart with her.

I wandered around, sat for a while in the gaming room which had whist and poker tables and roulette wheels, and finally bought into one game and was several hundred dollars ahead when I decided to get some fresh air. I bade my partners a fond thank-you. (Their contributions would

more than defray my expenses for the trip—gifts and
telegrams, tickets and tips and all—to Oneida and back to
Fort Buford.)

There was a fire escape in the rear of the house and an
iron catwalk which went across the yard to the second
floor of the carriage house. I moseyed across, my city
boots slick and gripless on the cast-iron grates. I let myself
in and watched the fights. There was a pair of reds in first,
a short quick fight, with the smaller cock kicking lucky and
piercing the other's heart. I watched about fifteen fights—I
have always liked cockfighting, ever since I looked into a
chicken's eye.

I drank too much, but for a man in my position quite
sparingly, and picked the Irish girl to spend the night. I
went to sleep, and woke to the sound of the church bells
ringing—which made me laugh.

As I was finishing my breakfast, Texas Jack hove into
view, and he looked like hell on the half shell.

Texas Jack held his head in his hands, and I finally had
the girl waiting on us bring him a concoction of raw eggs
and tomato juice and gin in a huge mug.

"Quit moaning, you stupid sonofabitch. Tell you what.
You drink that without comin' up for air, and keep it
down—no practicing, hear—and I'll come on your next
summer's Nob explorations."

Jack looked up, complexion all ruddy again, and said,
"Why, Luther!" Poured down the goddamn drink, wiped
his face, hollered for a beefsteak and some whiskey,
and said we'd meet in St. Louis on the twentieth of
June.

"Put 'er here, Kelly," he says, thrusting out a paw.

I shook hands. "Omohundro," I says, "I will not rest
until I nail you for this disgusting trick."

Stalking to the door in what shreds of dignity I still had,
I made the mistake of pausing.

"Keep your trap civil-like around the boss, Kelly," he said.

All right, Texas Jack Omohundro, you coyote, you . . . You want to play, we'll play.

I didn't stop shaking with rage until the train pulled out. And I thought and thought and thought all the way to my mother's home.

12

I'd not been home in more than a decade, and I got a mite more uncomfortable with each passed mile that brought me closer to the place I was fetched up in. I hadn't wired ahead. It ain't my nature to wander into any ambush, and believe me the past can be a patient bushwacker. I wanted to be a small target or none at all.

You can imagine my joy when I saw half the goddamn town, a brass band, and a large banner welcoming *Yellowstones* (sic) *Kelly* (well, they got that right). I suspected the black hand of Texas Jack Omohundro—and about forty others of my chums. All them long nights staring at the stars whilst listening for snapping twigs and the like seems to put in us an urge to play practical jokes upon one another, and if life or limb is lost, the laughter is even harder.

The mayor was there with a key made out of pine and painted with gilt, and my doting family with their assorted spouses, brats, infants, in-laws, out-laws, and hangers-on wasn't much above a couple hundred folks. They had newspaper reporters and a medium-sized Salvation Army band trying to match tootle for tootle and clang for clang the brass band of the local Odd Fellows.

My mother was standing a bit forward, smack in the middle of the red carpet. The engineer of the train got caught up in the festivities and tooted his horn and whistled his whistle. This was a signal for all of the menfolks in the crowd to whip their revolvers out and fire a raggedy-ass salute.

I stepped down on a gilded cast-iron railroad step, with the conductor reaching for my hand as if I was some goddamn debutante.

The mayor waddled over to hand me the key to the city (when I had left there was one general store) and beneath the undulating rolls of fat was the face of that goddamn lardy little weasel Arthur Tooele, whose block I had knocked off so many times it was beginning to look spherical from rolling—you know the type, the fat kid whose one talent is sweating and smelling bad. Must have inherited the General Store. Gave me a hand felt like a pint of oysters in rancid grease.

I graciously took the key and walked to my mother, straight as a young birch, hair all white now, and the same deep gray eyes. I bent to kiss her on the cheek, and as I did so she whispered:

"Luther, you behave yourself, for I have seen that look upon your face before. Starting at about two years of age."

"Yes'm," I whispered back. Then a tide of my brothers and sisters engulfed me. Two stout lads who resembled faintly my snot-nosed four- and five-year-old brothers lifted me to their brawny shoulders, and I was borne triumphantly down the street, waving and smiling and thinking I was going to nail Texas Jack Omohundro's balls to a fatwood stump and set the stump on fire.

Folks started hollering for a speech, and I am good at

nothing but a mumble-and-grunt (one of my nicknames
was "The Sphinx"), but nevertheless was deposited in a
sort of temporary pulpit nailed to the side of a chestnut
tree. I get eloquent when I get mad, and so with Jack
Omohundro's face dancing in the back of my mind, I
beamed and smiled upon the crowd and held my arms out
to my sides (wishing I could fly) and grinned back at the
throng like a damn ninny.

The whistles, claps, and hoots died down and I cleared
my throat and knotted my hands behind my back (thinking
of Jack's neck) and smiled like a loon, vowing never to set
foot in this goddamn place ever again.

"Friends, family, ladies and gentlemen, I am deeply
touched by your warm welcome (why can't you mind your
own damn business). When I left here twelve years ago I
never dreamed it would be so long before I was back
among you (and you ain't seen nothing in the way of
absences yet). It warms my heart (and I will warm Texas
Jack Omohundro's balls) and gladdens me that you would
remember me (and when I find the bastard or bastards
who sold you this pack of lies . . .) and turn out today to
welcome me. It has been a long journey but a worthwhile
one and I must repair to my mother's home and the
bosom of my family and listen to what has transpired in
my absence. (How many god damn nieces and nephews
am I hung with?) The Plains Indian Wars are over (we
poisoned and diseased 'em out) with the capitulation of
Chief Joseph."

Cheers! Horrahs! Huzzahs!

"Thank you friends for such a warm welcome." (I hope
Texas Jack fries in hell.)

I tried to make a run for it, but nothing would do but
these giants I remembered as grubby little buggers of
brothers must bear me in triumph to the ancestral hall,
nearly beating my brains out on the signs hanging from

the storefronts in the process. I smiled and thought of what I was going to do to Texas Jack Omohundro.

I was deposited in a disheveled heap on the front porch of our modest white frame house and I turned to wave to my admirers. There was one man on horseback at the back of the mob. He was so tiny he looked like a jockey on the thoroughbred he was riding. He waved at me, he waved a foolscap notebook. He took off his hat and waved that. It was George Hanks, correspondent for the *Hartford Courant*. He smiled and spurred his horse. I smiled and waved. All right, George, I thought, I deserved that.

Dinner was laid on. The house was crowded with people who were related to me, more than half of whom I did not know. Was this slender beauty with the sad brown eyes my little sister Dierdre? Yup. Had two kids and was married to a dull-looking fellow named George—had a hardware store and a sawmill. So forth and so on. There were several hundred copies of a pulp tract supposedly authored by me, and I was to sign it. I wouldn't, because it was a pack of lies. Sad faces, especially the young boys. I was about to set the record straight when I caught my mother's eye across the room. She shook her head no. (Dear family, for the last twelve years I have been slaughtering buffalo, slaughtering Indians, whoring, looking for stolen gold, poisoning wolves, and watching dyed-in-the-wool fools in Army blue hack to pieces people who hadn't any idea what we meant with those words on the treaties anyway. It's been downright ennobling.)

I was placed at the seat of honor at my mother's right hand, and long-thought-out arrangements for the kids were put into effect with only minor snags, like one of the four-year-old boys dropping a pitcher of lemonade and sending gouts of sweet sticky liquid and shards of ice into one corner of the sitting room like a cannon shot. I like that kid, I thinks; definitely shows promise. (I'd seen the look of evil on the little bastard's face before he faked stumbling.) Wonder who he is?

The room grew silent and everyone looked down the length of the main table. A cadaverous-looking parson, with a face that suggested he lived entirely on a diet of codfish with the bones in, rose to say grace. He cleared his throat and began a squeaky peroration which addressed the sins of the world while the food chilled. It took twenty minutes—and two sharp kicks from my mother, who caught me looking at a quart relish bottle in front of me and figuring elevations and trajectories—before he was done squawking.

When this vulpine leech had finished and the hubbub and clank and clatter of knives and forks on plates full of cold food began, I leaned over to my mother and said, "Ma, what in god's name is that?"

"The Reverend Dr. Spaulding," my mother said. "He is the head of the St. James Academy for young women here, and highly thought of in the community."

"Are any of my sisters in school there?"

"Yes, your sister Camille. And two of your brother-in-laws teach there. And he holds a note on the farm."

"Oh," I said, "how much of a note?"

"Three thousand dollars."

"Why did you mortgage the place?"

"We had a fire, and three bad years of crops, and your brother Robert was ill and finally died, and he was the only one old enough to do the work."

"I'm sorry," I said. "I didn't even notice that Bob was gone."

"Twelve years is a long time."

I looked down at the Rev. Mr. Codfish-with-the-bones-in and smiled, receiving a wintry grin in return.

So went the day and the evening. At last, all but Camille, my mother and myself were gone to their respective homes.

"I'm going to buy your note," I said, when Ma and me were sitting before the fire.

"I don't know if he will sell it to you, Luther," she said. "He's horrible, and he has proposed marriage to me. He came here about eight years ago, when the academy was founded. He has money of his own and Church of England money, too. His hold on the town is extraordinary. He seems to have an uncanny instinct for where his money will give him the greatest chokehold on the community."

"So that's why he was at dinner?"

My mother nodded.

"I'll take care of it," I said. The fire crackled low and I studied it long after she had gone to bed.

13

I bought the note from the Reverend Dr. Spaulding the next day, with no trouble. I thought the matter was over, and went hunting for grouse with two of my brothers. The matter was not over.

It seemed that both my brothers had opened their law practices without the usual beggaring partnership with an established attorney. The good Doctor had advanced them money at a stiff rate, and taken notes on their homes and some odd lots of property around Oneida that the family had owned since the first one of us showed up hereabouts in 1716. I was beginning to take a strong dislike to the man.

Curious as to why a man of the cloth should be so heavily involved in usury and such decidedly unspiritual matters, I moseyed on down to New York and paid a call on the Bishop. The Bishop concurred that yes, Spaulding was an ordained minister, and yes, he had founded the St. James Academy for Women, and as to the peculations he'd no idea and, since no church funds were involved, no interest in the matter. I was shown the door, wondering what his cut was.

I stayed in New York a week, looking here, looking there, amazed at the sheer energy of this most frazzling of our cities and ports. I went to Broadway and to the burlesque. I spent a great deal of time at McSorley's, eating white onions and good bread, and drinking a good deal of porter and Irish whiskey.

When an Indian goes hunting, he dreams of what it is that he hunts. He dreams buffalo, or deer, or wapiti, or birds. When what he dreams of comes, then the dream and the hunt are both finished. I dreamed of the Reverend Dr. Spaulding. I was not ready to return to Oneida. So I went to Lake George and spent a couple of days on the *Sagamore* eating and drinking and sleeping and watching the lake get ready to freeze.

The first morning that I was on board I emerged from my stateroom only to be promptly bowled over by a short young man with glasses a half inch thick and a display of ivory so dazzling I would fear for him if he were to go to the Arctic. This was the first time I met Teddy Roosevelt. We were groping around in the half light trying to find his specs. The specs had gone overboard, we decided, and so I led him back to his cabin where he kept a gross or so of the things for occasions such as this, which were frequent in occurrence.

I liked him. He had been asthmatic and sickly, and had built himself up by a regimen of exercise that would have killed me. He was forever braining himself with Indian clubs, or lifting weights until his joints cracked, or some damn-fool stunt. He fell overboard three times in one crossing of the lake, because the day was choppy and his glasses got blurred. I kept near him, to toss him life rings and life lines and such, and fetch another dozen pairs of specs as needed. He wouldn't drink anything with alcohol in it, but wouldn't say why. (Years later I found out that his older brother, Elliot, had killed himself with booze.)

Teddy came bursting into the grog shop one afternoon, wriggling like a pup smelling his first bird, and said, "You are laggard, sir, laggard in telling me that you are the famous scout, none other than Yellowstone Kelly. Laggard!"

"Theodore," I said calmly, "my name is Luther Kelly. I have on occasion scouted for the Army, and so have several hundred other men."

"I must come out west! You must guide me. Capital!"

I looked at the row of gleaming teeth. Oh dear god, I thought. Oh, shit.

"You simply *must* guide me on a hunting expedition!" he went on, his face a faint ruddy glow behind them monstrous choppers.

I had a bright idea. It was such a bright idea that I signaled for another drink. I'm even dumber than I look, and on those rare occasions when I can make a leap the size I was now looking at, it just makes me glow all over.

"Theodore," says I (one learned quickly that calling Teddy "Theodore" had a calming influence), "let's go back to the taffrail. I need some of your help."

"Just say the word," says Teddy, smiling, me thinking that if you just planted the fool's feet in concrete he'd make a splendid lighthouse. His damn teeth made my eyes ache every time a light hit them.

"I have this problem," I began, and I explained everything about Oneida, Spaulding, and my mother to him. He looked grave, very grave.

"Seems a bad business," says Teddy. "I shall telegraph Mr. Root at the next opportunity. A very bad business. Yes."

"Give me enough of a head start so I can be in Oneida," I says.

We parted at the dock of Lake George Village, and I caught the train to Schenectady, Utica, and finally Oneida.

It was well after dark before I stomped up the stairs at my mother's place. The house was dark above, and brightly lit below. I went in, stomping the wet and the snow from my boots. The floor in the hall sounded hollow as a drum. My moustache was wet from my breath, and I could still hear the wheels of the little inter-city passenger train, a double tunk-tunk so soporific that a smart dentist might have put his shop in one of the coaches, to save his customers pain.

It was the wheels must have done it, for I was putting my coat on a hook when it suddenly swum up through my brain—I could hear my mother's voice, breathless and angry, and some scuffling sounds in the parlor.

Spaulding had been pawing away at Ma, and was so far gone in the bug-eyed snorts that I could have knocked the door flat and he'd have paid it no mind. I stalked into the parlor and wrapped my arm around his neck with my fist in the back of his head, the way you take a sentry quiet-like, and he went limp in my arms in a few seconds.

My mother sat on the couch, and tried to remedy her mussed-up state as best she could, automatic gestures, while she made herself breathe deep and slow.

"Luther," she said in a hoarse whisper, "don't kill him. I know you have killed, I can see it in your face."

"I'm taking this bastard to the jail," I said, "and no, I won't kill him."

She nodded.

I carried Spaulding over my shoulder to the porch—for all of his height he didn't weigh no more than a sack of spuds—and I hitched up a little bay mare to the poles of a sleigh. Upstate New York gets more snow than the Missouri headwaters, if you leave out the mountains above nine thousand feet. It was sleighs from November to April.

There was one sleepy-looking Irish constable at the desk, and the sounds of a couple of drunks trying without much success to harmonize baritone and tenor pukings in

the marble disorderly conduct tank, or St. Pat's Cathedral,
as it was known in Oneida.

I explained what had brought me standing here with a
black clad scarecrow over my right shoulder, and the Irish
kid scuttled off up the street to fetch the sergeant, who
was thawing out his tonsils in McGillery's Saloon.

The sergeant came back at a run, and he had a fire like
Coran cor Amaran burning bright below his thick white
eyebrows.

"Molestin' that nice Mrs. Kelly, is it?" he growls. "How
like the Church of England. This way, sor, if ye don't
mind."

The sergeant led me and my offal back to a cell, and I
tossed the bastard down on the bare springs like so much
sour laundry.

"Ye'll bring yer mother in to prefer charges," says the
sergeant.

"You know Mrs. Kelly," I says. "By mornin' she'll have
forgiven him. But keep him in overnight, if you would,
since I'd gladly kill the bastard, except that Mrs. Kelly—
my mother—made me promise that I wouldn't."

I went home, and stayed up well past dawn, too angry
to sleep. Ma hadn't had liquor in the house since Pa left,
but I did have some emergency Tanglefoot in my Glad-
stone, and I made hot toddies and then cold with water,
and then straight out of the bottle. I still couldn't sleep,
drunk as I was. I stared out of the window and wondered
how soon I could go away to where I felt comfortable, out
where all there was to talk to was the wind and your
horses.

Ma got up, and looked as fresh as though nothing had
happened. She bustled about in the kitchen and made
coffee and sweet rolls and three kinds of eggs. I ate damn
near all of it, and went back to my chair and my brooding.
I felt the dread twitch.

"Oh, god," I said out loud, "damn it to hell. No!"

Gout. I may tell you that I don't drink out there because it spoils my distance vision (which it does) or makes me a bit less keen (which it does), but the real reason that I don't drink out there is that after a couple of weeks I have the world's most painful big toe. It swells up, and gnats coughing in the next valley over send jolts of pain like Morse pulses up my leg and into my brain. I keep telling myself not to blow the goddamn toe off with my buffalo rifle. I chant that like a canticle at times.

Ma heard my moans and curses and came quietly into the parlor, looking with concern upon my empurpled face and the murderous expression in my eyes. How do you murder your own toe? There is no god, gentlemen.

"Luther," she says, wiping her hands on her apron, "whatever is the matter?"

"I am . . . having . . . an . . . attack . . . AARGH . . . of the . . . gout, Ma," I says, straining the words through my clenched teeth.

"Mrs. Eddy says that it is all in your mind and you must have faith and tell yourself that it doesn't hurt."

"Why don't . . . you go ask this Mrs. Eddy . . . OOOOOH . . . if she's . . . ever had the . . . AHHHHHH . . . GOD DAMNED . . . GOUT!"

"Luther, you are swearing in my house. And to answer your question, I think that if Mrs. Eddy had gout she simply would not notice it and it would go away. Now I am going to make you a nice cup of tea."

Every time I talk to a woman about some things I am left gapemouthed and wishing terribly that I had a large dog with a heavily callused butt.

I sat seething, watching my toe swell and turn red as a switchman's lantern, and wondering in my present state whether I would have the stuff to be polite to my ma through all of this. She had my father and six boys to contend with before my two sisters came along, and she had lots of practice in setting us about each other's ears so we would stay out of her hair. At any given time in my youth a couple of the family males would be beating each other witless in the back yard while the others were splitting wood and shoveling manure to work off bad cases of enraged bafflement.

The tea she brought was red willow-bark tea. Be damned to Mrs. Eddy, I says; it was the only thing that would touch my infernal toe.

"This wouldn't happen to you if you didn't drink so much," said my mother, down to the arrows of advice in her quiver. "I pray every night that you don't turn out like your father."

That is an Irish prayer, and an Irish story is the one where the foolish young man cuts out his mother's heart as a gift for his demon love, and as he goes down the forest path to her bower he stumbles and falls, and the bloody heart in his hands says, "Oh, I hope you didn't hurt yourself, my son."

The willow-bark tea reduced the daggers of pain to dull throbs just about as bad on the weak fabric of my temper as the shooting twinges.

I had spotted a case of Saratoga Springs mineral water on the landing of the basement stairwell, and my mother brought me several bottles—gout has something to do with acid. Worst attack I ever had was after a drunken night in California where the tipple was a tart white wine.

There was a rattle at the front door, and I heard the rustle of my mother's petticoats crossing the Turkey carpet, and the slight squeal of the hinges, needing oil this winter.

Two sets of footsteps approached my lair, one my mother's, the other a heavy and methodical plod-plod. The plod was the sergeant of the night before, he of the bushy brows and the clotted-cream brogue.

"There has been a terrible tragedy," my mother says. "It seems that Dr. Spaulding has hanged himself in his cell."

"Really?" I says, to the first good news of the day. "Remorse is a terrible thing, they say. Well, that's that."

"If ye wouldn't mind, ma'am," says the sergeant, "I'd have a quiet word with yer son here—it's standard for the inquest procedure, ye know."

"Of course," my mother says brightly. "I'll put the pot on, and you just call when you are ready for tea."

"Thank ye, ma'am," says the sergeant.

My mother bustled off, and closed the door behind her. I was wondering what in blazes the sergeant could possibly want with me.

"He hanged himself in his cell, Mr. Kelly," says the sergeant. "With his belt it was."

My ears shot up. Spaulding had been wearing suspenders, but not a belt.

"Was he still breathin' when ye brought him in, Mr. Kelly?"

Ah hah.

"Yes," I says. "If you recall, he choked a couple of times when I threw him down on the cot."

"I didn't hear that—the chokin', I mean," says the sergeant, "so it will be hard to fix the time of death. Thanks for yer cooperation."

I grinned at him. He grinned at me. I pointed at the sideboard, where I had stashed a bottle of Rittenhouse Rye. The sergeant poured himself a generous dram—about a pint—and drank it like it was iced tea on a hot day. He made a perfunctory gesture toward me. I shook my head and pointed to my incandescent big toe.

"Sor," he says, "if ye don't mind me sayin' so, ye might try a bit of lighthouse keepin' with that—ye'd just have to sit with it in front of the Fresnel lens and do a few wee adjustments to the mirrors, and they could see the light from the Jersey shore to Liverpool."

"Liverpool is the capital of Ireland," I half snarls, "and

it sure is damned shameful old Spaulding took everything so much to heart."

"Oh, that it is, that it is, sor," twinkled Sergeant Swift.

When he left, he had the rest of my rye in his jersey pocket, and I had a good map of where the cowflops were, should the coroner feel obliged to get nosy.

I've never known if Teddy's message was sent to Root at all, but it might have been. If there was a favor done, it ain't the sort you write a grateful note on.

14

Me and my family had jawed each other to a draw after another week, and my toe got civilized again. I told myself a few hundred times to see Wolf Tail, the old medicine man who lived a few miles south of the Great Bend of the Yellowstone, and get an Indian herbal remedy for my treacherous toe. Always the right toe.

I had expected to hear from Theodore Roosevelt, but there was nary a peep or the sign of his gleaming molars and canines and choppers anywhere to be seen, which was fine by me. You ever meet someone you *knew* was going to be a whole hell of a lot of trouble, and there was no way in hell you could avoid it? Teddy hadn't a mean or devious bone in his body, but those of us who were tossed around in his wake all tended toward the same glazed expression and exhibited fearful scars and wounds of body and soul, the results of ricochets off Teddy's invulnerable self-delusion. Well, he was a great man.

The train ride to Chicago was uneventful, and the

weather on the southern tip of Lake Michigan had turned
to the raw bluster that was Chicago's climate from December until May. The streets still teemed with people, but
their faces was all wrapped with mufflers of wool and they
pretty much coughed and sneezed all the time.

I stayed at Sally's for a couple of nights, but the sheer
numbers of people was choking me. My dreams was bad
and confusing and I would wake up in the middle of
the night sweating something fierce, with the chippie
of the evening way over on the side of the bed to escape
the ponds of salt water that ran from my pores.

The last day I was there was a Tuesday, and I took Sal to
a late breakfast at the Black Hawk. We dawdled over
champagne and delicacies and like any good friends we
had a hard time thinking of things to talk about that would
avoid the unlucky subject of goodbyes.

"Luther," said Sal finally, "I can't stand this. Take me
home."

I had a cabbie drop her off—she asked me not to walk
her to the door, and I was somewhat confused as to what
was upsetting her. Now I know that it was one of them
itches you can't scratch, and that there was nothing to be
done.

The whole trip had been a puzzlement. My family was
strangers, Sal seemed put in a snit by my mere presence,
I was about half wild with one of them nameless fears
when I began to think about the sheer numbers of white
folks livin' in each other's pockets, and all in all I decided
that I wouldn't come back for a good long spell. The year
1877 was fast drawing to a close and good riddance. If I
had knowed what 1878 was holding for me I'd have gone
back to Oneida and taken up a good trade—house-painting
or saddlemaking or such, but the only kind thing about
the future is it ain't happened yet. And that's enough.

Jim Hill was stealing and lying to fund his railroad—
he'd sent a brilliant young prospector/engineer name of

Hamilton to the west, and the youngster had discovered Marias Pass, a railroad man's dream—easy slopes up and down and lower than any other in the Northern Rockies. I took trains as far as what was to be Bismarck—though it is true that the last two hundred miles was on huffer-puffers, tenders for the track-laying crews.

Fort Buford was just as squalid as when I left. Well, a little better, because the clean white snow had covered over a lot of the trash and offal and Indians who had died of drink, and none of that would show until April, when the soldiers would have to police the muddy ground to keep typhoid fever away.

I collected my traps and possibles, bought overpriced supplies and a few hundred dollars of good trade goods, and took my little string of pack animals out into the Big White (in winter; in summer, the Big Dry. In winter the snow could drift eighty feet deep, leveling the land cut by an arroyo or coulee—if you wandered out in one you would sink like a rock into feathers. Slow, too—a few fractions of an inch a minute until you suffocated) and headed for the spot where I planned to join up with Buffalo Horn.

The winter of '77-78 had come on hard and fast to the Northern Plains. Though the Yellowstone and the Missouri were still ice-free at Fort Buford (they join there) it wouldn't be long until both rivers was shut fast and tight.

The Army was through with winter campaigns. They weren't doing much in the way of Indian fighting, except down in the New Mexico Territory, where about ten thousand troops were trying to catch about two hundred Apaches, and having damn little luck. The Sioux and Cheyennes was broke, the Arapahoes and Blackfeet was being ravaged by smallpox. It was smallpox, syphilis, and trade whiskey done in the Horse Indians, not our gallant Army. Starvation helped, too.

My old friends the Crows had stayed pretty much away

from the white man's water-that-banishes-reason, but every other tribe from the Plains was represented in the
ragged filthy mob of beggars camped outside the fort's
walls. You could buy a woman for as little as a shot of
whiskey, kill her if you liked. It made me sick and it made
me angry. I have always liked the Indians, liked the way
that they treated their children and their way of looking at
the world and the heavens. There were toddlers half
naked and filthy, lice-ridden, and blind, their eyes covered
with whitish clouded scars from gonorrhea.

The buffalo hunters was working up from the marginally
milder southern Great Plains toward the north. A couple
of Pennsylvania Germans had discovered a way to make
good leather out of the hides—good leather meant hard
and stiff, for shoes and trunks and such, not soft-tanned
the Indian way—and there was hundreds if not thousands
of hide hunters killing buffalo, as many as three hundred
apiece in a single day, peeling the hides and cutting out
the tongue, and leaving the rest to rot. The scavengers
couldn't near keep up with the tons of rotten meat.

Old Bill Sherman had remarked that to subdue the
Plains tribes it was necessary only to kill the buffalo, and
he was right. I had met Sherman several times. He had
one of the strangest minds I have ever encountered. He
was soft-spoken and courteous, and utterly ruthless. Most
folks have heard the famous line "War is Hell" but very
few know that the next sentence was "And wars are won
and lost with the lives of human beings and no eloquence
or rhetoric can make it less so." He'd ground the Rebels to
powder on the Tennessee and then burnt the South's belly
out with his march through Georgia, and had been seriously thought of as a Presidential candidate to succeed
Grant. Sherman hated politicians and he would cheerfully
have hanged every newspaperman in the country, but he
did the bidding of both and chewed on his beard. He had

the mangiest looking beard I ever saw, for a famous man, I mean.

I made arrangements with a couple of teamsters, Reilly and Grogan, to follow along and pick up our peltries and cart them down to the pickup points along the Yellowstone. They come highly recommended—they would steal only the usual amount—and since they was paid piecework I didn't give a damn how much they drank. One of the two was sober enough to sign the contract with me—his partner was suffering the deliriums off in a lean-to near the stables. A steady diet of trade whiskey made a man crazy at first and then made him dead.

"When we takes off," says Reilly, blowin' breath at me smelled like the Devil's Privy, "Grogan will be shakin' so bad he won't be able to keep his hat on his head for the first few days, but he'll be right after that."

"Fine," I says. "Just remember where I told you to go and how I mark my pelts. Won't do you no good to try to sell my pelts—the housemen all know my mark."

True enough. Oh, they could try to run them all the way up into Canada, through a few hundred miles of hostiles and strange country, but that weren't worth the effort. I trusted the drunken bastards so much that either Buffalo Horn or me would check on them time to time anyway.

I left Fort Buford in the middle of the night, since that would put me at an odd place to camp when the sun come up. I skirted the mouth of the Big Horn proper and cast a wide circle looking for signs of Buffalo Horn. Our code is slashed willow tips, the cut ends pointing in the direction gone, the number of tips the days until returning. I followed along, until the tips numbered two, and I could see Buffalo Horn's fire signs and knew he was somewhere fairly close by.

There wasn't much snow on the ground yet. There was a crisp, wet, icy smell in the north wind, which told me it was snowing like blazes a hundred miles north. My weather sense told me it was going to get mean cold soon. About midafternoon I saw two sundogs appear, one on either side of the sun, and damn near as bright. I knew that meant that the temperature was going to fall like a rock through the air and stay at fifty below zero for a week or two. I commenced to look for a good place to hole up until the weather warmed and I could piss without sounding like a string of firecrackers.

I come up over a little rise and saw about twenty buffalo before me, pawing at the cured grass, hunkering their shoulders against a wind suddenly turned mean and cold. I looked to the north, and saw the wind that the Blackfeet call "Kas'sa'poo'intay," a high, cold tide of snow-laden air, the grains of snow tiny as sugar pounded fine, and deadly. The white dust would come with your breath into your lungs and freeze the tissue—and three days later you'd be dead of gangrene pneumonia. I thought of Sally's nice warm whorehouse and swore to bust myself in the chops for being so stupid if I lived through this.

I had two rifles with me—a 45-120 buffalo rifle good to over a thousand yards, and a little lever-action 35-40 to get camp meat with. It was still pretty warm out, maybe zero, so I hobbled my horses and sneaked over toward where the buffalo was. They had decided to stay and wasn't spooky, more afraid of the north wind than they was of wolves. The wolves was running belly-low to the ground for their dens right now, and wouldn't have stopped for a porterhouse steak if it was cooked right and left on the path in front of them. I rested my little 35-40 on a rock—setting my mittens on the ground—and drew a careful bead on a fat young cow about sixty yards away.

There is just two spots on a buffalo, shooting from the side, that will drop the critter for sure in its tracks—I didn't have time to trail a bleeder just now. I squinted down the barrel and put the leaf of the front sight on the spot in the neck and squeezed the trigger.

The cow dropped—dead before she hit the ground, likely—and the others snorted and took off and were over the hill in a minute. The wind was rising, and it had a nasty keening wail in it. I stood up and glanced behind me and there was six Indians around my horses and mules and every one of the six had a rifle, though out of politeness only one or two had their long guns pointed at something vital in me.

They was River Crows, and it was just my luck that they was from one of the far northwest bands I had never come in contact with, so they did what Crows do. The Crows are a peaceable people—hell, they'll tell you so, and they told me now—and all that they do is rob you. No self-respecting Crow will kill a white man, and they wish all white men well. They hope, after they have peeled you down to the last layer, that you will return to the white men's stores and get a fresh outfit and come back so they can peel you again. Third time they peel you, they admit you into the tribe because your mind's broke and they feel sorry for you.

They left me a pocketknife and my pants and shirt and woolen vest. There I stood in my stocking feet watching them ride off, with a Blue Norther blowin' down from Canada.

The last Crow rode my horse up to me and tossed my boots on the ground in front of me.

"You can have these back," he says, in sign lingo. "We don't have anybody with feet that big." He gave me a cheerful grin and followed the others.

I figured I had about one chance in ten of making it through the cold spell that even now was arriving. I commenced to skinning the cow out with my pocketknife. It took me nearly an hour and time I had the cow's hide peeled it was getting near dark and the wind was howling like the Furies. The wolves were howling from the doors of their dens and the coyotes' cries sounded like farewell speeches from old sopranos.

I dragged the stiffening hide over to a clump of sagebrush that would screen out maybe ten percent of the wind and I rolled up in the buffalo hide, hair side in, as tight as I could. My hands was too cold to use the flint and steel I still had, and anyway I was too far from wood to keep any size of a fire going. I buried my face in the woolly fur and went to sleep.

The Blue Northers, when they first come, don't blow along the ground like the wind before a summer thunderstorm. The howling is high overhead. Then the Blue Norther's bellies creep closer, and it sounds like an approaching army firing on occasion at skirmishers. Trees with water in them freeze and go CRACK. The reports woke me back up. I had a double layer of fur and hide, plus my clothing and boots. The reports stopped, and me and the fleas and the odd tick all went to sleep.

I woke up several hours or days later. Something was tugging at my improvised bedroll. I tried to move, and reached for the rifle that wasn't there anyway. My arm went about a good sixteenth of an inch. The god damned buffalo hide was frozen steel-hard. I had a wolf or two gnawing at the scraps of meat on the hide whilst the rest of the pack was tucking into the buffalo cow.

Jaysus, Kelly, I thought. I entertained myself for a while calling myself names, though there really wasn't much else that I could have done. I couldn't even hear much of what was going on outside, I was so tightly wrapped.

Yellowstone Kelly, I says to myself, Legendary Great Buffalo Crepe of the Northern Plains. Died with dignity as a side dish at a wolves' banquet.

I couldn't have been getting enough air, for I managed to go to sleep again.

15

My bladder woke me, as full as it felt like getting. I twitched and wriggled, and got about as much freedom of movement as I would have had if I had been dipped in thick varnish. By straining my neck and rolling my left eye damn near out of the socket, I could see a tiny patch of light. So I had slept through a long winter night. Then something tapped on my hide—not my own personal hide, the buffalo robe I was rolled up in. I had no idea who it was, but as it didn't sound like wolf fangs, who or whatever it was was just fine by me. I just wanted to piss once before I died.

Taptaptaptaptaptap. What with the buffalo hair in my ears and the wool scarf I had wrapped round my head like a granny with a toothache, I could feel much better than I could hear. There was a faint tearing sound, and the grip of the buffalo robe relaxed a tiny bit. Now that hope had returned, my bladder commenced to throb.

Taptaptaptaptaptaptap. Someone was using a knife or a

hatchet to cut the frozen hide. The hide gripping my head and ears relaxed, and I heard a snatch of song. Sung with a thick Bannock accent.

> *Oooooooh, the elders of the village,*
> *they was too old to firk,*
> *So they sat around the table*
> *and they had a circle jerk,*
> *'Twas the finest ball that Kirremuir*
> *had had or ever been,*
> *Hip hip hurrah*
> *and pass the brandy o-ver.*

It was Buffalo Horn, of course, reciting from memory one of the hundreds of verses to that wretched ballad he'd got off the titled drunks he'd been nursemaiding (along with Texas Jack, who drew no sober breath once out of sight of the white settlements). Old Horn had a marvelous ear for languages, rather like a parrot—no idea what the noises meant, and happy to repeat them.

Horn kicked me over—he wasn't overlavish with the sympathy, you see—and commenced to hack away at the other side of my *crepe de bison*. He had a cheerful disregard for whatever parts of mine should chance to be commingled with the buffalo's, the bastard. Presently the hide parted, sort of like a great hairy clamshell, and I was able to blink at the fierce light and wince at the fierce cold.

I didn't so much as thank him, and wasn't even fully to my feet when I began clawing at my flies to drag out my pecker and piss. It was still fifty below, and the yellow stream sounded like a tubercular Gatling gun—it literally tinkled on the frozen grass like glass shards on a stone floor.

"Ah, Kelly," says the Bannock son-of-a-bitch, "I shall long enjoy telling this tale around the fires of my people and to the English hunters, who will then give me good tips. Henh!" All of this was much muffled by the wolf-fur ruff on his heavy buffalo coat. He took it off and handed it to me.

"We must go, before we both freeze," he says, and sets off at a slow trot—it's fatal to breathe deeply in weather this cold. I followed, already shivering like a wet dog. My pecker burned like it was scalded.

Buffalo Horn had made a good camp in a coulee about a mile from where I damn near met my doom, a lean-to covered with brush and green hides, with a good supply of dry wood and parfleches of pemmican hanging from the poles that held up the roof. He built the fire up in a hurry and I got out of my duds and into some clean dry things he had. This damn weather will murder you with your own sweat and breath.

"The wolves had almost gnawed through the hide over your butt," says Buffalo Horn. "Haw, haw, haw."

"Don't take much to amuse you, does it?" I says. "And I am much obliged all of the same. You got any coffee?"

He nodded and plopped an enamelware coffeepot on the coals. I was still shivering, but the cold was lessening in me and my bones didn't feel like they was made of ice any more.

We hunkered down for the next three days, playing dice and an Indian game of mumblety-peg, and when those diversions palled we mended gear or told lies.

The cold snap lifted gradually, warmer air from the west came and things began to move on the land again. When we heard the screech of a Canada jay we knew it was time to have a look about.

Buffalo Horn had left his ponies in a little dingle out of the wind, where there was good cured grass and some brush to hole up in. They was covered with rimes of ice and had long icicles hanging from their lips—their mouths were chapped and bloody, but they were alive.

It took the rest of the day for us to tend the horses and

such—it was close on the longest darknesses of the year—
and it was still chilly enough so I had no notions of going
after the Crows in the dark.

"There were six of them and there are two of us, Kelly,"
says Buffalo Horn, as we munched our pemmican that
evening. "Do you think we can kill them?"

"They are already dead," I says. "And I'll bet not over
three miles from here."

Horn grunted and went back to his meal, and drank
about a quart of boiling hot coffee, and went to sleep. If
tomorrow was a battle, it was a good day to die in, and if
not, a good day to live in. Like I said, I have always
admired the Indians, and how they look at things.

The next day we circled wide and found some faint
traces of the Crow trail. Didn't need them, as it turned
out; from the hillock behind our lean-to we could have
seen the birds gathering—magpies and ravens and kites.
We rode cautious-like toward the Crow camp. Two big
loafer wolves was staggering around the camp, almost
dead of the strychnine in the Indians.

I always carried a couple of bottles of trade whiskey
laced with strychnine stuck innocent-like in my possible
sacks, for occasions such as happened with the Crows a
few days ago. The Crows had got a camp together and
celebrated, passing the filthy mixture rapidly around. Only
one of them was outside the lean-to—and not a pretty
sight. The birds had mostly pecked his face off, and died of
the meal, I might add. We gathered up my traps and
threw the bird-pecked Crow in with the other five and
piled brush on the lot and set fire to the whole mess. I
didn't feel any too good about what had happened and I
damn sure didn't want another Crow party puzzling out
the story, as they have long memories and once annoyed
are too damn single-minded for my taste.

Horn thought it all a great joke. He made up a long
song recounting my splendid treacheries, to sing for his

people when he returned, a wealthy and respected warrior and trader.

Buffalo Horn was a good friend, too, and I had saved his hair once or twice, so he expanded the story and made it just preposterous enough so that it wouldn't be believed, if it should be sung, say, in the lodges of the Crows.

16

The truth of the matter is that wolfing just isn't very interesting. We poisoned and skinned out nearly three thousand, and had about eighty Canada lynx (caught them with baited traps) and a few odds and ends of marten and sable. The wolves had multiplied something fierce with the slaughter of the buffalo, and since the hide hunters left them all of the meat it was a free lunch for old lobo. Buffalo Horn and me took the valuable peltries (everything but the wolves) down to Fort Buford, and left the baled wolf pelts for Reilly and Grogan to sledge out however they wanted to. I wouldn't advance them any money, just gave them some modest credit at Salomonsen's General Store in Fort Buford.

Buffalo Horn and me came away with about eight thousand dollars apiece for our winter's work, less expenses, which came to about fifteen hundred dollars, including the salaries of our Irish friends.

I left the agreed sum with the factor for Hazleton and

Moss, the St. Louis outfit which had purchased all of our furs, with instructions that not one cent was to be given over until every pelt was accounted for.

The factor was a pale young feller with a long nose and rimless spectacles.

"You've had dealings with those fair Hibernians before?" he asked, raising one pale eyebrow.

"No," I says, "but I've known a lot like them."

"If they get too firm in their requests, Zeke here will be glad to show them the door."

He jerked his thumb at a mountainous gent who was casually leaning against a stack of baled hides. The factor's office was a wood and glass cubicle in the front of a gigantic warehouse. With several millions' worth of pelts and robes waiting on the spring breakup of the Missouri ice, I suppose they had a bunch of Zekes here and there at all times. This Zeke was wearing four pistols and carrying a sawed-off shotgun for sloppy close-range work.

The factor wrote me a draft on Hazleton and Moss to their St. Louis bank, and another to the branch in Fort Buford, so that Buffalo Horn could get his money in gold and head for home.

I took the heavy sack of gold the bank manager gave me out to Horn, who was leaning against the front of the only brick building in Fort Buford. Horn refuses to enter white men's lodges, claiming that they stink so bad he gets dizzy.

"Well," I says, "this is our last time. So I'll wish you tall grass and deep water."

Horn just grunted. I asked him if he wanted me to ride a ways with him. He made the sign for no. Then he grinned. "Stay away from buffalo robes, Kelly," he says. He swung up on his Appaloosa and grabbed the towline on his two mules.

The ice was thick on the river. I watched him cross, over to the north bank of the Yellowstone, where the going is easier on account of the wind clearing most of the snow

off the ridges—it gets pushed into the river bottom. I ain't
a sentimental feller, to put it mildly, but I did feel a
twinge at seeing him go.

Spring on the high plains is just about the most miserable mix of weather you can imagine. Snow, sleet, warm
days, freezing nights, ice jams and floods, and no traffic on
the river at all. Fort Buford was out of whiskey, vegetables, newspapers, seegars, and decks of playing cards.
Damn near everything else, too. The soldiers was bored
and surly, and the guardhouse was standing room only. A
bit after I got there a sixteen-year-old private was hanged
for having struck an officer. Everybody in town but me
turned out for the hanging, as it was the first real entertainment to be had in months.

When the packet boats could navigate again, and the
first little sidewheeler pulled up to the near-wrecked
dock, I lit out for the hills and spent three boring, wet,
miserable weeks in a tent on Big Dry Creek. The new
arrivals brought news and seegars and whiskey, and they
also brought influenza. The influenza soon had caused a
stack of coffins to pile up in a shed next to the cemetery.
Crowds will flat kill you, take it from me.

There was a feller name of Jordan Phipps a couple of
creeks down from me, who had gone around the ban on
firewater—the packet boats was thoroughly searched by
the army—by bringing up a still and then buying grain
from the Gallatin Valley, upriver a bit over four hundred
miles. The army tolerated him because they didn't know
he was there, or what it was he was doing, officially.

The place reeked of mash and there was a pathetic
bunch of Sioux living in damp caves by the river. They had
traded everything for firewater—pelts, guns, squaws. Hell,
they would've traded their children if Phipps would've
taken them. I had fought the Sioux and I had helped to
hunt them down, but to see them reduced to this made

me gag. I resolved to make mention of Phipps when next I was in Fort Buford. The Sioux used to bury their dead wrapped in buffalo robes with their war trophies and such, hung high in the river bottom cottonwoods or set upon biers open to the sky. Now they just dragged them out on the river ice.

I rode on back one fine warm April day, still a lot of snow on the ground where it was shady. The night before the ice had gone out with a great roar. There was a few cakes of pan ice floating by, and I imagined one hell of an ice jam downriver. The army's sappers would blow the jam free, and I hoped that whatever diseases the first arrivals brought would by now have run their course. The Lower Missouri ice always goes out about three weeks early, getting everybody excited, and when the Upper Missouri and the Yellowstone go out a bit later there is hell to pay downriver.

In the time that I had been gone, Reilly and Grogan had struggled in with the last of the pelts. The factor had paid them, obviously, for I had to step over Grogan, peacefully asleep in the mud, on my way to the Post Office. I had a letter.

It was from my old chum Texas Jack Omohundro. He formally offered me the job of guiding some bunch of nabobs from England, who wanted to see the Great American West and by the by wreak a great slaughter on whatever game was handy. For Victoria, and Empire, and to add a few more sets of horns to the walls of the family castle. Jack was a well-spoke feller, but his writing looked like he done it with the pencil held like a stabbing knife and his spelling was a wonder to see.

As an added treat, Buffalo Bill would be going with us.

I thought for about two minutes. I thought about the thousands of rotting buffalo carcasses, the Sioux camped by Phipps's whiskey still, the Nez Perces ridden down to a handful. Crazy Horse killed while I was back east, and how different things was now than they was when I first came.

The next downriver packet left at six the next morning. I booked passage to St. Louis, where I would hook up with Jack.

Then I went to the army post, and asked to see the Officer of the Day.

I told him about Phipps. He thanked me and said that they would look into it.

17

It took twelve pleasant days to make the St. Louis docks. Coming down the Missouri, I was at first amazed by the spring green, and then it occurred to me that we had dropped thousands of feet in altitude.

Up in the Big Hole of Montana, I had once been trapped by a sudden blizzard which dropped three feet of wet and heavy snow in less than twenty-four hours. Two others in the party died of exposure, because they tried to struggle back to the camp. Me, I found a cutbank, threw my blankets and slicker on top of me, and curled them into a miniature teepee around the barrel of my rifle, which I held between my knees, and stayed in there, farting and cursing, until the snow stopped. Nothing unusual about the blizzard, except it was the twentieth of July.

We coasted through the junction of the Missouri and the Mississippi—the Big Muddy was the color of coffee with cream in it, while the Mississippi was darker and clearer.

St. Louis was booming and bustling in April of 1878, trade coming from all directions. There seemed to be the same sort of activity going on that you see if you kick over an anthill.

Finding Buffalo Bill and Texas Jack (I knew them both when they was Bill and Jack, before fame up and struck) was real easy. They would be in the most expensive hotel, located near the most expensive whorehouses, where they would be eating the most expensive foods and not paying a dime for all of it. And they would have those folks who remind you of animals that can't kill their own meat hanging on them like leeches, proud to pony up for the whatever. Yellowstone Kelly, I thinks, shit.

Bill and Jack was in the bar of the Ashley House, and Bill had got drunk enough to go up to his room and get Tall Bull's scalp (some scalp, anyway) and he was re-enacting his own valiant deed in killing this most redoubtable warrior. Bill had had a lot of help with the "re-enactment" from a squint-eyed, bandy-legged, teetotaling idiot name of Ned Buntline, who had published this pack of lies about Bill, most of which Bill now firmly believed.

"First scalp for Custer!" hollers Bill, waving Tall Bull's (somebody's, anyway) scalp. Not a dry eye in the house, except mine. I had come through the door just as Bill was throwing back his head and waving his golden locks. He gave a bit of a start when he saw me, but being a true showman he soaked up all of the applause and dashed to the bar to cool down.

See, I happened to be at the Yellow Buttes fight where Tall Bull was killed. Tall Bull was peacefully riding up the trail on the north side of the Buttes, and a fourteen-year-old kid named Obadiah Mertz got him right square in the earhole with a 25-20 peashooter. The kid hightailed back, scared as could be. His older brother, name of Increase Mertz, went back with Obadiah to get the scalp. Not having much experience in the scalping trade, first thing they did was saw off Tall Bull's head. If you ever need to scalp somebody, leave the body attached, as it makes a most useful counterweight to your enterprise.

The brothers Mertz were forced to skin out old Bull's noggin', which they did like they was skinning a muskrat, at which they had some experience.

While the brothers Mertz were thus occupied, the rest of us were engaged in a hell of a fight on the south side of the Buttes. The Cheyennes finally broke off and ran, but we had too many wounded to give chase. On the way back to the supply wagons, Bill spotted Tall Bull's horse, which he immediately appropriated (the horse was a magnificent one, seventeen hands, and the color of gunmetal), and when the brothers Mertz straggled in with Tall Bull's topknot, Bill offered five dollars for it. The brothers Mertz went off satisfied, and Bill went off to clean up a few of the ragged edges (they'd left the ears on, see, which is a serious breach of etiquette) as he could never abide sloppy workmanship himself.

"That was a mighty fine performance, Bill," I says. "I can't remember when I've seen a better one."

"Luther, old comrade," says Bill, giving me a mighty slap on the back, "what'll you have?"

"I was so dazzled by the performance I ain't had time to think," I says, coughing. "I guess I'll have some Scotch whiskey."

"Woog," says Jack in my other ear, "goo to see you, Lusser." Jack had been on a prod for some days, it seemed.

"Tell me about this bunch of nabobs," I says, "and what and where are we going." As if I didn't know what I was going along for. The two celebrities would drink and preen, and I would get to run the show.

"The Duke of Ironheath, his lovely Lady, the Duchess Lydia, four lesser titled Englishmen and their ladies, and an assortment of servants."

"How many all told?" I asks.

"Thirty, maybe thirty-five."

"Fine," I says. "I'll have them fit out the *Delta Queen* (she was the most opulent riverboat working) with wheels and then cable P. T. Barnum and lease thirty or so elephants to pull the damn thing."

"Kelly, you always were a joker," says Bill, throwing back his head and bellering.

"I ain't joking," I says. "They can shoot buffalo from one of them howdy things that they put on the backs of elephants. Then the elephant can pick up the buffalo and carry it back to camp, which will save a lot of work, and any skulking Indians sees the elephants they will die from the wonderment of it all right on the spot. I think it's a great idea."

"Luther," says Bill. There was a loud thud on my right. Jack had expired.

Bill and me each took a handy end and hauled Jack to the elevator, and carried him down the hall to his room. Jack wasn't a big man, even adding the thirty or forty pounds of Panther Piss he had taken on. We dropped him on the bed and went back down to the bar.

"I was about to say," says Bill, "that these folks are interested in investing in my Wild West Show. I met them in England last winter, when I was on the tour that Colonel Buntline had arranged for me."

"Sure, Bill," I says, "tell me how much I'm making and what I have to do to get it."

"Five hundred dollars a month and a bonus at the end to make up for anything extraordinary you have to put up with."

"What's that mean?" I says, smelling trouble.

"Ah," Bill paused, ". . . the titled English are sometimes odd."

"Well, I suppose that it will have to do," I says.

Bill and me went to dinner, finally, and about halfway

through our meal Jack came wobbling in. He ordered plate after plate of oysters and glass after glass of white wine. This time Bill and me took him back upstairs in a laundry basket we bummed from the kitchen help.

As I was falling asleep, I realized that I missed the sound of the river.

18

I had demanded a room on a different floor from Bill and Jack—they had adjacent suites—and I further demanded that the desk not divulge the room number to *anyone*. Pranks was a big part of our life back then, I suppose because of the somber loneliness of the plains and mountains. Some of the pranks turned off all wrong, and the butt of the joke was maimed for life.

I also propped a chair against the doorknob and turned the gas jets all the way off. You will notice even in the fanciest places that the doors either have a bunch of patched holes around the vicinity of the lock, or the doors are new. Rubes come to town and blow out the gas jets, thinking that they are just like the kerosene lamps at home, and the gas kills them, or there will be a sudden loss of pressure, which snuffs the flame, and the pressure resumes and the poor fools asleep never wake up.

I got up about noon and had a bath, and then

went down to the hotel barbershop for a shave and a haircut.

"Leave my moustache and my sideburns," I says, just before the hot towels got slapped on.

St. Louis was so damn noisy I was still starting at unfamiliar sounds, my hand reaching for my revolver, which was stuck in my waistband.

The dining room was open, and there was an enormous sideboard of delicacies on ice. I took a table, and the waiter took my order for about forty dollars' worth of ham and eggs. The ham was from some place in Germany called Westphalia, and the eggs was fresh. I hadn't had fresh eggs for months, and at first they tasted strange and then mighty good.

I had polished off my breakfast and was having another pot of coffee when Bill come in, looking a little worn. I figured he'd spent the night down at one of the fancy sporting houses.

Bill gave a careless wave to his gaping public and pulled up a chair. The waiter came, and Bill ordered himself some steak, eggs and champagne. He diddled a little with the damask tablecloth, and looked around the room. The walls was red velvet, the trim was white and gold, and there was mirrors hung all around.

"Long ways from the Sand Hills, ain't it," I says, by way of breaking the ice. Something was eating on him fierce.

Bill cleared his throat.

"I'm troubled about Jack," he finally says.

"Jack was always blind drunk in towns," I says. "They make him uncomfortable. Hell, they make me uncomfortable."

"It ain't that," Bill says. "See, Jack went with me to England, and he met this titled lady there, and I am telling you she ate him up and spit out the seeds."

"Few weeks out on the prairie will set him right," I says. "Always has before."

"She's one of the party that we're guidin'."

"I see."

"I wish I could get the sonofabitch jailed for a year or so," Bill went on. "He's crazy as a bull elk in rut, and I don't need the lady's husband as full of holes as one of them things you use to drain vegetables and such."

"A colander," I says helpfully, pouring myself some more coffee.

"So," I went on, "at best he's useless, at worst he could sink your backing, and by the by get himself hung for perforating a nabob. Hell of a fix. I'll think on it."

"I'm a real slow feller," says Bill. "It took me all of five minutes to think of the feller who had the right sort of mind for this particular tangle."

"Prides me right up to hear you say so," I says. "Consider it done." I knew exactly what I was going to do, which was absolutely nothing, and if Jack wanted to get himself hung for ventilating a gen-yoo-wine English Aristocrat, that was his business.

"I feel much better," says Bill. "Now, the Duke's major-domo or whatever you call it will be here sometime this week, to go over our arrangements."

"Sounds good. Don't seem to make much sense we do much much more than shop around for a little stock, and find a few good teamsters and drovers, and if we did our recruiting slow and steady we could find good men and keep the price down."

"I want you to find someone who will be watching Lord Tibble every damn minute that you are not watching Lord Tibble," Bill says, dragging the conversation back to the trail he was still stuck on.

"I'll look around," I says.

"Stand you to a drink?" says Bill.

"Sure, Bill."

Though it was only a little past two the bar was half full.

Full of the sort of portly, waistcoated thieves who like to get together over oysters and booze and figure out how steal a bit more. I had seen the same faces on the gents who headed south after the Civil War—I doubted a one of them had put on Union blue, and here were the same faces heading west, where there was lots of cheap land and lots of dumb, honest farmers to gull.

Somehow the leeches sensed that Bill was in no mood to put up with their antics at the moment, so we got a bottle and went to a table in a quiet corner and started talking about how things were back then. Oldtimers, we was. I was twenty-seven and Bill was thirty-three. Talk turned to a lot of friends who had lost their hair, and a lot of enemies who had met pleasing ends. Then Bill got a kind of puzzled look on his face.

"You remember Wild Bill Hickok?" he asks.

"Of course," I says. "Got his head blown off over in Deadwood."

"Well," says Bill, "I saw him here, in St. Louis, about three months before he got shot by Jack McCall—Jack was his half-brother, you know—and he told me that he'd just been to see an eye surgeon, and the man told him he would be totally blind within six months. Course he asked me not to tell anyone, since if that was known, every saddle-jammer in the country would be after him. I haven't told anyone, until now."

"We ain't drunk enough to be talking like this," I says. "Now tell me the route you plan to take."

"That's simple," says Bill. "We go up to my place on the North Platte, from there to Denver, up to Estes Park and the Red Mountain lakes, over Two Ocean Pass to the Grand Tetons, through Colter's Hell, down the Yellowstone to Pryor Creek, back down past the Big Horns and the

Wind Rivers, and fetch up at Cheyenne, where the duke's party can make rail connections."

"We'd best ship everything to Cheyenne and start from there," I says, "because you can't go by wagon to your place without a camphor-soaked rag over your face. The stink and the flies are hell from May on."

"The Duke wants to shoot some buffalo," says Bill.

"I'll find him all the buffalo he wants up on the Yellowstone," I says.

We were interrupted by a waxy-looking imitation of our old and true friend Texas Jack, who was of a pale clear green complexion and a shuffling gait not a bit like the springy step of the scout feared even by the great Comanche Chief Quanah Parker.

Jack let himself down gingerly, and then held his head in his hands.

"I ain't a well man," he says. "Would you order me some coffee?"

The coffee came, and Jack sniffed at it for a while, sort of suspicious-like, and then he managed to drink a cup.

"Bill and I have been talking," I says, "and we decided we would take off from Cheyenne. The Central Plains are an awful thing to behold."

"Uh," said Jack.

"So pack your traps and head for Cheyenne," I says, "'fore you kill yourself from whiskey."

Jack took a minute to take that in.

"Guess I'd best be moving."

"First thing you do when you get there is get us a cavvy of maybe forty head of good horses. We need well-broke, wind-sound, mountain horses."

"I'll go get him a ticket," says Bill, dropping some gold on the table to cover our breakfast.

I took Jack up to his room and helped him pack.

We deposited Jack in a suite in the Pullman car, with a

few bottles of champagne and a large jug of bromide of potash.

"I hope he don't see snakes all the way to Cheyenne," says Bill, as we watched the train go.

The wind had turned raw. We took a cab back to the hotel.

"Big doin's tomorrow," I says to Bill, "let's turn in early."

We had a good dinner, and did just that.

19

The next month was a dull round of going here to order this, there to order that, interviewing drovers and teamsters. I was pretty sure that what we would find in Cheyenne was the dregs not even the hide men would take. The British Army was buying buffalo leather in preference to any other kind. It was lighter in weight and held a polish better than cow leather. The hide hunters were working the year round now, and without Crazy Horse and Sitting Bull and Gall and their braves to scare them, they would soon be after the Yellowstone herd. With the Crees and Metis having done in the Canadian herd moving south to kill off the buffalo north of the Missouri, and every ragtag-and-bobtail of the hunters from the Red River, the Arkansas, the Platte, and the Republican heading north, it wouldn't be but a year or two before the only buffalo left would be stuffed and in a museum.

The majordomo arrived, ready to domo a moving mansion to hell and gone. His name was Oliver Johnson, and he proved to be pleasant, well spoken, efficient, and very humorous in that parched sort of British way. He was smart enough to ask when he didn't know, and between the two of us we pretty well had everything lined out by the middle of May.

My search for reliable men took me to some of the wagon trains—there were still a few, even though the railroads were reaching out farther each year—and I was able to hire eighteen of the twenty teamsters we would need. They all looked sound, without that twitchy paleness that the whiskey-bills have. I bought tickets to Cheyenne for all of them, and told them to meet me there no later than the twenty-fifth of May.

Oliver had brought a detailed list of the supplies that the Duke's party would require us to drag along. I doubt that the Duke had even glanced at the list. Oliver was to arrange, and god help him if the port was the wrong year or the seegars were presumptuous.

"Hmmm," said Oliver, a couple days before I left, "I do believe that we have attended to everything."

The wine and such that had been shipped from England had arrived the week previously, been placed in a boxcar which we then sealed, and sent on to Cheyenne. I wired Jack and instructed him to post an armed guard—with another armed guard to watch him—twenty-four hours a day, and further, if when I got there the seals had been broken, there would be hell to pay. The Duke's party had enough wine, champagne, liquor, porter, stout, and seegars in that boxcar to keep all of Cheyenne very happy for several days.

Oliver reminded me of a bittern. When he was thinking, he would tilt his head back and look straight up and then make a clucking sound, a half swallow, glumpick, glumpick, glumpick, until whatever item he was searching for in his memory floated up to within reach.

"Kelly," he says, "I would like a guided tour of the bars and brothels of this feckless American city."

"I'm a guide, all right," I says. "Let's get us a good dinner and then I will find a couple places to get drunk in and get our bellropes pulled."

"Bellropes?" says Oliver. "Oh, I see, another of your American idioms. They have the same . . . uuh . . . vigor as your country."

"You should have gone into diplomacy," I says.

"Actually, I was in the Foreign Service for a bit," Oliver says, "but they kept posting me to beastly hot places. The Duke was kind enough to offer me a position, and I accepted."

"What sort of feller is he?" I asks.

Oliver gave me a very hard look. "He is an English gentleman," he said curtly. "I wonder how Mr. Cody is faring in New York?"

"Hell," I says, "he's holed up in the Waldorf-Astoria concocting another pack of lies with Ned Buntline. In between temperance lectures from Ned, they should have three or four dime novels' worth by the time the party from England gets here."

"I had thought Mr. Cody's adventures extraordinary," says Oliver. "Both as to substance and to sheer numbers."

Oliver had been sitting at his desk in shirtsleeves. He was the skinniest full-grown human being I had ever seen, not counting outright starvation cases. He was shrugging himself into his coat when he burst out laughing. "Kelly," he says, "the thing that Mr. Cody understands is that your American West has certain . . . er . . . mythical properties. He's shrewd enough to understand how to sell that, using his own person. He will do very well."

"No doubt," I says.

"You do know that there is a book out about you?"

"I figured George Hanks of the *Hartford Courant* would do some damn thing like that."

"Have you read it?"

"No," I says, "I ain't. And I'm not going to. Now let's go get some dinner and then do a little serious carousing."

We had a leisurely dinner, and lingered over brandy and seegars until well after ten o'clock. Once Oliver got a bit of ankle-walking water into him, he let loose with a damn near unbroken string of funny stories about his service to Her Majesty's Government, and he had a lot of sly tales about growing up on a small estate in the Border Country of Scotland. I didn't know that under English law the eldest son gets everything, and the rest of the children get whatever crumbs he chooses to toss their way.

We went to Madame Patch's first—she was called that because she always wore a diamond-studded patch over her left eye. The whorehouse was nearby, and the girls were young and pretty.

Madame Patch greeted me with her usual warmth—I paid on the nail, you see—and after Oliver and me had plunked down our twenty dollars each the champagne commenced to flow. Madame Patch let us sit and listen to the piano player—a nigger in a silk shirt, sure played good—and then she sent down all of the girls that wasn't occupied for us to look over.

They was all young and fresh-looking, and none of them wearing enough to wad a shotgun with. I picked out a dark little thing, she had eyes as blue as the kingfisher's wing, and I don't know which one Oliver took, because my little minx took my hand and hauled me upstairs before the Englishman had given any sign that he even knew the girls were there.

My chippy told me that her name was Prudence, this while she was pulling off my boots, and by the time I had shucked the rest of my clothes—she'd taken off her few wisps of things, and insisted on hanging everything up, meanwhile stretching one long leg or the other, or waggling a tit my way—I was breathing deep and so ready my pecker was throbbing like a bullfrog's throat in courting season. We screwed like minks and I suppose it didn't take very long. It seemed like all of my worries about the upcoming trip went out when I come. I laid there for a bit, while she washed me, and then I went downstairs and waited for Oliver. I don't know how long it was—two big glasses of champagne's worth—and soon here he come down the red plush stairs, adjusting his necktie and looking at his cuffs. What with his accent and his funny round black hat and cane he did look sort of out of place in a medium-good whorehouse in St. Louis.

I stood up, and Oliver came over.

"I should like to see your St. Louis," he said. "I have done nothing since I arrived but deal with those infernal papers and even more infernal merchants."

When we marched out of the front door, with Madame Patch's cooing voice behind us and the traffic in front—St. Louis never really shuts down for the night—I naturally turned left, to head uphill to where the better bars and such were.

"Kelly," says Oliver grabbing my arm, "what is down there?" He pointed downhill, in the direction of the river.

"Well," I says, "that's first a desperate bunch of poor white folks' places—bucket-of-blood bars and gambling hells, cheap whorehouses with poxy whores, a couple thousand cutthroats, sharpers, and if you get through that in one piece you're in Darktown."

"Interesting," says Oliver.

"Oliver," I says, "you can get your throat cut for a few pennies down there. The clothes we are wearing say we got more than a few pennies."

"You have no sense of adventure."

"None," I agrees.

"Hmmm . . . then I wonder if you are perhaps the proper party to guide the Duke's tour?"

"I don't need the damn job, Oliver, so that ain't going to get you anywhere."

"Well, then," he says, grinning, "I shall hope to see you at breakfast." He began to walk down the hill, whistling gaily, god damn him, and he hadn't gone two blocks before I cussed myself clean out and went after him.

And a good thing, too, because by the time I caught up with him he was in the outskirts of Hellsport. I was maybe ten feet up the hill from Oliver when a couple of dark shapes rushed out of a space between two buildings, and one of them raised a long sap high over his head.

"Look out!" I hollered. The man with the sap turned to see what was behind him. I had my gun out and I hit him hard on the side of the head with it. The street was steep, and I fell and rolled quite a ways downhill before I could stop and get up and run back. The man I hit was on the ground, but another one had come from somewhere and the two of them was moving toward Oliver.

About the time that I'm thinking the headline in tomorrow's paper is going to read "Duke's Man Broke in Half," Oliver tugs a thin sword out of his cane, slashes one across the forehead with it, so that the blood will blind him, and runs the other through. Didn't seem to take more time than it would to strike a match.

The feller Oliver had spitted was staring down at his stomach like he couldn't believe what had just happened— an expression I have seen many times—and then he crumpled and rolled downhill, fetching up against the one that I had hit. The man with the slashed forehead was on his knees, frantically trying to claw blood out of his eyes.

"We should summon the police," says Oliver.

"Summon 'em all you want," I says. "We passed the line that they'll cross over about two hundred yards up the hill—after dark, that is. Daylight they might be tempted to come as far as we are now, if the crime was serious and going on in plain view."

"Hmmmm," says Oliver. "In future, I shall listen to you, Mr. Kelly."

We walked back to the hotel, and drank for a long time. It didn't take any kind of hold, so we finally gave up and went to bed. I had terrible dreams which I couldn't remember the next day.

20

Oliver didn't show for breakfast, and I had just remembered my promise to Bill about getting a bodyguard for the Duke and a foil for Jack, if it came to that. Oliver was a brave feller, but somehow a sword against a Peacemaker 45 didn't seem all that good odds to me.

I took a cab to a livery stable, hired a horse, and rode out toward the west of town, for no particular reason. It was late spring here, the trees had all leafed out, and everything was green.

I was loping along on a rutted country road, going nowhere in particular, enjoying being on a horse again. The air was soft. Truth to tell, I had had enough city for one lifetime, and taking it day by day I hadn't realized how much I had come to hate it.

It occurred to me that if I was in need of a gunman I could easier find him in little Cheyenne than in big St. Louis, so I put that out of my mind for the time being and just enjoyed the ride.

About two o'clock I turned round and headed back, feeling much better for the riding and for getting away from the city stink. It was about five, I suppose, that I come up to the ferry. It was on the far side of the Missouri and still had some wagons and passengers to unload. I got down and looped the reins over a hitching post off to the side, and then sort of half-sat against the rail. I bit off the end of a seegar and lit it, and looked up at the blue sky. Soon, I thought, I will be out of this grimy mess. It was grimy, worst I'd ever seen. Ash from coalfires in thousands of homes, ash from the gasworks down by the river, ash from the steamboats, the foundries, the railroad trains, and god knows what else.

The seegar was about half gone when a young man in homespun, wearing boots about to go bust, and carrying a little bundle of what I supposed was his entire estate, walked up to me and looked me square for a minute.

"Mister," he said, "I'll rub down your horse for you if you'll pay my fare across the river."

"Sure," I said. I went back to looking at the sky.

The kid rubbed on the horse in a practiced sort of way, and he even lifted up the horse's feet one by one to check them for stones.

"Fare's a nickel, Mister," he said. He kept looking me straight in the eye. I found it curious, usually someone who has to ask for a favor will turn away.

"What's your name, son?" I said.

"Tom."

"What do you want to go over there for?"

"I don't."

"Where do you want to go?"

"Out west."

What was bothering me was he reminded me of Luther Kelly in 1866, carrying the army mail, and telling the postmaster that "of course I could find my way to Fort McCloud even if it did look like snow." I was wrong. If a kindly old Cree brave hadn't seen my tracks and followed them (he had crossed them several times since *he* was going in a straight line), Mrs. Kelly's boy Luther would have been crowbait, sure.

"What are you going to do when you get out there?"

"I'm going to get me a job, and then I'm going to be a scout as soon as I can earn an outfit. Like Buffalo Bill."

I began to laugh, and then I howled, and gasped, and it was all that I could do to keep from pitching over sideways. Young Tom was getting redder and redder, and balling his fists. "I don't see what's so damn funny," he says, "and I'd sure as hell like my nickel."

I had laughed so much that my voice was hoarse, and I was still wiping a tear away now and again.

"Tell you what," I says, "I'll give you a job and your passage to Cheyenne. Job will last about six months, it's forty a month and found. I'll advance you enough to outfit yourself, and that will come out of your pay."

"You funnin' me or what?" he says. He looked like he was about to try and break my jaw.

"I ain't funnin' you," I says. I reached into my pocket and brought out what coins I had in there, and gave him a nickel and two fifty-dollar gold pieces. He stood there gaping at the money—and when I tipped the three coins into his hand it took him some seconds before he drew out a little leather pouch he had on a string around his neck and started to put all three inside.

"You'll need the nickel for the ferry," I says. The boat had started back. It was a donkey-engined sternwheeler, and had to keep its bows about forty-five degrees upstream to keep from being swept downriver by the current.

Some of the stun had wore off young Tom by the time we were halfway across the river, and he began to rattle off a bunch of questions, most of which I couldn't hear over the belching and hissing and farting of the donkey engine.

I shook my head and pointed to the shore. He understood. When we had debarked and begun to climb the hill he started to ask just what it was he was going to need, and why couldn't he get it in Cheyenne?

"Everything is twice as much in Cheyenne," I said. "Now, what I want you to do is go right on up this street here, and when you get almost to the top of the hill there's a clothing place. Get some good heavy shirts, longjohns, pants, boots, and a good felt hat big enough so you can jam it down far enough over your head so the wind won't take it. Then look me up at the Ashley House—Luther Kelly is my name—and I'll buy you dinner and we'll list up what else you need to get in the morning."

I swung up on my horse and took off uphill, leaving young Tom waving after me.

After I returned the horse to the livery I did something I had been working up to for some time. I rode a streetcar. For some reason they scared me, and it was interesting to find out that they just rocked along, like a train. The car paused in front of the Ashley House, and I hopped off and strode inside. I told O'Banion, the doorman, that a very young feller in new duds, about so high and dark, would be along looking for me, and he did have legitimate business with me, if you call guiding nabobs legitimate.

After shedding my riding duds and shucking on one of my Eastern disguises, I went in search of Oliver. He was in the bar, drinking Scotch whiskey neat, with Apollinaris water for a chaser, and eating slices of pickled buffalo tongue.

"Set for the morrow, are we?" he asks. "Do we carouse again tonight?"

" 'Fraid not," I says. "I don't much like the idea riding the train with a hangover." I told him what little I knew about Tom.

He shrugged. "It would have been cheaper, I suppose," he says, "to hire someone there."

"If there was someone there for sure," I says. "This way I am sure that he'll stay on for the whole trip. He's a stubborn little bastard. All you have to do is imply he can't do something, and he'll do it out of orneriness, even if it does cost him both hands and feet."

"Oh," Oliver said, looking skyward, "before I should forget." He handed me a slim wallet. "There is ten thousand dollars in there, for you to make purchases or hire. I shall require receipts."

Without a word I went to the front desk and got a pen and paper, and gave him his damned receipt then and there. He folded it and placed it in his wallet, filled with similar scraps of paper, bills, and such. As an afterthought, I counted the money twice. It was there. I felt a bit foolish and a whole lot angry. Oliver was toying with me, and I didn't like it one damn bit.

"Well," he said, taking his weight off the bar, "I have decided to dine elsewhere tonight. See you in the morning."

There had been a lot of times over the years when I have felt uneasy just after making camp. And when I do, I wait until it is dark, and then move off quietly a few hundred yards, after dousing the fire. Even with the city noises I felt uneasy now. I went up to my room and packed—didn't have much, I'd sent the bulk of my gear out in the sealed boxcar. I changed into my riding gear, which was nothing more than denims and a flannel shirt, and put on my buckskin jacket and comfortable old hat. I put the ten thousand in my moneybelt, pulled on my boots, and tucked a Colt in my belt and a derringer in my boot-top for good measure. I went down by the stairs, out the back door, and around the block. I come whistling up to O'Banion and asked him if he had seen my young friend. The words was no sooner out of my mouth than I saw Tom, walking slowly toward the Ashley House, looking from side to side at the buildings and lamps.

"You didn't see me," I says to O'Banion, pressing a gold piece into his practiced palm.

"Not since ye came back from yer ride," he whispered.

I hurried down to Tom and hissed, "It's me, Kelly, come on, we have to move."

He didn't gape or ask any questions, just spun on his heel and fell in step beside me. He was creaking like a ship at anchor, what with the new leather of his boots and the starch in his clothes.

I hailed a cab, and had him take us to another livery stable, some blocks away from the one I had rented a horse from earlier in the day.

We crossed the Missouri and rode. I aimed to catch the train at its second stop, a little place called Catersville, about twenty miles to the west and a little north. The roads were good, and just by navigating as I was used to—the stars—we come to Catersville about three in the morning. The train station was open, and I purchased two tickets to Cheyenne. We slept on the benches until dawn, and the stationmaster directed us to a boarding house across the way, run by a widow who served breakfasts and such to travelers, though few ever stopped here, so close to St. Louis.

It was one of the best feeds I have ever had. There was fresh biscuits, ham, steak, eggs, flapjacks, home-canned peaches, coffee, and cinnamon rolls. Breakfast for the two of us (actually, four, Tom ate three times what anyone else could hold) came to forty cents. The widow lady had looked upon Tom's gastronomical feats with that motherly smile women save for peaked-looking young menfolk.

Full of food and tired, we just drowsed in the chairs on the station platform. We'd dropped the horses off at the local smith's—the liveryman was sending a boy out on the train to take them back.

Right at one o'clock the train come in, and we got on, headed for Cheyenne.

And I still had the ten thousand dollars.

21

It took four long, boring days to get to Cheyenne, with Tom pestering me with questions all the damn way. We stopped for a two-hour layover in North Platte, Nebraska, to let the fast freights through. The seats was comfortable enough, the food in the club car was all right, and I felt like I'd been nailed to a rocking chair and had a magpie on my shoulder.

The General Store was a well-stocked place, and Tom bought blankets and a canvas bedroll and a slicker and a rifle and such odds and ends as appealed to him. He paid thirty-five dollars for a used Spanish-style saddle. At the end of this buying spree he had about ten dollars left, which was fine, because where he would be going there would be precious little chance to spend money.

About the time we come to due south of the Sand Hills a fearful stench assaulted us, and flies by the millions came in the windows. Ladies screamed as the little buggers got entangled in their hair. It was impossible to eat, the flies covered the food the moment the cook put it on a plate. The wind finally veered around to the southwest, and the stench lessened.

"Before you ask me," I says, "those are the thousands of buffalo killed last winter up north, maybe even as far as a hundred miles." I made a note—to wire Bill and make sure that every window and door on the nabobs' cars was tightly screened, which effort might reduce the flies to mere tens of thousands.

We steamed along for another hundred miles of prairie and a new wave of buzzing flies, and young Tom was silent the whole time.

"You sick?" I finally says, not having had a moment's peace since we left Missouri.

"No," says Tom. "It's just that ever since I was a tad I have wanted to go west, and now I am beginning to think that it is going to be pretty much gone before I get there."

There wasn't anything I could say to that, except maybe the only thing that was worse was having to *watch* the Big Lonesome shorn of its buffalo, Indians, and openness. Say what you want about nesters, they are just plain damn dull. There is no such thing as a pretty fence.

"Cheyenne is only about a hundred miles," I says. "When we get there we're going to be working more or less around the clock. Once we have all of the gear stowed and Jack's got his hands on the reins, you and me is going to take two weeks and do some hard scouting for game. There should be quite a bit left, but it will be in scattered places."

The train chuffed on, and we didn't speak much. I went back to the club car for a drink, but the twenty or so happily drowning flies in my whiskey discouraged even that, so I went back up to my seat, pulled my hat over my eyes, and went to sleep.

The slowing of the train woke me. We pulled into the station, and there was Jack, looking clear-eyed and healthy,

standing in all of his Plains finery. Tom's mouth dropped
open looking at this "pretty shadow." Not having mirrors
much, the clotheshorses out here like admiring their
shadows as they ride along.

The train had just stopped when I thought of something.

"Tom," I says, "it is impolite, I know, but do you have a
last name?"

Tom looked puzzled. "It don't seem impolite. It's Horn.
Tom Horn."

We swung down off the train and Jack ambled over to
us, never looking at me once. He just kept his eyes on
Tom. He was looking Tom over like you would a two-
headed calf or an honest politician—something simply not
to be believed.

"Luther," says Jack, "we have been friends for a good
many years, and I feel that I am entitled to an explanation.
What is this here creature?"

"I found it outside a whorehouse, crying for its mama,"
I says, "and I gave it a peanut and it followed me home."

"Is it human?"

"Barely."

"What does it do?"

"We can hang a lamp on it at night."

"That all?"

"So far."

Tom just stood there, and he got this big grin on his
face.

"I'm Tom Horn," he says.

"Texas Jack." They shook hands.

"Well," says Jack, "we got some work to do."

Jack had brought what is called a Cape Cart, a light
wagon with oversize wheels—bought to transport heads
back to the taxidermist which the Duke was bringing
along.

Jack had set up camp about five miles north of Cheyenne,
near a little spring, with a lovely grove of cottonwoods.

The flies had abandoned us at the Wyoming line, I don't know why.

There were twenty-two freight wagons lined up, ready to put the traces and teams on, and three lighter wagons. The cavvy of horses was off down the little stream, in a pole-and-rope corral.

The teamsters would start arriving in a couple of days, and then we would begin off-loading the boxcar. Until then, all we had to do was make sure that the horses was gentled, the merchants paid, and a few hundred other petty tasks seen to.

"Tom," I says, "you know how to ride?"

"Yessir."

"Well, there's eighty horses over there, and I want you to break 'em all."

Tom looked a little puzzled.

"How many horses you broke?" I says.

"Two."

"Time you learned," I says, picking up Jack's sea-grass rope.

22

Jack and me attended to the merchants, had the teamsters set up tents, off-loaded the boxcar, and from time to time we would go watch Tom fly gracefully here and there. Each time he'd eat dirt he'd climb back aboard, one of those who just won't let go. Well, that was sure in his favor.

Word came from Bill that the party would be arriving on the seventh of June, a week later than we had planned. Fine by me, there was always more to do than you would have thought. Tom was getting to be a good horsebreaker. He was bruised and pulled and strained every which way, so if he made a wrong move his body immediately screamed. Best tutor in the world, pain is.

One fine day, I believe it was about the third of June, I went over to the Cheyenne Cattle Club for a drink. Nothing much to it, but I heard a lot of pistol shots coming from around back.

"What's going on out there?" I asks the barkeep.

"Shooting contest."

"Anybody I know?"

"Red Buck—you know he's Charley Goodnight's trail boss—and some sawed-off little runt Shanghai Pierce found on a Denver gooseberry ranch. I think the wager is twenty grand between the two of them, and Lord knows what the side bets are."

Charley Goodnight and Shanghai Pierce were Texas cattlemen, and the sort of enemies who can't get along without one another. I'd never met either of them, but I had heard the stories.

Shanghai Pierce thought very highly of himself—so highly that he commissioned a fifteen-foot-tall statue of himself. He built a bandstand and invited everybody to come and listen to his speech. After which there would be free whiskey and barbecue. So, of course, half the folks in West Texas showed up. Only one ain't invited is Charley Goodnight. Shanghai being economical, he just sent out one un-invitation to Charley and bade everybody else come. The band played for a while, and toward the middle of their last number Shanghai rose and made his way to the speaker's platform.

Just as the band starts to play the final bars of whatever it is they are playing, a train blows its whistle, and here comes an engine, steaming backwards, with just two box-cars. The train slows and stops at the end of Shanghai's own private railroad spur. The whistle dies down, the boxcar doors open, and about a million pigeons fly out. Shanghai don't know that you unveil a statue after the speech, so there all fifteen feet of him is, with clouds of pigeons fighting to get on and take a crap. Shanghai is screaming for a Winchester by this time, but the train is pulling out, and Goodnight is hanging out of the engine, waving his Stetson.

I walked around to the back and saw about thirty gents in a group standing behind the two shooters and the thrower. The thrower was tossing glass balls about three inches in diameter as far as he could, and one or the other of the gunmen would draw and fire.

"What's the score?" I asks a gent I don't know.

"Ninety-six to eighty-eight."

"Out of how many?"

"That was the ninety-seventh."

"Didn't know Red Buck was that good," I says.

"Ain't Red Buck," the feller says. "It's that little dwarf Shanghai found."

I had only met Red Buck once, and he was about the most hair-trigger cowboy I have ever known. Thinking perhaps that Red Buck would probably not accept defeat graciously, I returned to the bar and had another drink, behind the club's thick walls. A great cheer announced that the contest was over. I waited. No shots. Later I found out that Goodnight had demanded that each contestant have a pile of exactly one hundred shells in front of him, though why he thought that Red Buck wouldn't use numbers ninety-nine and one hundred to do in the dwarf, I'll never know.

The mob trooped in, and Charley hollered that the drinks was on him. Some of the bettors had this little feller on their shoulders, he having made them richer than they had been.

Everybody was so jovial and determined to get drunk they did indeed manage to in a remarkably short time. Little knots of men drifted off to tables, some well-wishers left, and pretty soon I was able to go up to the dwarf.

"I'm Yellowstone Kelly," I said, sticking out my paw. "Are you in need of a job?"

He shook my hand, and then commenced to cough something awful. There was bright red drops of blood in the blue cloth of his kerchief.

"Marion Hedgepeth." He coughed a bit more. "Is it in a dry climate?" he said, after wiping his lips.

"Yes."

"I'll take it."

"Don't you want to know what the job is?" I says.

"You don't look like an idiot," says Marion. "I charge five hundred a month."

I told him where the camp was, and gave him a month's pay in advance. Then I rode over to the telegraph office and wired Bill. It was a short message. "Found one for Jack."

Things was ready, everybody was bored. The horses was broke, the wagons packed, and the teamsters and the two Mexican drovers and me and Tom and Marion hadn't anything better to do than braid two-color horsehair ropes, the Plains needlepoint.

23

The great day finally come, and the stationmaster at North Platte wired ahead to let us know if the train didn't fall off the track, our nabobs would arrive at 3:10. They were two minutes early. The train looked like an ordinary train, except for the two enormous custom cars attached to the caboose. Wouldn't do to have the peasants walking through, you know. The engineer pulled ahead far enough so that our customers and their servants and god knows what all could step directly to the platform, while ordinary passengers had up to three hundred feet of mud to wade through before gaining anything substantial to stand on.

Bill was first off, all in his buckskins and wearing the smile he used for encores. He strode right up to me and shook my hand, and while the loafers and bummers and cowhands cheered and he waved his hat, he hissed at me out of the side of his mouth.

"Where's Jack?"

"He's out at the camp, wanted to save himself some pain, I guess."

"Come on," says Bill, "I'll introduce you to our... uh... illustrious guests."

The Duke of Ironheath was first off, and he leveled a hand for his lady to lean on, and she stepped out into the bright Wyoming summer light and commenced to glow. I have seen a lot of beautiful women in my day, but never one before or since like Lydia, Duchess of Ironheath.

Tall she was, and wearing blue satin and white lace, with a huge flowered hat atop a pile of gold hair. I could have reached round her waist with my two hands.

"This is my friend Yellowstone Kelly," says Bill. "He's going to be your guide some of the time."

The Duke shook my hand without looking at me, but the Lady Lydia offered hers, and as I bowed and kissed it (I came from a good home, you see) she gave a little throaty laugh.

"To find such manners here, Mr. Kelly," she said, in a deep husky voice. And she laughed again. She was used to being looked at by thunderstruck males. She disengaged her hand and swept off, looking up at the sky and out over the prairie.

Next I met the Marquess of Wiggins, who was married to the Lady Lydia's sister, who was known as Lady Violet. Another gorgeous creature. After that there were three Englishmen with one chin between them. I never really did get them all straight, as they looked about as different from each other as a half-grown litter of prairie dogs. They was buddies of the Marquess. All that those three did the whole damn trip was stay in the big Sibley tent and giggle. Except for... oh, hell, I'll tell you later.

The Duke walked slowly down the station platform, and his head kept moving side to side, like a mechanical toy. I had taken one look into his too-pale blue eyes and decided that no one was home and the lights were out. If Bill'd had any trouble with any of them he'd be the one. I'd hear about it in due time.

The Union Pacific Railroad had built a special siding for the two custom coaches, and when the westbound train pulled out, having disgorged fourteen of what I presumed were the Duke's servants into the mud along the tracks, a little donkey-puller came out and shoved the cars off on the siding. There was even water lines and slop-pipes set, to hook up to the cars.

By this time most of the loafers had left. The Lady Lydia and the Lady Violet were down at the far end of the platform, the Duke standing stolidly nearby, staring off across the prairie at something I suspect that only he could see. There were clouds on the western horizon. Soon it would begin to rain.

The servants had managed to wallow out of the mire by the roadbed, and they trailed off in the direction of the hotel, a medium-good place, since the bedbugs was of a very high order.

Oliver Johnson sauntered out on the smoking platform at the rear of the first car, and when he happened to glance my way—I knew damn well he'd been watching everything from behind a curtain—he waved real offhand-like, and then looked out over the prairie.

The two ladies came swaying back to Bill and me, twirling their parasols.

"You two must come to dinner," said the Lady Lydia. "Shall we say at eight o'clock?"

Bill and I accepted. Some time in the next three hours maybe Bill will tell me what it is that's eatin' on him, I thought.

"Buy you a drink?" I says to Bill. He nodded.

We squelched through the mud to the Club, and wiped most of the dirt off before walking on the red plush carpets. We might as well not have bothered; the carpet by the front doors looked like an otter slide, and was damn near as slick. There was about thirty fellers in there, including Shanghai and Charley, who were glaring at each other from opposite sides of the room, and no doubt thinking of new ways to make each other miserable.

I bought a bottle, and Bill carried the glasses. We went to a table in one of the bay-window alcoves. There was quite a bit of light there, so I pulled the curtains.

"What happened?" I asks.

Bill poured himself about four fingers and tossed it down. "The Duke killed one of Madame Patch's whores. He was doing something made her scream and to shut her up he hit her alongside the head with a champagne bottle, and caved her skull in."

Bill was silent for a minute. "Patch had her thugs drop the girl's body in the river. The Duke departed as though nothing was amiss, and when Patch sent her attorney to try a little genteel blackmail, he beat the man half to death. Oliver Johnson paid out many thousands of dollars to hush everything up. I knew the Duke was a wrongun', but I had no idea..."

"You still need his money, right?"

Bill nodded.

"All we have to do is take them on this tour, and then we bring them back here, to Cheyenne, and wish them well and goodbye. There ain't that many places for the Duke to get into trouble out there." I gestured toward the mountains.

Bill began to cheer up some. I reminded him of all the times we'd come upon the whoremasters with their wagononloads of chippies, headed for the next gold town, the girls half dead of whiskey and hopelessness. Sometimes that was a whore's life.

I got up and bought a fresh deck of cards, and Bill and me played dollar-ante seven-card stud until it was time to go to dinner.

Not knowing just which door to knock on, I let Bill take the lead. We went to the coupling that held the two cars, and then up the left-hand stairway. Oliver was acting as doorman or greeter or whatever you call it, and he took our coats off to somewhere.

We was the first to arrive, and Oliver took our orders for drinks and in what seemed no time at all we were sipping fine old Scotch and admiring the paintings on the walls of the dining saloon. Oliver made a little jerking movement with his head, and I followed him into the cloakroom.

He looked at me steadily for a moment. "Kelly," he said, "you were smart to leave when you did. Your room was ransacked that night. It seems that the clerk had connections with some footpads. The police had been watching him for some time."

Well, I didn't know but what Oliver wasn't in on it, but I smiled and thanked him. "Wondered why they didn't forward my trunk," I said.

"It is right for you to suspect me," said Oliver, "but you are wrong. When they were done with your room they came to mine." He fingered a barely healed welt on his left temple.

There not being much to say to that, I rejoined Bill.

The Duke come in and nodded to us, and when the Lady Lydia and the Lady Violet had been seated the servants began to scuttle in, and I settled down to a ten-course meal. I had found my card next to the Lady Lydia's, and one of the chinless dudes was on my right. She asked me all sorts of questions about where we were going, how many men I had killed, were we likely to encounter hostile Indians, and would there be plenty of game for the Duke to shoot.

I told her a mild pack of lies. Dinner over, the two lovely ladies departed, and seegars and port was passed around. The Duke held us enthralled with accounts of his slaughtering expeditions in Europe, Africa, India, and Australia, where he single-handedly halved the population of kangaroos in a matter of a few weeks. He talked about partridge and pheasant hunts on his estates, where the tally of birds went into the thousands. All in a monotone, one more wholly unnerving thing about this strange feller.

The evening ended abruptly with Oliver bringing Bill and me our coats. We shrugged into them. As I was going out the door, I reached into my right coat pocket for my kerchief and found a short note. "Come to the rear door of this car at one o'clock. L."

"What's holdin' you up?" Bill said.

"Oh, nothin'," I said.

24

Bill and I had a couple drinks, and then he took off for the camp, winking at me and rolling his eyes.

"Mind you don't turn out like Jack," he says, grinning like a dog with a fresh cow turd.

He'd read the sign, all right.

A few minutes before one I left the Cattle Club as quiet as I could, not wishing to be remarked upon by the loafers, most of whose eyes had long since been crossed so far over the whole world looked flesh-colored.

The rear door of the coach opened silently, and Lydia, wearing just a mite more than nothing at all, grabbed my hand and pulled me inside. I wasn't slow in shedding my boots and duds, and we commenced to screw on every available flat or inclined surface and a couple times swinging from the chandelier. Lydia had obviously made a study of the subject—she said, once when we had paused for breath, that a lot of her ideas came from some carving on the walls of a temple in India, a place she went to often whilst the Duke was off slaughtering tigers and leopards and panthers and the occasional beater.

We plumb wore out each other, and whilst we was waiting for our second wind Lydia started fingering the various scars my hide has picked up over the years. I was lying on my stomach, and my back is where most of the scars is, on account of how I refuse to stay over-long where I'm not wanted.

She seemed satisfied with my explanations, and we had another hour of acrobatics. I was worried about the noise, but Lydia told me that her "class" was trained from birth not to notice anything, which I guess explains the imbecilic bravery of Her Majesty's soldiers and sailors—and especially the officers.

Lydia was purring like a tabby cat on my shoulder when there commenced a bit of glow in the east, and I rose and dressed and slipped out before there was anyone up to remark upon my early rising, and further, upon my early rising from—gasp!—the rolling mansion.

By the time I come to the camp everybody was up and about. The teamsters had the oxen hitched, and were lumbering off toward the northwest. Tom had caught and saddled seven of the best horses for our dudes—with many choice comments about the English saddles, which are called pancakes out West and considered as sightly as turds in a punch bowl.

"There's no place to sit on these damn things," said Tom. "I can't see how they'll stay on."

"Well," I says, "aside from the fact that you put them all on backwards, you have done a real good job. Now take that string in and tether them near the Pullman, and me and Jack and Bill will be along shortly."

"How can you tell they's backwards?" Tom asked, reasonable enough.

I sent the three teamsters with the Cape Cart and light wagons to pick up the servants at the hotel, and run them to where we would make our first camp, about twenty miles to the northwest, five days by wagon from South Pass and fifteen from the Grand Tetons.

Bill and Jack put on their best duds, pale doeskin trousers and dragoon boots, silk kerchiefs, fringed and beaded buckskins, and great big sombrero-looking Stetsons that looked like they ought to have come equipped with tent poles and guy wires just to stand up.

Bill had hired a few tame Indians, and they was to make a mock attack on the Pullman cars. They was to swoop down just as Bill and Jack and I rode up, and we were to playfully fire blank cartridges at them, eventually knocking all of the savages off their horses—some sort of re-enactment of something or other. Well, hell, here it was the wild west.

The nabobs had taken an early breakfast, and were variously lounging on the open deck at the rear of the last coach, or walking on the roadbed. The ladies were nowhere to be seen.

The three of us dime-novel heroes rode up, and then reared our horses—they was show ponies, trained to stand on their hind legs and paw the air—and when the horses set down we all swept off our hats, and the horses made curtsies. If I'd tried that with what I usually ride, I'd have been kicked halfway to China, out of the horse's embarrassment.

The hats was the signal for the twenty or so mostly drunk braves to commence whooping down, all painted, waving their lances and decorated shields. The Indians commenced to circle, while Bill and Jack blazed away at them—me, I had got off to check the saddles that Tom had by now got pointed the right way.

The blanks from Jack's and Bill's revolvers made a kind of a loud pop. Suddenly I heard the unmistakable crack of a strictly-for-business cartridge. I run toward the sound, and there was the Duke, with one of his double-barreled guns, drawing down on one of the Indians. He fired again before I could reach him, and the slug tore into the horse's ass and knocked both horse and rider back about twenty feet.

The Duke's loader handed him another double-barreled gun, and I leaped up to the platform in time to shove the barrel skyward just as the Duke pulled the trigger.

"Sir," I hollered, "it's only a joke, they're only funnin' you." The Duke looked at me with those flat blue eyes, and he was fair foaming at the mouth.

Oliver come out of nowhere and helped me subdue the Duke, who seemed to be having some sort of fit. As soon as he was prone he commenced to bang his head on the floor. Oliver stuck his foot under the Duke's head, in a practiced sort of way, and Bill and Jack come up. The Indians had wisely departed.

The seizure didn't take very long. The Duke sat up after a minute, then grabbed a chair and hauled himself upright.

"Will we have sport today?" he said to Bill, as calm as though nothing had happened. Maybe for him nothing had. He went into the Pullman, and when he come back, the two ladies was with him, all decked out in riding habits.

"Luther," says Bill, "Jack and me will take the men and go do a little bird hunting, and if you would be so kind as to take care of the ladies, we will meet for supper at the camp."

The two ladies tripped down the steps and Tom brought two horses over for them. I stepped down from the platform and made a stirrup of my hands, to give them a leg up. They was riding side-saddle, of course.

"You ride herd on the Duke's chums," I grunted. "Camp's twenty miles past our present one, due northwest."

"I suggest that we ride fairly hard a bit, and then do some sightseeing," I said to the ladies. "That will leave the Duke's party with plenty of unstirred-up game."

I swung up on my horse and started to move at a brisk trot. The Lady Lydia whipped her horse into a gallop, closely followed by Lady Violet, just like they was riding over a groomed course instead of a plain studded with prickly pear cactus and perforated with prairie-dog and badger holes.

I cursed plenty, and rode after them. They went about ten miles, passing the teamsters with the ox-drawn wagons, and they didn't pull up until their horses were just about winded. They knew the business of riding, though. The three of us walked the horses to cool them, and then we remounted and headed for the place that we would camp that night.

Herds of antelope dashed off to both sides of us, and I saw a couple of wolves, quick dark flashes between clumps of sagebrush and stunted cedar.

The ladies approved of the campsite, and they chattered like sparrows as we watered our horses.

"Mr. Kelly," said the Lady Violet, "this is such... mysterious country. Do you know its secrets?"

For my money, the country was flatter than piss on a plate, and there wasn't much interesting until the Big Horn mountains, but after a bit of carefully posed head-scratching I said that I knew of a spot not too far off where the Indians had been making arrow points since before Moses took to the weeds.

They thought that was a good idea, so we rode over to a water-cut, which had exposed a small cliff of obsidian. The Indians would build a hot fire against the base of the cliff, and then throw water on it, which made the volcanic glass shatter off in useful sizes. Over the centuries the Indians had tunneled in about fifteen feet. The cliff base was littered with flawed arrow points and broken spear points and little flakes of glass popped off the points by the maker's elkhorn flaking tool.

They each filled the dainty saddlebags they had on their

horses with such rocks as they could find, and then they remarked how nice it would be to have luncheon.

"God," I said, "I'm sorry. I forget to get anything, and all that I have is some jerky and dried fruit."

"Let's go back to the campsite, and have your... jerky," said the Lady Violet.

"And with the dried fruit and spring water it will be a feast!" continued the Lady Lydia.

We rode back to the spring, and sat on fallen cottonwood logs and ate jerky and dried apricots. The way those two ladies tucked into my travelin' rations, you'd have thought it was fooey-grass and horse doovers.

"Most interesting," said Lydia.

"It'll do you if need be," I says.

"Is that a blanket tied up behind your saddle?" she asked, looking innocent. "Do fetch it. Violet, should anyone come, do whistle, won't you?"

I took the blanket and followed her into the dogwood bushes that grew thick on the hill behind the spring.

25

Things don't take long to become routine. I spent the days guiding either the ladies or the chinless three, and the nights in my tent with Lydia, who arrived in the dark and left each morning before first light. I was beginning to feel a mite tired, but Lydia seemed to thrive on no sleep. Violet had taken up with Jack again, and Bill and me wondered when she'd drop him. I'd told Marion my worries, and the poisonous little dwarf was never very far from Jack. Marion blended well, he was about the same color as the prairie dust, except for the red blood in his kerchief.

One day I felt I couldn't take no more, so I went to Bill and proposed that I take young Tom Horn and go for a quick look-see in the Tetons.

"Could you maybe tether a few elk and buffalo and grizzlies for His Lordship?" Bill asked. For the sorry truth had emerged. The Duke couldn't have hit the ground with his hat if you gave him three tries. And everything that

moved was a target—Bill had had to pay off several irate
nesters who'd had their mules and milk cows and hogs and
such blasted into eternity by his Lordship's custom cannons. The Duke had even winged a camp-boy that was
walking a bit too ape-like. Took him ten shots.

"I'm worn down to a nub," I says.

"Maybe the blacksmith could help," says Bill, "and I
hear if you chew soaproot it's almost as good as oysters."

Tom and me left in a cloud of hurried dust. Free of his
job as a wrangler, he had the whole wide world before
him, and he commenced to explore, at top speed, country
which was much the same for a hundred miles in any
direction that you cared to point.

We did nearly thirty miles before we stopped to rest our
horses and eat a little of the hardtack and jerky we carried.

"Next day we'll be through South Pass," I says, "and
then we can turn north and head for mountain country."

Tom looked hard over west. "I don't see no mountains,"
he said.

"South Pass ain't a mountain pass," I said. "I am never
quite sure just at what point I'm over it. It don't look any
different than what we're riding through now."

Tom shook his head, in wonder or disbelief.

"I'm going to rest up a while," I said.

Tom took that as an excuse to do some exploring. He
took off with a whoop and a yell, and before long he was
just a little speck on the endless brown plain.

He'd get his lesson later. Right now I was thinking
ahead, to our evening meal, and so I hobbled my pony
and left him to graze by a little spring, and took my 35-40
and climbed up a low hill that still had me gasping for
breath by the time I had got to the top. I have never been
able to really grab hold of the scale of things out here. I
knew it was sixty miles to the horizon because I had been
over it so many times, but I couldn't *see* it.

Antelope are the fastest animals on the plains. And the

most curious. To hunt them, all you have to do is tie a
white rag on a pole. The fluttering white attracts them,
and all that you have to do is sit and wait and not make
any sudden movements. I put up a pole with a white rag
tied to it.

In about an hour a young antelope buck come in sight. I
pulled the hammer back on my 35-40 and broke his neck
with the first shot. Dressed out the liver and the back
ribs—we had plenty of jerky and dried fruit on the two
pack horses—and left the rest for the scavengers, who
were likely having a thin time of it. There was a few
buzzards way up, and I did spot one coyote—rare you'll
see one; they are so shy of man.

"S'pose that they could run cows on this," I said to my
horse, "but it just ain't going to be the same."

I could see young Tom headed my way, so I knocked
down the pole and took off my kerchief—I'd wrapped the
antelope in oilskin and tied it behind my cantle.

"Hallelujah," he says, reining up, his pony all lathered.
"I never liked a place better than this."

I just stared at him, my eyes narrow. Finally it broke
through his wooden skull that I was displeased with him.

"What's wrong?" he finally asked—and I'll give it to him
that he looked me right in the eye.

"Listen, you farina-faced little glob of puke," I says,
biting off the words like I was chewing jerky, "your horse
is near windblowed and you pulled a tendon in his front
leg. He's lathered and blowing and up here in the wind.
Now I strongly suggest that you get down off him, and rub
him down with some of that bunchgrass over there—the
reddish stuff—and then you walk him to camp."

Tom got down and off-saddled, and began to walk the
horse in a circle, and Tom's head was hanging.

I grabbed the pack string and rode off.

He hollered, "Where's camp?"

"You wanted to be a scout," I hollered back, "so do

some tracking." I rode off, and managed to make it out of sight before roaring with laughter, but nonetheless I rode nearly twenty miles, because that was one lesson that had to sink in. You're only as good as your horse out here—he's dead or crippled, then so are you.

I made camp by a sweet spring that bubbled out of a gravelly hill. I doubted that there was any Indians in the hills at all, but still I cut dry willow and peeled off the bark, so that there would be no smoke. Saw to my guns, and made rope hobbles for the horses. They could graze in the meadow above the spring—plenty of grass, and the gravelly hill behind was too poor of footing to allow them to climb with two foot-hobbles on.

This particular spot was new to me, so I wandered around on foot, looking at the prairie flowers and the grass, almost to full growth. Soon it would be blistering hot, the grass would seed and go dormant until the next year—the only green would be in the little creek bottoms and along the river.

I found another spring, and sitting in it was a bone so big I wondered if I'd been napping and missed herds of elephants among the buffalo—and decided that I didn't drink *that* much. The spring was cutting back into a clay-and-sand hill. There were several more bones poking out, and something looked suspiciously like the end of a tusk—gone all cracked and brown, but a tusk. I got a stick and scraped away what I could, and several teeth as large as a brick fell out. I scratched my head, and wondered about it. The bones were too big to pack, so I just took three of the teeth.

It was late afternoon by now, and I was hungry. I was going to save the antelope to share with Tom, whenever he limped in, so I had a can of sardines and tomatoes and made my customary rounds, memorizing bushes and boulders. If I was to see a new bush at night I would commence fire right then, as a few hours was too short a time in this harsh climate for a bush to grow that much. I had killed quite a few Indians who were creeping my way, bushlike, thinking how nice my hair would look on the war pole back to home. Learned that from Fergus McDonald, who was about eighty when I knew him—I was a kid in Oneida. Old Fergus had the most perforated hide I have ever seen—one eye, bullet wounds, one ear gone and the other sort of tattered, all manner of limps and staggers, three fingers missing off his left hand. ("I's leein' face doon," he said, "while this Arapahoey is sawin' off me fingers to get me rings. Rings is a bad idea out there. I was disinclined to protest at the moment.")

It got dark, and the bugs commenced. I lathered my face with trade whiskey—makes the skeeters sing with rage and never come nearer than six inches—and began a fire to cook the back ribs. The meat began to sizzle and the first stars was coming out. Well, things looked the same up above.

About midnight I heard the jingle of harness—no offense, but I was into cover and circling, and it was Tom, walking in his socks with his boots under his arm.

"Luther?" he called, real hoarse. He pitched face down on the grass.

I walked over and took his pony off to feed and water, and dropped his saddle over a log. Then I drug his stupid young ass over to the creek and gently laid him face down in it, which brought him to right now. He sputtered and choked and reared up to his hands and knees.

Then he shoved his face back in the creek and commenced to suck in water like a shaft pump.

I shook my head and went off to eat liver and back ribs and drink black coffee. I had finished my meal when Tom began to lose the ten gallons or so of water, dragonfly nymphs, bottom mud, horseshit, small minnows, frogs and salamanders he had swallowed. It went on for some time.

Finally a very pale young feller stumbled into the

firelight and sat down heavily on the ground. He breathed hard for a moment.

"Kelly," he said thickly, "you are the most copper-bottomed bastard I have ever known."

"Some folks has mentioned that," I says. "Have a nice walk?"

"OOOoooooohhh," he says, and puts his head in his hands.

"Along with the horse," I says, "I might mention that when you are as thirsty as that, it's best to take four palmfuls of water, and wait a few minutes, and then take another four palmfuls. If you are really dry—and you don't got the notion what real dry is yet—you keep taking four palmfuls till you can piss. Then you drink all you want. Horse gets six gulps. A Blackfeet would have just padded up and put his foot on your skinny neck and stood there, feelin' virtuous for saving ammunition and a lot of washing time on your hair for his squaw."

Moan.

"How're your feet?" I says.

He peels off his socks and displays a fine and numerous set of purple blisters.

"Kids these days," I snorts, taking the folding canvas bucket off to the creek for some water. I come back and he was lying on his back, eyes half open.

"Put your hoofs in this," I says, and he looked blearily at the bucket, and put first one and then the other in. He winced from the pain, and then the cold took that.

"Aaaah," he says, just as I poured the quart of trade whiskey in.

The next aaaah was of a different nature.

"You get infected, I'll leave you out here for the skunks and the birds. Grit your teeth and keep them in there, goddamn you."

He did it. Me, I went to sleep.

Next morning I was cooking the leftovers and coffee

when he come to, looking a little pale. He tucked into the back ribs, and he left teeth marks on the enamel plate I served it on. He topped off his monstrous gut with four cans of tomatoes, two of peaches, and one of canned Boston Brown Bread, which was about the color and shape of a can of axle grease, and about the same texture, too.

"Lecture's over," I says.

He nods.

"I'll get the ponies, and pack up. You can ride, even though on a horse you look like a turd hit with a club. We got work to do."

I got us packed up and we started along.

"Mr. Kelly," he says, about a mile along.

"Yes."

"Did General Sherman get rid of the Plains tribes by letting you adopt them?"

I had to laugh.

26

The next day me and young Tom Horn did nearly forty miles, running off most of the grain-fed flesh that was on our horses. We could see the spires of the Tetons in the high maze to the north. Tom gaped open-mouthed at the pale silhouettes. I know of higher mountains, but they are tucked into windrows of lesser peaks. The Tetons are about the prettiest mountains I've ever seen.

Game was abundant—we were a long damn way from any mining camps or budding towns. I saw sign of another party that had been through maybe two weeks before. Other than that it seemed that we would have the place all to ourselves.

Tom had settled some—he would never again abuse his horse, I was sure of that—and he picked up on what I was doing as quick as any I have ever seen.

We had been five days on the scout when I decided to turn back. Tom looked wistful—he'd have kept on going north till he was out on the ice if it was up to him.

"We're being paid to find game for the Duke to shoot," I says, "and I don't like it either."

We rode hard for two days, and about midmorning on the third day I saw the dust from some wagons—regular wagon trains was a thing of the past if you were going directly west on the U.P. route, but most of the lands that were available for homesteading had to be approached the same as before the railroad.

It turned out to be Bill, Jack, and the rest, everybody but the ladies, coated with a film of dust—the trail was worn so deep that once the wagons was set in the ruts it was impossible to get the wheels out until you come to a wallow or some rocky ground. There was all manner of moldering furniture beside the trail, some of it thirty or more years old, and quite a few graves, covered with stones, the graveboards long since ground to dust by the endless wind.

This was the only dry camp—it was nearly another full day to the nearest good water—that there was on the whole damn journey. To hear the chinless ones scream you'd think we was in the middle of the Jornada del Muerto with our feet cut off and the sun rising. The Duke and the ladies didn't let out a peep.

We had a cold supper, and then Bill and me walked out on the prairie, to confab a little about what was ahead.

"Violet's still bangin' Jack," Bill says, "and Lydia has been sneaking out to the teamsters. Happiest crew I've ever ramrodded. The Duke has managed to hit several things, including two of our horses. You wouldn't know anybody who has an out-of-work Gila Monster, would you?"

"It's going to be a couple of months before the elk have any decent horns," I says, "and the bears is all mangy."

It was nigh onto dark. I was looking forward to a good night's sleep, and by God if I didn't get it. I was awakened only once by a chorus of enthusiastic cheers from the teamsters' tents.

In order for the Duke to best have his sport, he decided, after some consultation with Oliver, to ride ahead carrying only a bedroll and a few thousand rounds of ammunition. The train would catch up in two or three days. The Duke was very bored with the available game here—prairie dogs, eagles and hawks, the occasional horned toad. He felt that something larger would be in order.

The next morning he announced his decision, spoiling my breakfast. He wished to have young Tom, myself, and Oliver for guidance and company. Bill nodded.

We set out, with Tom dragging two pack mules along back in the dust-eater's seat, at the rear of our party. The Duke kept forging out in front. I was damn sorry I hadn't come on any grizzly sign that I could steer him to. The damn bears was all the way up in the high country, digging up marmots and white pine roots.

With the horses fresh and all, we made the low hills to the south of the Tetons by nightfall, and made a pleasant camp close by a little stream that would one day meet the Colorado, and so flow to the Gulf of California. It was a chilly night, and in the morning there was a bit of ice in the water pails. The Duke had never slept under the stars before. He kept sitting bolt upright at every mouse scratch and bat fart.

"Egad," he would say, "what the devil is that?"

"A bat farted, sir," I would say.

"Quite so, quite so."

We ate pan bread and bacon for breakfast. I told Tom to pack the mules another forty miles north to a spot we had camped at during our quick survey of the area. It was due west of the Tetons, in the foothills. A large grassy meadow with plenty of feed for the stock, ample good water, including a trickle spring near to camp that the stock couldn't muddy up, and firewood just for the picking.

The Duke and me would take two days and describe a loop to the east, and I told him that with any luck we would find a trophy grizzly.

"Capital," he said.

"I hope so," I muttered. "Then we can hang the bear."

The Duke was a fair horseman, considering his bulk and that silly pancake he was riding on. We had a good trail for the first twenty-five miles or so, and after that we had a choice of skirting the high country by following some old mountain buffalo trails—the mountain buffalo was taller and rangier than his plains cousins. There never was many of them to begin with and as far as I know they all went for meat early on, in the 60s. Or we could zig-zag up the switchback trails and try to find Old Ephriam, what the mountain men called the grizzly.

The Duke has just the one rifle, a double-barreled big game gun, and I had just my little 35-40. Without his shotgun he was considerably less of a menace to the hawks and owls and chipmunks and such. We saw some mule deer far off, and when we did, the Duke would scramble down from his horse and wrench his rifle out of its boot and then look bewildered. The deer by this time were two miles away.

That evening we come to a trail that went up, over the top of the short hills, and it was the way up to Jackson's Hole proper. I told the Duke that if he liked we could go on up and maybe get a bear. The Duke thought about it for a long time, and then he decided to wait until Bill and Jack and the rest of the party were nigh on. Since he was the worst shot any of us had ever seen, perhaps in some dim corner of his mind he knew that Bill and Jack were firing at the same instant he touched off powder, and that further I was probably not going to do the same. Jack and Bill wouldn't have bought my letting a grizzly eat him anyway.

I knew the country well, so we traveled most of the

night, north and some west, and come to the camp that
Oliver and Tom were at a couple of hours before dawn.
Oliver had packed several bottles of whiskey, and the
Duke finished two of them and fell into a sleep so deep he
wouldn't have awakened if a pair of porcupines was fucking
on his chest.

Oliver had adapted well to the rugged life. He had been
sleeping with just one blanket since we left Cheyenne,
and he was now used to the cold and slept comfortable
without all of the truck we was packing for the others.

The three of us drunk coffee and chatted until dawn,
and then Oliver turned in for a little sleep.

"I ain't liking this much," says Tom.

"None of us like it."

"Sure is pretty country."

I drifted off myself. The hot sun woke me in the late
forenoon. Oliver was up and stirring the fire. The Duke
was still out cold and would be for some time.

"I'm going to take Tom and search out some game," I
said to Oliver. "Jack and Bill and the rest of the party
should be here late afternoon tomorrow. We'll be back by
then."

Oliver just nodded, his face flat. He didn't like what this
had turned into either, though he at least had known what
to expect.

Tom and me rode up to the top of the ridge behind the
camp, and from it we could see the Tetons rising up in
the gold sun. White snow gleamed on the blue peaks,
and the air was so clear the blue of a jay was visible to
a half a mile, sapphire upon the dark green of the pines
and spruce.

"Where are we going?" asked Tom.

"Up there," I said. He grinned at me and we hit a fast
lope. I already knew where the game would be, I just
wanted to keep my contact with His Lordship down to a

minimum. Oh, Bill was going to pay for this particular shit-covered biscuit, for certain.

They are sudden mountains, the Tetons, they rise off a plateau, blue and bleak and cold looking. Nothing but rock and snow, and jagged as a smashed bottle.

We rode right up to their bases, and Tom started up a goat trail. He made it only a few feet when his horse balked. The busted chunks of rock that the trail was made of was footing enough for a mountain goat, but no self-respecting horse would have anything to do with it. Tom just laughed, and got off and backed his skittish pony down. The trail was too narrow for the horse to turn round on.

There was a sort of lake just a bit to the north and west of the biggest peak—a bog, really, filled with old beaver dams. This area had likely been trapped out by 1825, but the dams had held in some places for over fifty years. There was even some fresh beaver sign—repair work on some of the smaller dams, and cut poplar and willow stems, peeled to the white wood.

"Goats and sheep will be up on those," I said to Tom, pointing to the mountains, "sheep about halfway up, and the goats about three-quarters of the way up. Way to hunt either one of them is to get seven-eighths of the way up and hunt down. It don't occur to them that anything can climb higher than them, so they never look up, only down."

Tom nodded. I don't think he ever forgot a thing I told him. I had been right, he took to this life as though it was his own.

We scouted a few bands of elk—the bulls was just beginning to bud their horns. In another month they would be rubbing the velvet from their antlers and fighting one another for cows.

We had come maybe ten miles north and twenty miles west from where the Duke and Oliver were parked, and I was thinking on killing three or four of the grouse that looked at us with their stupid eyes from perches in the spruce. Then we heard a rifle shot, and then another. The reports come from over the next ridge.

We rode quick up to where we could see the valley below, and it took a moment to spot the fellers who had been shooting. Two men in dirty buckskins was chasing a young Indian girl up the creek. She stopped for a moment at a little sandbar, and grabbed a handful of sand and then lifted her skirt and rubbed the sand in her crotch. Then she ran on.

"What the hell is she doing?" Tom says.

"Those fellers are going to rape her, and she's spoiling their fun," I says. "Indian girls learn to do what she's doing real young. Course those fellers may be so mad about it that they kill her."

Tom took off without so much as a word, and he was dragging his saddle gun out of the scabbard before he had made fifty yards down the hill. The men chasing the girl was so preoccupied they never even looked up our way.

The first feller got a slug in the small of the back. I saw him fall off his horse and then try to drag himself away, using just his arms. His legs had lost their usefulness.

The second feller heard the shot, and glanced back at where his partner had been. He reined up, unable to see back because of the willows. Tom come busting right through them and shot the man in the head at a distance of about fifty yards, no mean feat from horseback. He was dead before he hit the ground.

The exhausted girl was slumped in the grass a hundred yards upstream. I saw Tom dismount, and watched his hands make sign lingo, and he pointed back downstream. Then he got on his horse and rode back up to me.

"What did you tell her?" I asks.

"Where the feller with the broken hunkers is," says Tom.

The Indian girl was walking deliberately downstream, and the sun glinted from a knife in her hand.

"I've had it with the Duke and such," says Tom. "If a feller wanted to fight Indians and see some wild country, where would he go?"

"Arizona Territory," I says. "Go and find Al Sieber. He's the scout to learn from."

"Obliged," says Tom.

I flipped him a fifty-dollar gold piece.

"I figured we was just about even," he says.

"We'll be drinkin' whiskey and telling lies someday," I says. "Don't worry about the horse, either, I'll square that off."

Tom nodded. He rode off to the south.

Terrible screams started coming from the valley behind me. I headed back to the camp.

27

The Duke was getting fidgety, what with all of the songbirds around to shoot, and him without a shotgun. I had told him about the mountain goats and sheep, and he muttered that he wanted to wait until the wagons come up, as he had a special gun for that sort of work. So to pass the time he went down to the creek and tried to shoot the trout, this with a gun designed for elephants and rhinoceroses and such. The cartridges was the size of a Havana seegar. When the bullet hit the water it sent spray fifty feet in the air. He killed some fish with the concussion, and we had them for dinner. It made a nice change from the bacon and pan bread.

The main party arrived just at dusk—they had sent one of the drovers up to make sure that we were where we said we would be—and the servants and the chef scuttled around and served a splendid eight-course meal in the big double Sibley tent. One of the odds and ends being packed along was a huge "Peerless" woodburning cookstove

that took four of the teamsters to lift out of the wagon that
carried it.

Jack seemed in decent spirits, so I assumed that the
Lady Violet was still slipping into his tent of nights. The
Lady Lydia looked right through me, which as you may
well guess did not upset me one bit.

Jack had a badly sprained knee, got when he was
helping heave one of the freight wagons over some hump
or other, so I was detailed to guide the Duke on a hunt for
sheep and goats.

The Duke had a special gun, the kind that is called a
Mauser needle gun. It shoots a very slender, long slug at
high velocity. He had had a telescopic sight fitted to
it.

The two of us took off before first light. There was an
outside chance that the sheep might be feeding low
down, so I told the Duke to be as quiet as possible. It
was hard to see. Wisps of mist were wandering this way
and that, and the rising sun gave a back-glow to the fog.
I had us halt by a big meadow. The wind was right, it
was coming toward us, and we waited to see if when the
sun burned off the fog, anything would be feeding out
there.

When the fog burned off it did it all of a sudden-like.
There weren't any sheep, but there were a couple of
moose gobbling up huge mouthfuls of water weeds. Just as
I turned to tell the Duke we'd have to sneak up on them,
he fired. The moose raised their heads at the noise, and
then went back to feeding. We crept closer. I had tethered
the horses back in the lodgepole, and we were creeping
through grass that was waist high and soaking wet. Going
on our hands and knees got us soaked clear through in the
first ten feet that we crawled.

It was slow going. I inched my eyes up, and we was
only about two hundred yards from the grazing moose—
two cows, each with a little calf. The Duke shot all four of

them, first the cows, and then the calves, who didn't have the wit to leave their dead mothers. With his usual fine marksmanship, he managed to break one cow's front leg, and she lurched and stumbled off into the timber at the far side of the meadow. The Duke fired a few dozen shots at the trees.

I followed along, and I stopped to slit the jugulars of the three dead moose. The Duke had gone after the wounded cow. I waited for a shot, and when I didn't hear one I started after him, following the oafish prints of his feet.

I had gone maybe a hundred yards into the timber when I saw the Duke. I went up to him. He was lying on his face smack in the middle of a game trail. About an inch of blade and the handle of a Green River knife was sticking up out of his back, high on the left side, where the heart is.

"Oh, shit," I said.

I whirled around, looking for who done it. He was standing maybe fifty yards behind me, arms folded.

"Luther, old chile," says Liver-Eating Jack. "I been hearing about this sportsman you been guidin'. What Indians are left don't think much of his huntin' ways."

Jack had a nasty scratch on the side of his face, and was missing part of his right ear.

"When he done shot me, chile," he went on, "that was too much. Even if he didn't mean to."

The scene I was looking at sort of moved away, like my eyes was running back into tunnels in my head. Jack standin' there lookin' sorrowful, the Duke where someone should have put him long ago, the bright mountain light. I remember a Canada jay cussing from a tree.

If the Duke had shot Jack it was a one-in-a-million ricochet. Jack was a man the size of a Durham bull, able to hide behind small thises and thats and sometimes nothing at all. I suspected that Jack had sawed some of his face with his firesteel for my benefit; he was always sensitive to the feelings of other folks except when he didn't like them.

Well, I owed Jack my life a couple of times and hadn't had the pleasure of returning the favor, and truth to tell I didn't mind the Duke in his present condition.

"Well," I says, "we got to hide what's left of His Lordship and then go straight up in the air."

Jack walked over to the Duke and picked him up like he was a sack of bubbles and sort of casually tossed His Lordship on one shoulder.

I had this funny prickling feeling right in the small of my back, which only happens when there's someone back behind me staring and thinking bad thoughts. I turned around slow, because I didn't know just how bad the thoughts were.

There was eight of the ugliest Blackfeet Indians standing there—they was all ugly to me, on account of how they felt about whites.

Jack coughed out some words and they commenced to wiping out sign.

"Time we headed north," says Jack. "All them other directions smell bad when the wind comes from them. I like north fine."

"Sounds good," I says, swinging up on my horse. "By the way, how do these Feet here feel about that little thing with the leg and all?"

"Wal," he says, "these boys grew up hearin' the story, but after a little palaver I convinced them that it were my big brother done it while I was still back in Iowa sloppin' hogs, and besides they like the story so much that they are happy to know the brother of a man who could do a thing like that. They are curious as young folks are about ways and means of doin' things. I has taught them a marchin' song to ride by and a few things here and there. They's plum attached to me."

Off we went, headed north through the old war trails, and one of the most striking experiences I have ever had is bein' escorted by eight mean, ugly Blackfeet singing "Jesus Wants Me for a Sunbeam." It had to be heard to be believed.

28

I was fairly sick of "Jesus Wants Me..." before we were more than three days or so down the trail. Jack had stuffed the Duke down one of them black mudholes that goes down about a mile and is only three feet wide at the top. Jack cut a nice long lodgepole about six inches through at the base and poked the Duke down about twenty feet and then he pulled the pole out and washed it off good and carried it another ten miles before we burned it. I have always admired a thorough man.

We run the Duke's horse up into a draw and shot it. We skinned it out and cut off the hooves, so that there wouldn't be nothing but maggoty meat and no way to tell whose horse it was. In three days the carcass would be so bloated and stinking, no one could get within a half mile of it. We stuffed the hide and hooves and all of the Duke's traps—his saddle and such—down another mudhole.

"Whar you thinking of headin'?" says Jack.

"I think I'll cross the big water," I says. I still don't know why I suddenly thought that.

Jack grunted and went to sleep.

We headed north, crossing trails, sometimes seeing little clusters of houses where a few short years ago there had been a whole lot of open space. We kept to the doghair lodgepole, and crossed the Gallatin Valley in the night, for there were lots of farmers there. North of the Judith Basin we headed a bit east, and two days later we swum the horses over the Missouri.

The Blackfeet departed, headed west and then up into Canada, and Jack left the next day. He left like he come, and I never heard him slide off. I wasn't to see him again for a long time. I headed east to Fort Buford.

I slipped in and out of town quite early in the morning and spread a little money over the factor, who was used to folks tipping him for the favor of not being seen. Honest man, he was. My ten thousand in gold made two nice solid ballasts in my saddlebags and I still had over five thousand dollars in currency that I hadn't turned back to Oliver. So I dry-camped and slithered out of the good old U.S.A., loaded down and outward bound, as my crazed uncle, the retired sea captain, used to say.

He was the one who explained to me at an early age all I needed to know about the Westward Course of Empire. If the Americans sewed up the continent, they won. If they didn't, they lost. Inconveniences like the Indians would have to be dealt with.

"History is a depressing avalanche," he said, gulping Irish whisky. "Make sure you stay on top. Don't be a noble idiot."

When I come to the border I turned and waved to him, though he'd been in his grave for a long time.

I rode about fifty miles up into Canada and headed out across the great Canadian prairie, eventually coming to a little town so small I have even forgotten the name. I sold my horse and saddle there and bought a train ticket to Montreal. The train chugged and puffed across the grassland, and then it come to be forests of birch and cedar, and after six days I found myself walking down the streets of Montreal, my ear picking up the French spoke like French, not like the pidgin Frog I heard in the mountains from the Crees.

I asked around, discreet-like, and bought a British passport in the name of James Adendorff, off a one-eyed sailor I supposed was a great friend of the late J.A.

"Hullo," I says to myself in the mirror in my cheap hotel room. "Good old Jim Adendorff."

From Montreal I took the train down to Quebec City. It was French, too, and a busy, bustling port. Oneida was down south a ways, and one good thing that came of the Duke's demise was that I didn't have to go see my damn family. Lawyers. Kayrist.

I spent a couple of days prowling the docks, looking for the right sort of ship, that being one that had a captain who wasn't much of a mind to ask questions.

The second day, late in the afternoon, I saw a whole bunch of mules and oxen being drove down toward the docks. The drovers were a mixed lot of bullwhackers and British soldiers in red coats. The oxen and the mules didn't want to go much, and the herd, which was bellering loudly, was finally got up to a makeshift corral and then one by one cut out and slung from a cargo boom and lifted up into a dirty, rusty steam transport, called the *Forbes Castle*. There was a red-faced Army Captain standing by the sling chute bawling something at a tall, coffin-faced feller in a black frock coat.

"Damme, man," said the Army Captain, "we must make haste. Chelmsford needs these beasts and he needs them soon."

"Hull have 'em when the Looooorrdd sees fit, Captain

Reilly," says the coffin-faced gent. "I canna have tha'
saylers carry them abooooorrrrdddd one under each arm."

"South Africa is a long damn way from here," yelled
Reilly.

The coffin-faced gent waved at him patronizingly.

"By Jove," says Reilly, "when in the name of Hades will
we sail!"

"Faster if ye quit upsettin' the beasts with yer blas-
pheemin'," says the Scot. "I am Master of this vessel and
we'll sail as soon as God wills."

Reilly stalked off, to amuse himself by cursing the
troopers, who were wearing thick wool tunics buttoned to
the throat and white gloves. It was about a hundred
degrees, and as I watched Reilly giving hell to a pale-
faced, scrawny youth, the boy pitched forward on his face,
making a squelchy thump in the manure in front of him.

"Have you a cabin?" I says to the Scot.

He pulled his long chin and looked at me with the
palest blue eyes I have ever seen. He looked at my boots,
and at my stained buckskin jacket, and then at my eyes.

"A-yuh," he says. "Are ye to South Africa for the gold or
the diamonds?"

"Diamonds," I says.

He snorted and looked up at the decks of his ship.

"Be a hundred Yankee dollars one way," he says. "If
ye've the money ye can go up yon plank and seek out the
purser, Mr. Tavistock, and he'll see ye right. Or I could
always use another hand, if ye no mind muckin' after the
beasts."

"I'll pay," says I, sure in my mind that working for this
gent would make slavery seem a decent career.

Tavistock was a small fussy man who constantly dug at
things in his ears, which things I did not inquire about.
He must have cut his own hair with nail scissors, for it
stood out in tufts here and there and reminded me of
grazed-on winter grass. I paid him in Yankee gold, one

hundred dollars, which he didn't bat an eye at. The coins—big double eagles—disappeared, and he didn't offer me a receipt.

He showed me to my cabin, a cramped, smelly cubicle with a short bed built into the wall and a large basin and a water jug in a stout rack. Tavistock disappeared after saying to me that sailing time was "late the day after tomorrow or the one after that, if everything goes well, which it won't." The mules and oxen were bellering both on the docks and below decks.

I went ashore and passed the Captain, who stared at me for a moment and nodded. He stuck out a bony paw, which I shook.

"I'm Captain Macneice," he says.

"James Adendorff," I says.

"It'll do," he says. "We'll sail late tomorrow night. I'll keep the crew at it till they drop."

"I'm sure that you will," I says. "Any suggestions for supplies I might need for the voyage?"

"Ye been to sea before?" he says.

"No."

"I'd take a case or two of Scots whiskey and some towels," he says. "This old tub wallows like an Irisher at his mistress out on the sea. But the Loooorrd will see us through."

"What are all these beasts for?" I says.

"Her Majesty is going to war with the King of the Zulus," says Macneice, "and there is a sad lack of beasts in all Africa."

"Who are the Zulus?" I says.

"Damned heathennnnnn niggers," says Macneice, "ignorant of God and presumptuous."

I walked up into the chandlers district and arranged for two cases of good Scots whiskey and several changes of stout cheap clothes and rifle cartridges and a long list of things which I might need. Seasick cures, soap, razors.

"The gentleman is bound for. . . ?" asks a clerk in a dry goods store.

"Africa," I says.

"Oh," he says, "then it's ready money, is it?"

I paid him and arranged to have him deliver my purchases. I was beginning to get a little nervous. Crossing the ocean was one thing, but crossing the ocean on the *Forbes Castle* with several hundred seasick oxen and mules promised to be sort of long in the aroma department.

The next night the last of the protesting stock was hoisted aboard, the lines were slipped from the bitts, and a couple of tugs shoved us around and then we moved up the broad St. Lawrence.

I was seasick before we ever got to the damn ocean.

29

By sundown on the second day if any sonofabitch had said to me the word "sea" I would have thought very nasty things about him indeed, and further I wouldn't have been able to do a damn thing about it. I had heaved up whatever it was I had et for the last week, along with what I hoped were not vital sweetbreads and small glands. There was a pattern of roses in the porcelain in the bottom of the basin in my cabin. I was beginning to hate roses. I was thinking about cutting Tavistock's throat. He kept coming by and saying, "Not doing well, are we?" and like that.

Then we got out into the ocean, and I was fine. I spent a lot of time up on the bows, where the wind was fresh and salt, and I even slept up there when it wasn't raining, since my cabin smelled like the Kansas City stockyards on a hot day. I drank a lot of Scots whiskey.

The sea was gray and the clouds were gray and it took us twenty-four days to round the Cape of Good Hope. We did it at night, and I saw the lights of Cape Town off to the north. We were headed to Durban, farther up on the eastern side. Most of the mules and oxen had done pretty well; we only began to lose stock the third week. The critters that died were tossed overboard, and so was the garbage, and when I was feeling particularly brave I went back to the fantail and looked out at the ship's wake. They had just tossed an ox over the side, and it was bobbing in the bubbles behind. There were two big triangular fins near it, and all of a sudden the whole ox went under and didn't come up.

"Ye'd best not fall oooooverrrboard," said Captain Macneice. He had come up by me while I was still waiting for the ox to bob back up. "Fearful great gurries they have here. Saw one bite a man in half once. They get much more common and bigger as we go up the coast to Durban."

One of the sharks heaved his head out of the water and looked around. I thought I could throw a grand piano down his mouth without bumping the sides, if my aim was good.

"Well, Mr. Adendorrrff," says Macneice, "ye'll see Durrban soon and be glad, I am sure. Course, they'll draft you."

"Draft?" says I.

"Ye're an English subject sound in wind and limb and they'll be needing such," says this damned old Scots buzzard. "And ye'll take the widow's shilling, sure enough."

"Widow?"

"An expression we English subjects have, Mr.—cough—Adendorrrff. The widow is the Queen. Her name's Victoria. Or you could tell him you are an American and then only have to explain why ye've anooooother man's papers."

"How much you want?" I says, fingering my moneybelt.

"I am nae blackmailer," says Macneice, "and I went to sea a long time ago because I'd be hung for murther on the shore had I stayed. Keep the name Adendorrrff if ye like, but cast the papers to the sharks. They're not much for questions in Durrban; 'tis a young place, like your West."

"How 'bout a drink, then," I says.

"Fine."

The old bastard put away a full bottle of my Scots whiskey, and he told me about himself. I had known a lot like him, they were up and down the Rockies after gold, or foremen on the cattle ranches, or merchants. After he had made a big dent in a second bottle he excused himself and went back to the bridge. I went back to the fantail and tossed Adendorff's papers to the sharks. There were five big fins following the wake now.

The next day the wind brisked up and the seas ran across our course, and the bucketing of the boat got bad again, and I got seasick. I laid in my bed, moaning, and time to time I stared at the roses in the bottom of the basin, and when I was feeling blue I wondered if I could walk back home over the polar ice.

Macneice stuck his head in the door and said something choice about the crew having voted me the strongest stomach on the voyage, as I had been throwing farther than anyone else, and would I care to enter a contest and like that. I tried to throw a bottle of Scotch at him—full, too—but rather than duck he caught it one-handed and smiled and nodded at me.

"Temper," says Macneice, "temper, Mister Adendorrrff. It is one of the holy virtues to bind your anger."

I unleashed a string of blasphemies—the useful part of the catechism classes I had been drug to as a kid—and Macneice rolled his eyes and said, "Tut tut," and I finished up telling him that now I knew why all firearms had to be surrendered to the purser and kept under lock and key during the voyage.

Our arrival at the entrance to Durban's harbor was announced most emphatically. We ran aground on the bar—there was a good-sized river there, and it shoved out the sand which built up where the current of the river lost to the ocean. The ship heaved and shuddered and scraped and I scraped myself off the wall of my cabin.

I went out on the deck—the ship was shuddering forward a bit—and looked out at the coast of Africa. It looked lovely. The boat pulled free and slid slowly into the harbor, and a couple of little tugs, belching black smoke, rushed out and stuck their bows into the side of the ship.

Twelve hours later we were tied up to the dock. I bade Macneice a fond farewell and gave him the rest of the Scots whiskey. He told me that the Durban Inn was a good clean place and promised to have my things sent on. When I wobbled down the gangplank and put foot to the quay I fell over. I had totally got out of the habit of walking on things that didn't move. Some loafers sitting on bales nearby laughed and pointed. I staggered up and sort of tacked and yawed my way up the street, and about a half mile up the street I saw the Durban Inn. I stumbled inside and made way toward the desk. The clerk, a pimply youth, looked for a second and then went back to the newspaper.

"I need a room," says I, holding on to the counter for support. The clerk wrinkled his nose, no doubt at the smell, or rather, smells, I gave off. My nose had give up long since.

"You'll be off the *Forbes Castle*?" he says, dabbing at his nostrils with a handkerchief. His eyes was watering.

"Yes, thank god," says I.

"You'll be all right on the morrow," he says. "Shall I have the bellman carry you up to your room?"

"I'll crawl," I says. "Send me up some breakfast in the morning and right now I'd like a drink."

"The bar is closed," says the clerk.

I slammed a gold double eagle on the counter.

"Take a week's worth for the room out of that, find me a

bottle of good whiskey, and keep the damn change," I says, knowing that room clerks are the same everywhere.

He nodded and whirled the register around. I scrawled on it, making no legible sign, took my key, and went on all fours up the stairs. There were roses in the damn carpet. The wallpaper in my room was covered in roses. I fell on the bed, and when there was a discreet knock at the door I said, "Come in" and didn't even bother to get up. It was the clerk, of course, with my whiskey and a silver soda siphon and glasses. He put them down on the nightstand without so much as a nod and went off.

I had a few drinks and began to feel better, actually even walked over to the window without falling through it. I looked out on the small town of Durban, it being preferable to the roses.

A milkman went by, singing about he was a weaver and roving blade. His horse's shoes tapped on the cobbles. I went to bed.

30

The next day I peeled one eye open, winced at the sight
of the roses, pulled the bellrope, got a bellman, paid him
to go get me some clean clothes from my gear, which had
arrived, and went to the baths. I soaked in hot water for a
couple of hours and all of the time I had a feeling that
something wasn't right.

Oh, I finally said to myself, my guts ain't playing cat's
cradle anymore. I haven't been seasick for hours. Horray. I
got dressed and went down to the dining room and put
away a lot of eggs and steak and tomatoes and other things
I had given up on ever seeing again. I drank coffee. I
could walk.

The hotel manager was on duty now, and he hovered
around me, having had news, no doubt, of my generosity
with the night clerk. Not being desperate anymore, I
fended off his questions and finally scraped him off me and
went out into the bright sun to walk a little. After you
haven't been able to walk, walking is very interesting. My

head still felt like it had a big hole through it, and one look in the mirror convinced me that I ought to let other folks look at me for a few days but spare myself. My eyes looked like two pissholes in a snowbank. My clothes flapped about me. But I was on blessed, solid earth.

I went down to the docks and watched my shipmates being slung over the side. It was gratifying to see that most of them fell over, too. The oxen tended to sink down and put their heads on the ground, while the mules splayed their feet out and then, finding dry land, looked around for someone to kick. I was glad I wasn't having to work that bunch. There were soldiers running here and there and officers and sergeants talking or screaming and several more ships unloading wagons and crates.

I ate lunch in an open-air restaurant, with good wine. It was hot—the seasons were reversed here, and though it was snowing by now in the Rockies, it was hot as hell here and the flies gathered in big clouds. There were hedges of dark green with big, sickly-smelling flowers in them, and the traffic on the streets was heavy, though all of the horses looked poorly—old and tired, or not fed well. Of course, I said to myself, all of the good ones have been taken by the Army. There were little knots of turbaned fellers walking by, chattering, and holding hands. Indians, I guessed, the ones from India, where Columbus thought he was.

Durban was a funny mixture of substantial, well-built houses and buildings and rude shacks, all cheek by jowl. It was a lot like Denver, actually, new and thrown up overnight and then getting all respectable. The streets was clean, and unlike Denver, there weren't packs of mangy dogs everywhere, not that I could see, nor pigs rooting about in the streets. People didn't wear guns much. The women all wore big bonnets and uncomfortable-looking dresses, and were followed by a couple of black servants, barefooted, and usually dressed in white.

While I was walking down the main boulevard late in the afternoon a troop of Irregulars rode by. They was dressed in uniforms of black corduroy with red stripes and facings, and they all wore slouch hats with a long bird feather sticking out behind. They was riding well, but not in columns like Army troopers.

There was a big, bluff-looking British officer leading. From time to time he'd look back at his troops and then look forward again and start muttering. They went by, chaffing at each other, like all youngsters who haven't ever been in a war and think it is all going to be great fun. I thought that was what the officer was probably muttering about.

I ate again, early, huge portions of beef and salads and fruit and good wine—the waiter told me that Napoleon himself had preferred this South African wine to any from France, which, knowing Frogs as I do, must have made them scream a lot.

Full and feeling fit at last, I went out for a walk again. I heard a funny, sort of German-sounding babble behind me, and then there was a great thump on the back of my head and everything went to stars.

When I came to, back at the hotel, there was six people in my room. Actually, there was seven. The father, Piet Uys, was snoring under the table and out of my line of sight.

"It seems that when in his cups Piet likes to roar down the streets of Durban and butt a likely stranger in the back of the head with his own very hard skull. In England we call it the Liverpool Kiss."

The face of the hotel manager come up behind his god damn fruity voice and he smiled at me sort of like he didn't think that this could have happened to a more deserving feller.

Greetje Uys, the only woman in the room, was bathing my forehead and speaking softly to the manager, who translated. He introduced the four Uys sons, who had taken this opportunity to clean their guns, except for the one who was stropping his knife on one of my boots. Time to time they would look fondly at dear old daddy, who was snoring like a steam engine with a bust cylinder.

"They wish to apologize," said the manager, above the din of all five conscious Uys's Afrikaans, "for their father's butting you. They are also thrilled to meet the great Yellowstone Kelly."

"What?" I bellered.

"Just a moment," said the manager. He listened to the five of them for a while, and nodded, and then came over by me.

"Mister... uh... Adendorff," said the manager, "these people are convinced that you are Luther Kelly, whoever that is. It seems that an itinerant Jewish pedlar once became quite ill while near their farm. They nursed him back to health. He had a copy of a book about Yellowstone Kelly, written by one George Hanks, and the pedlar read a story to them aloud each evening. There was a picture of... Kelly... in it, and he looked like you."

I started cussing, in a general sort of way.

"Mr. Adendorff," said the manager, "they wonder what you are saying. If I should translate what you are saying the Uys boys will tear you in half before throwing you to the sharks in Durban Harbor. They are devout people. This is their mother."

I looked over at the four cheerful louts, all of whom were smiling and nodding at me, and showing lots of big white teeth. That could, I thought, change real fast. They had the flat, clear gaze of critters that eat other critters.

"Tell them that I am James Adendorff, and that I once *met* Yellowstone Kelly," I says. "And by the by would you find a copy of that blasted book for me?"

"Surely," said the manager.

Having seen that I was all recovered, the Uys family

rose and took their leave, the largest son throwing dear old daddy over his shoulder—Uys weighed maybe two-forty—like a feather comforter. The boys all shook hands, and poor, tired-looking little Greetje smiled and nodded.

"They say welcome to Africa, and they'll be by for you in the morning," said the manager.

"What?"

"Mr. uh . . . Adendorff," said the manager, "you apparently, when delirious, said that you were here for ivory, so they are going to help you get ivory. If you would like to explain to them that you don't wish to take up their offer of hospitality, that's fine, but you can find another interpreter and another hotel to do it in."

"I see," I says.

"And I might inform you that the Army is needing horsemen and men of military experience, and if you don't wish to go hunt Zulus, you may wish to go hunt ivory. The Army knows you're here. *They* will be by late tomorrow afternoon. My best guess only."

"Please tell the Uyses I will be delighted."

The manager beamed, I beamed, the Uyses beamed.

They stomped down the stairs.

"If you go with them," said the manager, "I would warn you not to denigrate their religion or bother their women. The only book they ever read is the Bible, and I suspect only the earlier books of that. They are a fine and honorable people and they have a true Old Testament God."

"Meaning that they'd have my liver and lights is what you are saying if I piss on their religion or chase their skirts."

"I hope that you do," said the manager. "I detest Americans. They are so . . . second-rate."

My reply resulted in my being assisted to the street by a couple of burly lads. My baggage landed beside me.

"Kelly," says I aloud, "this is not working out like you hoped."

Whilst I sat on my luggage thinking on clever rejoinders, the manager came out and dropped the stout leather valise with the very stout lock on it, that had my money in it.

I paid a loafer to watch my baggage while I hunted up a bank and rented some safe space. Say what you will about the English, they do respect money. The clerk didn't bat an eye, gave a receipt and assured me that my gold was safe and would be sent on to me if need be if I included a coded number in the request letter. I took a thousand for ready money.

Then I got a bottle of brandy from a pub and went back and paid off the loafer and sat out in front of the hotel, saying nasty things about the accommodations to those who looked like they might be headed in there. I had an enjoyable evening.

The Uyses came by for me at four in the morning, which is the normal waking hour for all good Boers. They had a Cape Cart drawn by four fine bay mares. We went west out of the city, to where their two wagons were held for them.

There was a small passel of nigger retainers—on the Boer wagons a black runs along beside the lead oxen and guides them. An old white-bearded man, one of the ancestral Uyses, spent a few happy moments kicking the blacks awake. His eyes was covered with cataracts and his vocal cords sounded like they was covered with warts.

A young boy, maybe fourteen, with hair so blond it was almost white, ran circles around the little train on a dapple pony. He rode right up to me and stopped and looked down for a moment.

Dik Uys came over, laughing, chattering at the kid. He then spent a few minutes going over his limited store of English, and finally pointed at Greetje and then at the kid.

"Oh," says I, light dawning. "This is your little sister."

"Ja ja ja," says Dik.

"Ape turd," says the little sister.

"You speak English," I says.

"Yaas," she said, and then turned to her dear brother, and smiling very sweetly, she said, "You stupid baboon."

"Ja ja ja," said Dik happily.

"Want me to translate?" says I.

"I would look very innocent and my brother would beat you into the ground like a tent stake," said the girl.

"Marieke," said Dik. "Ja ja ja."

"Nice to meet you," says I.

Marieke smiled sweetly and put spurs to her horse. She cantered off into the dark.

I got up on a wagon seat.

We lurched off toward a distant blue range of mountains. The mosquitoes were godawful.

31

This part of Africa looked a bit like most of Wyoming—dry, gravelly hills with sparse grass, buttes, and I could tell that there were high mountains far off by the way the clouds stacked up on the horizon in the evening. They were scrubby acacia trees along the little watercourse, and though the country was in some ways familiar, in others it was strange, and I was uncomfortable. I didn't have no Jim Bridger to draw me maps on a square of sand.

The family Uys took turns chattering at me in their Afrikaans, and I was able to pick up a few words the first day and more the next. They dragged their wagons with teams of sixteen oxen, all matched reddish and white on one wagon, dirty brindle on the other. The wagons themselves were longer than the Conestogas, and the whips the boys used to drive the oxen were nearly forty feet in length. A young nigger ran beside the lead animals and tugged on a rein to guide them around this and that. The wagons were pegged and a lot of the fittings that would have been metal on an American wagon were rawhide.

We drove all night, and let the oxen rest and chew their cuds during the day. The Boers have a saying—"Never let the sun shine on spanned oxen"—and I thought that a lot of our immigrants were fools to have insisted on driving during the day, since it was harder on the stock.

Little Marieke spent her time riding hell for leather here and there. She'd lather up four horses in a day. When she was in camp, she argued with her mother constantly. I couldn't understand what she was saying, of course, but I suspect that it was what all mothers and daughters argue about. Anything handy, favorite subjects being the loose comportment of the daughter, who is no doubt headed for a house of ill repute, and counter-accusations of fossilization and pecksniffery.

Marieke took enough of a shine to me to stop by where I was every once in a while and beg some new cuss words. It pleased her to describe in loving detail the shortcomings of her brothers, using words common to buffalo skinners and folks what just hit their thumbs with hammers.

She was very pretty. Certain of her parts would now and again fetch up against the loose shirt and britches which she wore and then disappear again. Once she give me a level stare which has but one meaning and I felt most encouraged before I thought of having a whole passel of Boer in-laws. I could see myself croacking out things I swore I would never say in front of a minister with six elephant guns leveled at my vitals.

Marieke would no doubt be leveling one of the guns. She went on at some length about what a stupid passel of unwashed dolts her brothers were and how she warn't going to settle for such as they. She lived her young life like she rode her pony—straight for the fence and be damned to the possibilities.

It took us five days to get to the Uys farm—it was one of

ten owned by the family. Boers feel that they need two
large farms, one for summer grazing, and one for winter,
and of course each son needs the same number for his
family, and so on. A lot of the green, lush places we passed
was infected with lung disease, so even though Africa was
big, I could see how land was dear—one Boer family who
produced the customary number of sons would need
upwards of a million acres for the next generation.

The Uys house was a low, one-story mud-brick house,
which rambled all over. New wings had been added as the
sons got married and about four hundred small children
came boiling out of everywhere—little white kids and
little niggers, all mixed up in a mob. And there was a
native camp—they call them kraals—about a mile away.

We had got the oxen off the tows and so forth and I was
trying to help without getting in the way. A rider appeared
on a ridge to the north, and I could tell by the way that his
horse moved that the animal was lathered and hard rode.
It was another Boer, and he come trotting up, swung down
and give his reins to a black groom, and launched into a
speech, with a lot of hand gestures.

Piet Uys and his four sons went up to him and they all
commenced to talk at once. They talked louder, and then a
couple of them went off and the old man began to beller
and point and order the black servants this way and that. I
didn't have the faintest idea what was going on.

Pretty soon the two sons who had gone off returned and
not long after some black herders brought in some fresh
oxen.

Oh, Kelly, I says, this don't look like no ivory hunt.

Old Piet was thundering along at the top of his lungs,
and the servants were throwing some things out of the
wagons and throwing other things in—lots of boxes of
ammunition, I noticed, and bags of the coarse meal the
Boers bake bread with—and Greetje was flying back and
forth with jars of this and that and chivvying her servants.

By sundown we was headed north again, lurching along what I supposed passed for a road. They had given me a horse and I had the use of a saddle, and my rifle was stuck in a rawhide boot. I felt strange. Here I was, going off to war, it now seemed, with a bunch of folks whose language I did not know and into a country I had never seen. I wished I had some maps.

There was someone following us. I don't think that the others took the bother to look behind, but I couldn't get out of the habit. A couple of times I would see a flash a couple of miles behind.

I slipped out of camp at midnight and followed my nose to a little cooking fire and found Marieke washing her hair in a folding canvas bucket. Then she washed the rest of herself. Soon as she began to dig the soap out of her eyes I padded in and took up residence on a near stump.

When she saw me she started a little. Not much. Then the little minx finished her bath and rubbed herself dry with a couple of small towels and stretched like a cat.

Then she come over and stood in front of me with her hands on her hips and a grin on her face.

"Bastard," she said.

"You ought to go on home," I says. "There's a war up ahead."

"I go home now, there's a war with my mother."

Not much I could say to that.

"Let's fornicate," she said.

Not much I could say to that either. Couple hours later I went back to the rest of the family Uys, who was all sleeping. A nigger boy give me a big white grin and I almost kicked him. I went out again the night after but she was gone and there was no sign of her.

Three days later, after crossing a lot of watercourses and gullies, we come to another road, one which had had hard use recently. We turned a little west and come dawn, camped. I could see dust far forward of us, and another big cloud behind us. One of the boys—I think it was Dik—pointed to the dust cloud and then pointed to the wagons.

"Rooinek," he said. It meant redneck, which is what they called the British.

Along about noon a train of wagons hove into view, some drawn by oxen, and some by mules. The wagons was driven by civilians, with a few red-coated soldiers riding in front and to the sides. They went on. The mules looked all in and starved to boot, so I figured that it must be some stock recently bought. The Army was in a hurry, if they couldn't wait even to let the animals gather their strength. One span of mules was in such bad shape I knew that they would be dying before long. Their flanks were bloody from the whips and they were wheezing.

I rode along with the soldiers—a young Lieutenant (subaltern) named Smith, and he told me what little he knew.

The General, Commanding, Chelmsford, was up ahead, and he had supply dumps for three columns which he was going to shove north into Zululand.

"We need to provoke the Zulus into attacking us and this is the way," said the youngster. He said a lot of other things of the sort you hear from lieutenants who just got out of school.

"And you, sir," he said finally, "will you be riding with those filthy Boers?"

"At least till I get to Helpmakaar," I says. "And who do you recommend that I see when I arrive?"

"Buller's your man," says the kid, "a jolly fellow."

I didn't reply to that, but what I was thinking was why a jolly fellow would be at the end of the damn earth buckling up to get perforated by a lot of spears. I had spent some time in the soldiering business, and found it largely run by idiots adept at sacrificing great numbers of morons. I had known some great soldiers—Miles, for instance, who for all his foolishness kept his eye on the prize—and a lot of others, usually low enough in rank that some imbecile up the ladder made sure they got slaughtered before they got enough rank to do anything about it.

We got to Helpmakaar, where the main supply dump was for Chelmsford's army. All of the grass for ten miles out had been chopped down. There were trains of wagons bearing nothing more warlike than hay. Apparently Chelmsford had given up on the hope of having enough oxen and was using mules, Army issue, and these mules, like most soldiers, had to be fed. They was unused to grazing and weren't about to start beating up their own living if there was cut hay.

The Uyses found a big mob of their kind and commenced to having a real nice bellering match, encouraged by some dirty old brute in a dog collar who must have been a preacher, who had a big old Bible he read from in a voice like a foghorn.

Dik Uys was standing toward the outside of this festival, leaning on his big old muzzle-loading elephant gun, and looking sort of bored. I rode up to him on the bay horse they had given me, fished out a couple of gold double eagles, handed them to him, and rode off, leaving him looking bewildered. I would no doubt see them again, at which time I could either pony up the rest of the money for my rig or get change.

Old Piet was matched up with another white-bearded old pirate, and they was alternately stabbing each other in the chests with horny forefingers or hollering to the heavens, so it seemed a bad time to dicker with him over the saddle and tack and stock. I got my spare ammunition from the wagon and my bedroll and slipped off, looking for the tent that must be headquarters and maybe a nice soft job over west, where I had heard the gold and diamonds was, and the Zulus wasn't.

Military encampments is all alike, especially the ones

back of the lines, where all of the stores is piled up and the damn clerks are running here and there hollering and begging signatures off of officers who are hoarse from shouting. The accents was British, and there was hundreds of potbellied niggers carrying things or being kicked and cursed by civilians.

I asked directions, was pointed to a cluster of tents up on a little hill, hard by a big corrugated iron shed. I was told I would find Chelmsford there and the rest of the staff. It was about noon.

My first sight of Redvers Buller was unfortunate, as it made me like him right off and if I hadn't seen him as I did at that moment, I might have reacted a little more sensibly later in the day.

The big tent off to the right was the mess tent, where Buller and the rest of the officers ate and in the evenings got drunk and such.

A little sandy-haired feller came flying out of the tent, and he was follered closely by a shower of notepaper and pencils, and then by a tall, broad-shouldered, red-faced Major who took one long stride from the tent door and gave the sandy-haired feller a hell of a kick in the arse as he was struggling to his feet. As the sandy-haired feller flew by me, he looked up at me. It was George Hanks of the *Hartford Courant*.

"Kelly?" he gasped, just as the red-faced Major—he was so damn mad that his moustaches were sticking straight out to the sides like a longhorn steer's horns—gave George another mighty kick, and when George didn't get up he stood over him and stuck his hands on his hips and bellered at him for a while.

"By Jove, you double-damned lying sneaking scummy little berk of a bloody journalist, if I ever see you in the mess tent again I will . . . ," and he trailed off and run out of words.

I couldn't think of a thing to do but clap and shout horray.

The officer turned and looked at me and blinked, sort of like a bull who has just turned an opponent into a bloody smear and wishes to crunch something else soon as his head clears.

"Do you know this bastard, sir?" says the Major.

"Ain't there a nice anthill we could peg him out on or some crocodiles we could toss him to?" I says. "That lying little bastard ain't never written a single truthful word."

The Major stared at me for a moment and blinked, then he walked over to me. I swung down off my horse.

"Buller," he says, sticking out a huge hard-cased paw.

"Adendorff," says I. His hand sort of swallowed mine, crushed several bones, and spat back the little that was left.

"I've not seen you before," he says. "Are you with the Light Horse?"

"I just got here," I says. "I ain't with anybody."

"That your horse?" he says.

I nodded. I was later to wish I had said something intelligent, like no.

"Cobbett!" Buller yelled. "Cobbett, damn you, get your arse over here."

A harried-looking Leftenant came rushing out of the tent so recently abandoned by Hanks.

"Enroll him in the Light Horse," says Buller. He looked me over for a moment.

"Make him a sergeant," says Buller.

"Right, sir, very good."

Buller went back to the mess tent. Cobbett pulled a pencil from a leather case on his hip, took out a form, and cleared his throat. I took the opportunity to go over and kick Hanks a couple of times. Hanks groaned and passed out again, or maybe he was lying doggo.

"Name?" says Cobbett.

32

The Frontier Light Horse was a collection of what passed for the gentry of Natal. Youngsters and a few choleric men in their forties who had seen action somewheres else and would no doubt try to fight Zulus like they fought wogs or Ayrabs. They didn't have any uniforms, and a great deal of not very good thought had gone into the design of their individual duds, no doubt by mothers and wives and sweethearts who wished to have their boys stand out and be prominent.

I have always wished to blend in and be a part of the landscape, as it attracts less in the way of bullets and spears and arrows and other expressions of interest from whoever you are fighting. The one uniform thing we all had was this great goddamn feather from something called a cocky-olibird. The feather was white and about two and a half feet long and mine was going to last right up to the point where we headed into Zululand, when it would disappear and be damned about it. My clothes was yellow-brown stout canvas denim and I had a hat of a color I call anonymous.

It was true that I didn't know the country at all, but I'd had a few years of wandering around in the landscape when it had folks in it who would dearly like to make Mrs. Kelly's son Luther into maggot food, and I had learned how to go silent, how to blend in, and how to stay out of the way of trouble as much as I could. It don't always work, that, but it goes with the job and I have never liked clerking.

I bought a bottle of brandy from a sutler and went around the encampment, looking for some scarred older feller with shifty eyes who might know something about these here Zulus.

As I ambled along I spotted a table which had a big pile of pamphlets on it, and as I looked through them I saw one that said "Fighting Kaffirs in the Seventies," by a Colonel Steptoe. I picked it up.

"That arsehole couldn't find the balls on a bull," says a deep voice behind me, "and what he don't know of the Zulus would get you killed."

I turned around and looked at the critic. He was a giant man, near on to six and a half feet tall, and though young, his eyes had those crowsfoot lines you get from squinting hard into the distance. Also one of the eyes was glass. The other was a bright blue and it never quit flicking here and there.

"Care for a drink?" says I. "As I am prepared to trade good brandy for a little information about these here Zulus."

The stranger snorted and nodded, and we walked away from the worst of the uproar and found us a couple of unused crates in the shade of a blue gum tree.

"I'm James Adendorff," says I, "and you know of the Zulus?" I handed him the bottle of brandy and he took a long pull.

"John Dunn," says he, handing me the bottle back. He had two pistols stuck in his belt, and his back to the camp, and while he talked his good eye never stopped flicking this way and that. There wasn't anything to see, but it is a good habit, one I admire and have myself.

"They are a great and noble people," says Dunn. This took me aback for a moment, as I was expecting a list of atrocities. "And this war is unjust as all such wars are. These damn fools"—here he jerked his head toward the encampment—"think that the Zulus are a bunch of cowards like their Kaffirs, who are farmers and slaves to wages. The Zulus made them cowards. The Zulus so despise the Kaffir that they kill them with rocks, they being unworthy of the iklu, the assegai. I have lived among the Zulus for many years."

And that is how I met John Dunn, the White Chief of Zululand. He had forty Zulu wives and was the scandal of the entire colony... the women, anyway. The men was green and dripping with envy. He talked for two hours, about how the Zulus form for a battle, how they divide into regiments so proud that they have to be quartered very carefully, for there are grudges between certain regiments and if they are camped together, they will fight each other.

The Zulus when attacking, he said, drawing figures on the ground, use a formation shaped like the head of a bull. The center of the formation is the bull's forehead, and here the Zulus are concentrated, with other regiments corresponding to horns, which as soon as the forehead collides with the enemy, race out to each side and surround them. The reserves are seated behind the center, some distance away, with their backs to the fight, so that they don't get excited. They fight with big oxhide shields and a short, five-foot spear called an assegai. Any Zulu who has a wound in the back is killed. Any Zulu who hangs back from a charge is killed. Their generals are called in Dunas.

They raise cattle, he said, and they seldom hunt, and when they do they just march out the regiments and surround an area and then close in.

"How are they at tracking and such?" I asks.

"Poor," says Dunn, "but some of them have Hottentots for slaves, and a Totty can track a bee through the air. No white man can ever track as well as a Totty—and *they* are amateurs compared to the Bushmen. But the Zulus can track some, and they can run sixty miles in a day. If you are being chased by the Zulus, care for your horse and give them the slip. If you just ride, they'll run the horse down."

He gave me a pamphlet written by a Bishop, of all people, name of Colenso, which described how the Zulu regiments was drilled and ordered, their tactics, and it had a phonetic dictionary of some of their language.

Dunn and I finished off the brandy. We parted and he went off, and I went to find something to eat—it turned out to be embalmed bully beef and some strange boiled greens.

I gave up on the dinner provided by the Frontier Light Horse, and went off to Helpmakaar to buy some tinned grub or what I could find. There was a couple of open-air cookplaces going full blast, and I got a dripping hunk of beef and a half a dozen ears of corn from some stout Boer woman who was doing a land-office business. There were some other stalls set up here and there, and I bought about ten pounds of jerky—they call it biltong in Africa— and some tinned honey.

By the time I got back to the camp of the Frontier Light Horse, Buller was bellowing orders and advice, in a stream of short words. We were to move out in the morning. I had yet to find out which of these jolly lads would be my responsibility—didn't want to seem pushy and overbearing, what with my new sergeant rank and all. Buller concluded his speech—we were moving out in the morning, to go west and then north, ahead of the western column. We would be scouting. This was fine by me. If I have a choice between skulking and a pitched battle I will always take the skulking. I'm good at it and had good teachers.

"Adendorff!" I heard this beller, and though the voice was different it had the same note of gleeful authority I had come to hate in the voice of Colonel Nelson Miles. It was a voice which had decided something, something unpleasant for old Luther, er, James Adendorff.

Buller come striding through the camp, glancing this way and that. He saw me as I was starting to slide under a wagon. He bellered "Adendorff!" and stopped me cold. I managed my sickliest shit-eating grin.

"When I first saw you I thought to myself that here was a scout," says Buller, beaming down at me, "and I have sent four junior officers to look for you. They couldn't find you, although some of them were near to you. You had just left. You had just been seen. I am encouraged, sir, encouraged. Vastly encouraged. If a man can disappear in a camp one step ahead of four officers and god knows how many sergeants, why, how much better will that man be able to disappear in the countryside. You are leaving tonight. You will take a companion. You will ride west and north to the vicinity of the Zunguin Mountain, and scout for Zulus. You will find bivouacs for a large force, with ample water and wood. You will map the country. You will meet me at the upper Drift of the Tugela in three weeks to a month. If you are late, I will assume that the Zulus have skinned you alive and draped you over an anthill."

"They do that sort of thing?" I says. "That's not friendly at all."

"Lieutenant Harford will go with you," says Buller, beaming and red. "Draw your rations and ammunition."

"Got my own," I says. "Yours ain't fit to eat."

Buller laughed.

Buller sort of nodded his head over to a thin wisp of a feller who was standing in Buller's considerable shade. This youth looked to be about fourteen on a good day. He was wearing a monocle. His hair looked like a bunch of grama grass been gnawed on by a big buffalo. He was wearing a canvas suit which was covered in buttoned pockets. He had on a sun helmet which was about six sizes too large for him.

He was holding a butterfly net.

"Now just a goddamn frost-fingered pluperfect fucking minute," I began, preparatory to remarks of a more specific nature, "I am not . . ."

Buller slammed his eyebrows together so hard they went thunk.

"Are you disobeying an order from a superior officer?" says Buller. "I hang men for that."

"Well, goddamn it, it beats gettin' peeled and the anthill. This pimply kid couldn't find his way to the bathroom from the goddamn library, and I am damned if . . ."

Buller beamed at me, he looked positively benevolent.

"You are very wrong, Mr. Adendorff," he says, "but you will have to find that out. Arthur . . ."

"Sir," chirped the youth.

"Adendorff will be your companion."

"Oh, dear," says Harford. "Is he fit?"

Buller snorted and grinned and stomped off.

We saddled up and stowed map-making gear—pencils, paper, and a compass—in our saddlebags. Then Harford got a mule, and put a large packframe on it, and then he began to unpack a lot of tin boxes from a wooden crate.

"What in hell are those?" I said, not believing my eyes.

"For the specimens," says Harford. "I am sir to you,

Adendorff, and I will damn well have you address me thus."

"SPECIMENS? WHAT IN THE HELL ARE YOU TALKING ABOUT?" I screamed.

"I am an entomologist and a Fellow of the Royal Society," says young Arthur Harford, "and you are a sergeant and a lout."

"Christ on a bent dingle," I says, "this is . . ."

Harford walked over to me and stared hard at me from down there somewhere for a while. His gaze was level and his voice had gone very soft.

"I know what I am doing," he said, "and we have a great deal to do. Shall we?"

We rode out, past the encampment, and picked up a road that wound off toward the Drakensberg Range, the Dragon Mountains. We rode all night.

Arthur rode very well. Sometime before dawn I trotted up beside him. He was asleep in the saddle.

I turned my horse.

"Do check the pack on the mule," said Arthur. "There's a good fellow."

I did. Wouldn't do to have Harford's goddamn bug-tins clanking. Wouldn't do at all.

Jaysus kayrist, Kelly, I says to myself.

33

Appearances is deceiving things, and by the end of the second day I was admitting to myself that I was dead wrong about this little feller with his monocle and bug boxes. He missed nothing.

We were headed far to the west of Zululand, and when it come time to turn north Arthur pulled up and hopped off his horse and commenced to sculpt a map in a sand patch. He modeled the mountains we would be going through—just like Jim Bridger had done for me a dozen years before—and he explained the rivers, how the clouds bunched when it was going to rain like hell, and how to spot the dry watercourses which would have twenty-foot walls of water moving down them a few hours after the rain fell in the faraway mountains. I knew how to see that anyway, but I was damn impressed with his simple explanation of what we were likely to see. I have a good sense of distance and proportion, and I could picture the sand map in my eye long after we had left it. Part

way through the lecture, Arthur spotted something in
the sand, plunged his hand in, and pulled out a beetle.
He gave it some Latin name and pulled out a small tin
he had in one of the hundred or so pockets of his
suit.

"How nice!" he said. "Jolly good!" The beetle was busy
trying to chew off a finger, with some success. The bugger
was about four inches long and had a set of choppers
would of done credit to a weasel.

"Do the Zulus leave you alone because they think you
are crazy?" I said. "Some American Indian tribes do, I
know that."

"Unwise to assume that," said Harford. "I was raised
among them and we are, after all, at war. I think perhaps
that they should not see us at all."

"Raised among them?" I says.

"My parents were missionaries," says young Arthur.
"The Zulus regard a converted tribesman as a spoiled
Zulu, and we were on the fringes of the kingdom, and our
Zulu were the disaffected ones. Still Zulus they were, and
fine people."

"Except for a few bad habits, like skinning folks alive
and pegging them out on anthills."

"Or throwing them alive into crocodile pools, or pounding
stakes up the rectum and leaving the unhappy victim to
scream for a day and scream more when the jackals come
at night, since the jackal or hyena always goes for the groin
first, or perhaps impaling the victim—again through the
rectum—on a thin stake, so that the weight of the body
drives the point ever deeper, or giving the unfortunate to
the women, who skin one slowly, or perhaps sewing the
victim up in a raw cowhide and leaving it in the sun,
or..."

"Nice friends you got," I says.

"You see why I prefer that we not be detected."

"Couldn't agree with you more," I says.

"We will, of course, travel at night," he says, "and you will do as I say. Or I'll kill you. This information is of great value to the Army. The lives of many depend on it. I will meet any insubordination or even mere clumsiness with death. I didn't want you along, Mr. Adendorff. I obey my orders. You obey yours."

"Fine," I says. "What do we do first?"

"We shall have to ford the upper Tugela. I will not, of course, take us to a crossing that is used often, since there will be Zulus watching it. Since it is late spring, the river rises late each day and then falls about the middle of the night, when the snows in the mountains freeze up. We shall have to get across and get away and erase the evidence of our passing and be well hid by daybreak."

"That I know how to do."

"Do you, Mr. Adendorff? And where did you learn?"

"Here and there," says I.

Harford snorted. "Not in dime novels, I hope."

We were stopped near a small rivulet which cut through a bank of clay. I scooped up a few handfuls and began to smear it on my horse, dab here and dab there. Harford raised an eyebrow.

"The plains here let a man see for many miles," I said. "If you break up the lines of a horse or yourself, it might mean not bein' seen. And if I were you I'd put a big dollop of mud over that damn monocle. Known quite a few fellers died 'cause the sun flashed off their field glasses or a bright bit to hardware. This gun," I drew out my pistol, "has a soft, dull finish—and a bit of charcoal on your face is, I am told, the latest fashion among all good scouts."

Harford nodded. "Not necessary to do that until tomorrow night," he said. "We'll cover the beasts' feet with rawhide. Also if we have to make a run for it I have several pairs of horseshoes. We may have to reshoe our animals."

We spent a few minutes trying to top one another and

then gave up. Harford was small and thin, but wiry and strong. The one item of gear which he kept near to hand was a braided rawhide whip, thin, and from the way it hung in its coil, it must have been weighted.

At dusk we began to move, starting late, Harford said, because the Zulus could well have sent some Hottentot scouts out to live in the bush, pissing down a straw and living on a mouthful of water and a small shred of dried beef each day.

We traveled all night, keeping off the ridges. There was no moon and a cold wind came down from the Drakensberg, and the starlight was so dim that I once almost rode into a gully. The horse sensed it and stopped. We weren't making good time, but then we were being cautious, and saving our stock. It might come to making a run for it later.

We spent the day in a cave halfway up a flat-topped mountain, a small cave where water dripped into a natural basin just inside, in the shadows. We had hid the stock below in thickets. For hours, we took thread heavy with beeswax and wrapped every bit of tack that could clank or jingle. Harford was thorough. I watched him and he watched me. We didn't have much advice for one another, and I was by this time thinking that he would do to run with.

I could just make out the silvery flow of the Tugela River about ten miles away, lush and green on its banks, the sun shimmering on the water. The banks was deep-cut, as dry mountain rivers always are, and it was a considerable river, with a mixed rock-and-sand bottom, most likely, and too fast and high for crocodiles. The crocs don't kill many folks, I had heard, but the hippopotamuses accounted for a fair number—more than all other animals combined—and it seemed that folks didn't take them seriously because they were so funny looking. Me, I took them seriously.

Harford was snoozing, his hat over his eyes, and I walked toward the cave entrance. I kept well back out of the light. I was staring off in the distance when a movement caught my eye off to my left. I swung my head, and looked at a huge black snake which had reared up its head and was looking at me and swaying.

The snake and me stared at one another for what seemed a long time. I don't like snakes, and this one's head was a good six feet off the ground and god knew how much coiled on the flat. Then, moving so quick I knowed I could hardly get my gun out it rushed at me.

I was raising my pistol, trying to sight on the head. The snake reared back and lunged at me, and as its head snapped forward a thin brown line flashed by me. There was a wet crack, and the snake's head fell off the long black body. The snake flopped and thrashed for a moment, and then arranged itself into quivering coils.

"Black mamba," said Harford, behind me. "Bad snake. Dead in three minutes, if one bites you."

My hair was standing straight up and I could feel cold sweat pouring down my spine. The damn thing looked to be fifteen feet long.

"They are the only snakes which will charge," said Harford. "Very aggressive. In some tribes, a boy becomes a man only when he either kills a lion alone with a spear, or a black mamba."

"They like any particular kind of country," I says, "or do you come across them any old place?"

"Open, grassy savanna," said Harford.

"We are not in an open, grassy savanna, Harford," I says, my voice a little raspy.

"Well," says Harford, "all of the ones I have seen have been on open, grassy savanna."

"I suppose that most of the country we will be going through will be open, grassy savanna," I says.

"Quite," says Harford.

"Got another one of them whips?" I says.

"Under the tins we packed on the mule."

"Why didn't you tell me earlier?"

"Well, old chap," says Harford, "had you been a little less keen and had you disappointed me a bit more I should have let the mamba strike you. Apologies, and all of that, but this is, after all, serious business."

34

Most folks would have brooded about what Harford said, but since it was just the sort of thing that I'd do in a similar situation I didn't waste any time thinking black thoughts. I had to admire this skinny pup.

We took off an hour after dark, walking for a while, then riding when there was enough cover. We come to the Tugela River about two o'clock in the morning, and swum across without incident. The water was icy cold from the melting snows high in the Drakensberg Mountains. We brushed over our sign where we come out, on a gravel bar, and moved off halfway up the side of the hills. Each time we would come to the end of what we had seen a mile back, Harford would stop and wriggle forward and stare real hard at the shadowed hills ahead of us. There was no moon and a high haze which cut the starlight. We found no sign.

'Long toward dawn we made a dry camp in a thicket of acacia trees, watered the stock out of an India-rubber bag, and took turns sleeping and keeping watch. Nothing moved on the dry hills but a couple of antelope. Harford had said that we likely wouldn't see anyone until late the next day, as the border area had been in dispute for three generations and neither the Boers nor the Zulus pastured their cattle where they were likely to get stolen.

At this rate, ten or twelve miles a night, we would be a long time drifting in and coming back out. On the other hand, if we rode hard in broad daylight we would no doubt find all sorts of excitement, and I am a dull, peaceloving soul.

Four nights later, as we padded along toward the north and east, I spotted a fire maybe five miles away. We found cover for the beasts and went forward on foot. The wind changed and I could smell cattle stink.

"If we can get in front of them, the cattle will obliterate our spoor," Harford whispered. "We are headed for the military kraal at Nodenwendghu."

We made a long, wide circle, coming to rest finally in a grove of little poplars by a small stream. There was one large tree, a poison tree, the kind that drips sap that will take your skin off at night, Harford said. They don't drip during the day. Harford climbed carefully up and scanned the countryside with a blindered telescope.

"Royal cattle," he whispered. "Some of Cetshwayo's own herds. All of the white cattle in Zululand are the property of the King."

We still moved at night, just ahead of the cattle, which, when driven in the early morning, would trample away our tracks. The herd moved from seven to ten miles a day, and straight for the King's kraal at Ulundi. We began to see scattered kraals and once a long file of Zulu warriors trotting over a ridge of hills to the east. The sunlight twinkled on their spears, and the heat made the flashes shimmer. I thought that maybe Solomon's soldiers had seen that flash. The Zulus had been making iron for close on to three thousand years, and we were, as Harford pointed out, where it was thought that Solomon had sent his miners to dig for gold. And to find peacocks, apes, and ivory, if I remember it right.

It took four more days for us to come to the big military encampment. There were hundreds of huts surrounded by a thornbush fence about a mile across. There was a couple of hundred men there, but the Zulu regiments were elsewhere. Harford and I made notes and maps and wondered idly where the Zulu army was. It was coming on to high summer now, the second week of December.

"I suspect that they are harvesting and won't rally until next week, when the rains will stop," said Harford. "There were other scouts sent to Ulundi, so we should return and give Buller what we have, since the left-flank column will have to come through the Zunguin Mountain area, and I expect that the Zulus will give battle someplace in the vicinity of Hlobane Mountain."

Well, I had seen plenty. The country was pretty and I had about got used to the damn lions roaring all night and the pepper ticks, which I preferred to the giant mosquitoes closer to the coast. Those bastards would leave you a dry and bloodless husk. The only thing I could compare them to was the Alaskan mosquitoes, which are far worse.

We snuck back, making better time now, since we more or less knew just where we were heading, fording the Buffalo and Tugela Rivers and swinging wide to the east and then making a single daylight dash for Helpmakaar.

We got there late that night, and found Buller. I got to stand outside the tent while Harford made his report. Buller asked a few penetrating questions and then I was hauled in and grilled as to my version of events, which was no different than Harford's.

"Well, Adendorff," says Buller, even offering me a generous glass of Scotch whiskey, "good job. You leave first thing in the morning. Head down toward the road from Dundee and find Chelmsford. He has a job for you."

"What job is that?"

"Look, you insubordinate scoundrel," roars Buller (a good judge of character), "Lord Chelmsford will tell you that. Don't be here when I get up in the morning, and since I do not plan to sleep tonight, that's now."

I rode south and west by the light of what the 'Pahoes call an Eaten Moon.

35

That damned Buller had sent me off and not told me even how to find Chelmsford. Lord Chelmsford was the General, Commanding, and I was more than a little worried how he had come to know about me at all. I have had a lot of experience with Generals, Commanding, and the sonsofbitches have to a man been too damn willing to send Mrs. Kelly's son Luther off on errands which might result in same's loss of life or numerous bodily parts to which I have fond attachments. I didn't like this one bit, and so I was thinking hard of ways to skulk around and maybe get lost, and ways I would come down sick or just how damn far was it to Portuguese East Africa or if I'd like Australia.

Finding Lord Chelmsford turned out to be easy. I was riding along asleep in the damned saddle, for I was fairly tired and there wasn't anything dangerous about, unless I counted my friends and allies, which I should have, when there was a sudden flurry of hoofbeats, and my horse started dancing, and I was too groggy to act quick, and six horsemen run into me on a narrow place in the road. Three of the horsemen went down, along with me, and there was a real nice horse wreck there for a few seconds, which I got out of and two of the other men did too. The third had a horse step on his face, slashing his left cheek open to the teeth and popping out his eye like a grape. I washed off my thumb with water from my canteen and poked the eye back into the socket before he came to.

They was troopers sent on an errand to get some remounts left back at a farrier's wagon. The undamaged ones directed me up the road. I left them to patch themselves up as best they could.

Chelmsford, it turned out, was up toward the mission station at Rorke's Drift. He was going to command the central column in person, and I suppose that he hoped that just the fact he had invaded Zululand would cause the Zulu army to seek him out, and that then there would be a jolly set-to, with the Zulus breaking themselves on massed breech-loading firearms fired by disciplined troops. The British had been quite successful at this, except for Afghanistan.

Being single and well mounted, I could cover a lot of ground, and the track that the central column had made toward Zululand and which had caused them weeks of anguished, sweaty effort was little more than a hard day's ride for a man alone. I galloped up to the top of the corduroy road that the Engineers had built on the bank, weaving around wagons driven by Boer contractors and once a bunch of rocket-tubes being hauled along, though for what purpose I couldn't say. A Congreve rocket was fine for celebrating a nice holiday or such, but it was useless as a weapon. They were well thought of by the British, who thought they scared tribesmen, which seemed to me not to be the point. I have never really understood the military mind.

The leading elements of the column was strung out far

ahead, across the river, and there was a lot of dust and confusion, which is to me the hallmark of armies everywhere. The British had a huge amount of gear, and I guessed that the scouts sent here didn't report that a gully (they call 'em dongas in Africa), which a mounted man wouldn't much notice, might mean that it would take a whole day with double teams of oxen to drag the wagons down and up.

On a good day when everything went right the central column would make ten miles, and from the track they had left—the earth was plowed up something fierce—I supposed that they were going on like the dogged Brits they were, hoping for a good day sometime. If they had only had the time, they would have made a fort out of the wagons each night. The oxen, for one thing, could pull only eight hours a day, and they needed a further sixteen hours to graze and then rest and chew their cuds. Between the thirteen hundred or so Imperial troops, and the few hundred Natal Kaffirs, and the wagons, and the limbered guns, and the spare oxen, and the bakeries on wheels, and two Gatling guns, and the rocket batteries and a couple of troops of Irregular Volunteers, and a lot of Boers hauling commissary supplies, and the hospital wagons, and the four tons of tents, and god knew what else, this whole thing looked to me like disaster coming. For one thing, all that the Zulus really had to do was wait until the troops were maybe thirty miles into Zululand, and then run off the oxen, and after the oxen were gone then the Zulus could sort of sit in a large ring around the hills and watch the English die of starvation. All while singing "God Save the Queen," of course.

And the British, no doubt, were hoping that just the mere sight of all the troops and such would make the Zulus so mad that they would attack and obligingly die by the thousands in front of the breech-loading guns, and after that Cetshwayo would give up his savage ways and maybe take up needlepoint or something. All in all, I didn't like any of it.

I come to Rorke's Drift, which had about a hundred troops at it, and they obligingly took me across on one of the punts and sped me on my way, since I claimed to have vital messages from Buller for Chelmsford.

Late in the afternoon on the twentieth of January, 1879, I found Chelmsford and his staff having high tea. They was out ahead of the main force, which strung out for several miles, and had decided on the campsite for that night. It was on a long, sloping saddle between a couple of low mountains—wind-worked mountains, like you see in Wyoming or the Southwest. He had vedettes and pickets flung out far to each side of the column, and there were a few Irregular troopers out ahead, riding in twos and threes, looking for signs of the Zulu army. You could have hid several armies in this country—it was filled with deep gullies of a huge size.

Chelmsford kept me waiting a good long time, which was fine by me as the less important I was to this enterprise the better, and I toyed with the notion of having an attack in the gallbladder and gallantly groaning back toward Helpmakaar, not wishing, of course, to add to the load of the surgeons, who were worked to a frazzle treating blisters from the heavy ammunition boots that the troopers had been stomping across East Africa in, and the normal run of dysentery, wounds caused by being kicked by animals, and the various injuries sustained moving a huge column of men across country that they knew nothing about.

When he finally had me brought in I made a quick report to the effect that Buller was riding around madly some sixty miles or so to the west and that we had seen no recent sign there of the Zulu army, and that we would keep looking.

Chelmsford looked fit and well. He gave me a glass of

claret and bade me rise early on the morrow and look around out in front for a good campsite. Also the Zulu army. I said I would leave before dawn and be back as soon as I could. Why, I thought, they'll hardly know I left as I just may not.

I was tired, so I went off and made up a modest little camp out of the way of the ox herds, the sort of place you would likely pass by, my preferred sort, after handing my horse over to a groom who said he'd rub him down and grain him good. Rather than line up for the meat, bread, and greens that the soldiers got, I ate from a loaf of veldt bread—a half-and-half mixture of meat powder and flour. I had some dried fruit, then rolled up in a blanket, and went to sleep to the sound of harness, bawling oxen, bawling sergeants, hoofbeats, shouted orders, and other loud noises.

At about two in the morning I got my horse back, after kicking the groom awake in the mannerly custom of the country, and slipped out of the camp, past the pickets, and headed generally north and east. There were clouds off to the east, moving toward me, and they were flashing a lot of lightning, so I picked a place halfway up a butte, and settled in to wait for the storm to pass. The wet ground would help with my tracking the Zulu army, and from where I was I could see ten miles or so toward the direction of Ulundi, where the Zulu army was leaving from, no matter if they attacked Chelmsford, Buller, or the column down by the coast, or just walked right between them all and went on to massacre Durban.

I set to work in the rising light, and carefully stared at the country. About ten in the morning I saw a few natives on horses far to the north, but no sign of a large party. The natives were riding west slowly, and then they disappeared into the country and I didn't see them again. I headed back for the camp in the early afternoon.

Chelmsford was looking troubled. The camp was

recovering from the effects of the storm of the night before. Lightning had stampeded some of the oxen and horses, who trampled some of the Natal Kaffirs, and there were injuries, and worse yet, two of the wagons had been struck, and the rain which hadn't been that bad a few miles to the north had made the ground a mess and soaked the tentage to four times its dry weight.

I told Chelmsford that there weren't any really good campsites up ahead for more distance than the central column could make in a day, and that the country got a little worse than it had been generally. Also that I had seen no sign of a large force, only scattered horsemen far to the north, and that they seemed to be heading west. Chelmsford nodded and sighed and said that the confusion caused by the storm the night before would take the rest of the day to repair. He meant that by the time the oxen were hitched up, the wet tents dried a little, and some order brought out of the mess in camp—the ground was slick and fast turning to a mire—and everybody was on the move, it would be dark and time to make camp again. Better to rest up and get an early start the day following.

One of the irregular cavalry officers, a great big brute of a man name of Browne, came with the news that he and a couple of his fellows had caught a young Zulu who had been spying on the camp.

"Bring him in," said Chelmsford. "I want to question him."

"I questioned him already," said Browne, "and he unfortunately died."

Chelmsford stared at Browne for a moment, the muscles in his jaw rippling. I slipped back out just as Chelmsford began dressing him down. This Browne was a bad 'un, no doubt about it. Rumor had it he had killed several of the Natal Kaffirs he had been leading, which is a poor way to get folks to follow you, if you ask me.

I got some food at one of the mess wagons and spent the

rest of the light checking my horse over carefully and
cadging grain for the animal, and waiting again for the
night. Chelmsford sent for me again just as I was about to
go off and get some sleep.

"I shall ride out with a large escort on the morrow and
select the camp myself," he said, "so please indicate
where you think it would be best to look."

I pointed out a spot on a map I thought had looked
likeliest, somewhat to the east and north. Chelmsford
bade me a good night and asked me to spend the morrow
looking for the Zulu army, doing a picket's work, a job I
purely hate as you may well find yourself warning the
main body of troops that the enemy is here by expiring
spectacularly some distance away from them. Hell, Kelly, I
says, let us find a good spot sort of out of the way.

I slept fairly late, and by the time I had got up and
pissed and had a big cup of coffee and some bread with
marmalade, it was about eight in the morning of the
twenty-second day of January, 1879.

36

Chelmsford rode off with an escort of about eighty men. They took the direction that I had suggested. One of the officers attached to Chelmsford was a young Navy Lieutenant, who was obviously much more used to striding the quarterdeck than sitting a horse. He made his problems worse by hauling a big brass telescope with him. A few men in the camp snickered as they watched him go, but he just ignored them and bounced out of sight, riding his horse in the manner Ol' Liver-Eating Jack had always called "fuckin' the pumpkin."

Just as I was leaving camp, there was a halloo from the trail back to Rorke's Drift, and a band of about a hundred horsemen showed up, mostly natives—unusual to see niggers riding, they rode with their big toes in little stirrups—and led by a one-armed officer I had never seen before. When he dismounted I saw that he had both arms, but one was badly withered and stuck in a pocket in front of his tunic.

Colonel Pulleine, who was commanding the camp in Chelmsford's absence, came out to greet the new arrival. They was standing being all jolly with one another, the way two dogs will just before all hell breaks loose, and after a few moments Pulleine waved me over and introduced me.

"This is Colonel Durnford," he says. "I wanted you to tell what you know of the whereabouts of the Zulu army."

Well, that didn't take long. I said I was going to poke around to the north, and as I was finishing there was a shot up ahead of us and a few Zulus went racing across the side of the mountain, to the north and west of us. Some of the Irregulars gave chase, but it was bad terrain for horses and the Zulus were long gone. The Irregulars straggled back, with two lamed horses.

Durnford and Pulleine glared at each other for a moment, and then they talked at each other for a bit, and agreed to send some of the troops here and there out to the north and east, to screen the main encampment which was moving in orderly confusion and getting ready to move up to wherever Chelmsford decided.

Orders was passed to captains and majors, bugle signals began to squawk, and the men fell in. They were dressed and had been eating breakfast mostly. I noticed that though they had the one pouch with the loose rounds for their Martini-Henrys, the other pouch with most of the rounds was missing. I began to feel the hairs on the back of my neck prickle up, for the troops were falling in and racing on the double out away from the camp, with not much ammunition.

I slid out of the camp and went north, quartering—it was too hard to bother with trying to get out unseen. I kept squinting at the distance, trying to spot birds suddenly flushed up. The ground was damp enough not to give off dust, and the racket in the earth made by the camp was too loud and too close for me to do my ear-to-the-ground, which is a terribly overrated way of figuring out anything, anyway. So I rode on slowly north. The Natal Kaffirs was being bullied out of the camp behind me, headed for a little knuckle of land right up ahead, maybe a mile from the main camp.

A wind come up, and leaves on the bushes rattled, and there was something about the landscape in front of me that didn't seem right. Nothing moved. Not an antelope, not a bird, nothing. I got a sort of crackling sound in my ears, and it is a sound I remember from Abode Walls and other places, just before the Comanches and Kiowas and Cheyennes attacked. It seemed like the whole earth was waiting for something.

I quartered forward slowly, keeping well away from anything big enough to have someone hiding behind it, my head swiveling, and I was even trying to smell what was around. I saw a big black bird riding motionless in the air about a mile ahead, and moved that way, for the bird was a vulture and the vulture was looking at something.

There are places where I have been where you can ride along and suddenly the whole earth seems to fall away from in front of you. The land doesn't give a hint about what it hides, no clearly defined rimrock, and the lines blend so perfectly you can't see it even if you know it is there.

I was riding very slowly, rifle cocked, and the silence got so heavy that I stopped my horse and slipped forward, straining every sense. Whatever it was it was here and it was close. The bird held motionless up there. I went along the ground on my knees and one hand.

I peered through a bush and the sight I saw was so outlandish it took some time to take it in. Below me, stretching as far as my eyes could see both to left and right, sitting as orderly as you please, was the whole damn

Zulu army. I stared for a moment. Some of them were standing, and they had ostrich plumes sticking up from their heads, so I figured them for officers. But most of them were squatting on their haunches, in neat rows, arranged by what appeared to be regiments—they had different colored shields and their dress was different from group to group.

That is not a mob of niggers, Kelly, I says to myself. That is an army.

At just that moment a black face stuck itself up on the other side of my bush, and we blinked at each other, and then I shot the face and raced for my horse. I swung up, and heard orders being shouted in what I guessed was Zulu, and then the first warriors came boiling over the top of the lip of the big gully. I cantered back, stopping to look from time to time.

They came up over the lip and charged to each side and took up the bull's head formation. It took maybe twenty minutes for all of them to scramble out, and they dressed right and left and formed into regiments. The proudest and best warriors in all Africa. Some with red shields, some white and black, some ochre, and combinations of those colors in stripes. The inDunas were mounted and one raised a stick with feathers on it, and then the whole Zulu army began to trot forward, the sun flashing on their spears.

I shot one inDuna off his horse and tried for the bird who had given the order to advance, but my shot went lost when my horse shied at the flashings of the sun on the iron assegai heads. All of this had taken maybe half an hour.

Rather than get shot by folks supposedly on my side I turned and cantered back to camp, hallooing and waving my hat—not that I thought that there was a soul there who wasn't absolutely fascinated by what was coming right along behind old Luther, er, Jim, but to remind all that I was definitely not a Zulu. Some of them wasn't too bright, I knew for a fact.

The camp was stirring like a kicked-over anthill—some red-coated men was racing to each side and a few mounted men were riding toward me hell for leather. I glanced back and saw two miles breadth of Zulus headed our way. Well, they'd soon learn what the fire of packed rifles meant—hell, the slug the Brits used for arguing with natives weighed more than the one I used in my buffalo rifle. At close range it would go through three or four men before stopping in one.

I passed the troopers who had been headed toward me and pulled up just before the camp. Durnford was going off to my right, leading several companies, and the Natal Kaffirs were standing about, while their officers cursed and kicked. At last they began to move forward. They passed me and took up their positions. The Zulus were a twinkling line, maybe a mile and a half away, and coming on.

It was just about then, as I saw the troopers going to my left and to my right, that I began to get real uneasy. Some of the men were shirtless and a lot of them didn't have their ammunition pouches on, just the little expense pouch that is sewn on to the belt. I looked over to where Durnford had gone and then I looked back. Durnford was spreading his troops out! There were weak places showing in the line. And a lot of the men were carrying only ten to twenty rounds apiece, not the sixty that they should have had.

I blame Durnford for what happened in the next half hour. There's been a lot of books written on the subject, by folks who weren't there, and retired Colonels (enough said). That battle was lost while the Zulus were still a mile and a half away.

I looked off to my right and saw a column of Zulus peel off and go around the flank of the mountain. I couldn't figure this, it would take them two hours to come round behind us, and the battle would be decided long before that.

Usually, in situations like this, I run. I had seen enough, but there was still some time and I thought I might try to do what I could. I raced into the camp and found the Quartermaster—he was stripping the canvas off the ammunition wagons. Well, he wasn't, but some of his men were. I pulled up and jumped off my horse—keeping a tight grip on the reins, mind you—and began to scream at him to get every man jack to work carrying ammunition to the troops in the line.

He looked at me for a moment, blinking.

"I see," he said. "And you have a requisition?"

"I haven't a goddamned requisition," I yelled. "If you don't get your arse to work running ammunition to the lines we're all dead!

"I really can't even open the boxes without a receipt for noting when the screws in the lids were first taken out. Have to account for the screws."

It ain't often I was speechless, but I was then. There was two soldiers to a wagon, with rifles. I knew I would be shot if I tried to open one of the ammunition boxes. Well, Kelly, I says, I ain't getting shot for that.

The camp wasn't deserted—there were grooms and orderlies and such wandering around, and the bakers were working on the day's bread. Business as usual. I saw Pulleine and his staff gabbing in front of his tent, then they broke up and Pulleine went in, no doubt to attend to some more paperwork.

The artillery just in front of the camp opened up, and I got to a place where I could see the battle and stood there, rubbing my horse down and graining him. I gave him just a little water.

The firing commenced, a steady aimed fire, and I saw the Zulus mowed down. There was plenty more. I watched for maybe ten minutes, looking up now and again from checking my horse's feet. And then I heard a strange noise.

The Zulus was humming like a gigantic swarm of bees.

I rode over to the wagon where I had seen a rifle like mine, and after looking about to see if the owner was around, I rooted through the likeliest duffel and came up with another fifty rounds, and another pistol and a hundred rounds for that. I put the bullets in the pouches to the front of my saddle and swung back up. Off to my right there was a sailor standing on a pile of mealie bags, watching. He had a cutlass in his hand.

All of this time I was keeping a sharp eye for any Zulus off to either side or behind me. Nothing.

The fire began to slacken a little, not much, but then I have been in a lot of battles. It slackened, and that's a bad sign.

The firing fell off a little more. A little antelope, what the Boers call a dik-dik, ran by me, chased by a little black and white terrier.

I suppose it was ten minutes more, I couldn't really say. Then the Natal Kaffirs broke and raced back toward the camp, leaving a gap three hundred yards wide in the front of the line.

The Zulus began to pour through it, and then I could hear the firing rolled up side to side—the men often must have been taken in the back before they knew anything was wrong.

When the Kaffirs got to perhaps fifty yards from me I turned and made for the riverbank, picking my way carefully around anything that might damage my horse. Now was not the time to have a lame horse, so I went down the beaten road, making for the river. From a high place I looked back. The Zulus was in the camp, and the artillerymen had had time to limber up and were cutting their way through. There was two big columns of Zulus going past either side of the camp and heading straight for the river.

I went on, down to the ford, and crossed and pulled up on the far side, got off and awaited events. The first fugitive Natal Kaffirs came, and then a few conductors, and a red-coated soldier or two. None were mounted. They dove into the river and made it across and passed me. Then the Zulus plunged into the river a mile above me and a mile below. I got back up on my horse.

I saw a compact band of blacks—it was they who'd come riding in the day before—walking, not hurrying overmuch. They stopped above the drop to the ford and spread out and began to give covering fire to the soldiers in the ruck coming behind them. It seemed far off, the river hid most of the noise.

When the niggers giving covering fire on the far high bank scrambled down and swum across, I checked the sights on my rifle and began to scout for targets. Before the fellers were halfways across I had two, a Zulu chasing some poor barefoot bastard—I did take time to wonder what the hell he'd been doing—and a redcoat being chased by three Zulus. I fired at the three, figuring whatever the poor bootless bastard had been doing it hadn't been fighting—and knocked one down with the first shot. The others drew up, so I fired at them again and then all three were down, though to be truthful two of them was crawling pretty good and the third was just limping. If you want rapid-fire head shots from atop a horse you should hire Buffalo Bill. Have him tell you about it anyway.

The barefoot feller was still making pretty good time, and his friend wasn't closing too fast, and then I thought that I hadn't better be mean and so I cleared his companion away—this one went down and didn't move.

The nigger company was coming out of the water now, and while I looked for more targets and slammed more shells into the magazine, they scrambled up and formed a line in front of me and waited.

It wasn't long in coming. There was a lot more Zulus than there was fugitives—I thought most of the Zulus had stayed to loot the camp, but there were twenty thousand, after all—and me and the company gave what covering fire we could. The Zulus was stabbing away pretty good, and the crowd kept getting thicker. A couple of big gray birds flew by low on the river.

And then suddenly there was a mass of folks, mostly Zulus in the river, and when I looked up and down I could see Zulus on my side of the bank running my way. I figured I had five minutes.

The only cannon that made it as far as the river was pulled off a low cliff by the maddened team, down to my right. Two red-coated officers reined up and then took the cliff, and the legs of their horses broke on the big rocks below. Then a wave of Zulus came over after them. The redcoats had sabers and pistols, but it was all over very soon.

"Would you have spare ammunition, sir?" said a deep voice.

I looked down. It was the sergeant from the nigger company in front of me.

"None for Martini-Henrys," I said. Then I handed him my spare pistol and he thanked me and went back to his men.

The mess on the far bank was so close now—I couldn't shoot for fear of hitting who it was I was trying to help—that I thought it high time to leave.

Then I saw a couple of officers upstream, and they was carrying the Queen's colors. There was a big party of Zulus after them. One of the officers was hobbling and the other helping him. I rode up to where I was across from them and fired the full magazine at the pursuing Zulus. It slowed them down a little, but the two winded fellers with the Queen's rag were too tired or wounded to make much time. They was caught before they was halfway down to the river. There was a big knot of Zulus around them, and a brief hacking flurry, and then that was over, too.

I jammed shells in my magazine, and turned to leave. There was several Zulus back of me now—they'd been moving up on me—and I dropped three and rode through them and got on the trail to Rorke's Drift.

About five miles down the tail I come across some Boer conductors, and I explained as best I could that where they was headed was an unhealthy place. I could see that they was old hands in this country, for each of them had a saddled horse tied behind the ox wagon. After they got the gist of what it was I was saying they promptly pulled off the trail and commenced upspanning their oxen, and then they mounted and rode off, without so much as even thanking me.

I had been so caught in the horror behind me that I had forgotten the Zulus who had gone behind the mountain before the battle. If they had made straight for the river they could be headed anywhere. I was pretty sure that they would be headed for Rorke's Drift. As near as I could remember, there were two thousand or so.

"Kayrist, Kelly," I screamed, "how I hate being noble. I can't remember when I have been so happy. Shit." I then went into a lot of curses I picked up from an old camel driver the Army had imported in some misbegotten attempt to use camels to chase Apaches or Sand Papagos— horses are so terrified of camels that they will climb trees to get away from the smell—and then the Army, being the Army, had abandoned the camel notion and old High Jolly, the Ayrab driver. Anyway there ain't no better curses than Ayrab ones.

So I set my horse off as fast as was smart, and headed for the south.

I didn't see a soul on the way. I clattered down to the

punt, which of course was on the other side, and after a few more choice dispraises of Allah I headed across the river and emerged below the punt station. A few troopers were waiting on the bank, and they helped me haul my nag up.

I figured it was no use even talking to the men, since they wouldn't shit without an officer told them, so I snarled that there had been a disaster to the central column and where the hell is whoever is in command? They directed me toward the mission station. I barged in on tea. I know it ain't done, but I thought I had an excuse.

The commanding officer was a short, bearded feller name of Chard, who listened to my news, slurping his tea dainty-like the whole damn time. He was one of them slow-to-act types, the sort you could set on fire and he'd sniff for a couple of minutes wondering what in the hell was that godawful stink, and was it polite to notice it.

"Are you serious?" he finally says.

"No, not a god damn bit," says I, ragged and dusty. "I just thought it would be great goddamn fun to ride here and tell you that the central column has been wiped out and there is two thousand Zulus headed your way. My idea of a joke, it is. Not to worry, ain't that what you say?"

Chard stared out of the window, and I could see the air going out of him. He was an engineer, not a line soldier. But then he snapped to, and rapped out orders to assemble the officers and non-coms forthwith and in great haste.

He asked me to tell them what happened, and I did, in two sentences—I clearly believe that had it been Bill Cody there instead of me, the Zulus would have been on us before the end of the speech, so you can credit me that much for saving Rorke's Drift.

They hemmed and hawed for a while about whether to run or to fight. I finally put a stop to that, too, saying that flight was suicide and if that was the idea I would be leaving now. They had a couple of dozen wounded and some sick, and the Zulus would overtake laden wagons and marching troops before they had got two miles, given the time that it would take to get hitched up and going.

I said I would stay to help. Me. Fool. I *could* have gone on to warn someone farther—much, much farther, say Cape Town—of the approaching storm, and to this day I don't know why I stayed, except perhaps I felt bad in some fool way for what had happened at Isandhlwana.

I touched it off, shooting that Zulu full in the face. Oh, it would have happened eventually, but there it was.

37

Every soldier remembers the waiting before the battle. During the battle things are so confused, and what one feller can actually see amounts to so little that virtually everyone will have a different version of what happened. I well remember frantically lugging boxes of stores to form a perimeter and blistering my hands with a pick to make loopholes in the walls. There were only about seventy men in good enough health to fight, for the others, twenty or so, were in the hospital.

A few stragglers from Isandhlwana passed, but not one stayed. I couldn't blame them. Some were two to a horse, with that dazed look that men get when things were just too much for them. Two were boys from my Natal Light Horse. They weren't singing now.

I was counting on there being not a lot of enthusiasm for attacking the station, because though the Zulus had destroyed most of the central column, they had also taken a fearful mauling—at least three for one of ours—and though they were brave, the bravest men can go only so far. Zulus go farther. They got no sense.

We were still frantically trying to make the place defensible when the two sentries Chard had sent up to a high place came pounding down and clambered over the wall of boxes and bags running from one of the outbuildings to the station itself. Chard had listened to me long enough to make sure that every man had more ammunition than he could possibly use, and a chaplain had volunteered to carry more ammunition wherever it might be needed. He was a tall, long-jawed man in his forties, name of Smith, and even during the heat of the battle he scolded the men for cursing.

Still I stayed, and if you are wondering why, my so disliking getting mangled and all, I have a perfectly reasonable explanation. While I was bellering at Chard, some sonofabitch stole my horse. There were some casuals at Rorke's Drift, and I had to admit that in his place I probably would have done the same.

I still hoped to kill him someday.

When the sentries came in, one of them screamed, "Here they come, boys, black as hell and thick as grass," and it wasn't but a few minutes until rifle fire started. A column of warriors crested the near hill, dropped into the seven-foot-high tambookie grass, and when they emerged a rippling line of fire went along the wall and many warriors went down, only to have the ones behind them leap over them. This black wave smashed into the wall, some of them grabbing for the muzzles of the rifles, to try to drag them over the wall, and a few Zulus leaped right up on top of the bags and boxes and stabbed at the defenders.

We were jammed into a fairly small place, and the smoke from the blackpowder cartridges soon made everything more than twenty feet away mostly a matter of guess work.

We fought for hours, late into the night. The Zulus had some rifles now, taken from the troops at Isandhlwana, and from time to time a shot would strike home. The man next to me leaped up on the wall to bayonet a warrior, lost his balance, and fell outside. I stuck my head up to see if I could help, and watched in horror as the warriors spread-eagled him on the ground, ripped his belly open with slashings of their spears, and then literally tore him to pieces. I shot four of them. Then the wall of boxes fell outward and me with it.

Battle is noisy. And I was always getting myself into the damnedest scrapes. Myself, I'd like to avoid them all, but my life ain't worked out that way. While all of this was going on I was looking for a way out—kayrist, there was four thousand of them and only one of me—and then I had this cold feeling, the one that you get when someone is sticking a bayonet in your back and suggesting by eloquent gestures which way he wants you to walk. As a conversation opener there is nothing like it and it always grabs my attention. Grab yours, too, if there was a few inches of cold steel right there by your left eardrum.

I looks over and I addresses the gentleman which has the bayonet and, so to speak, is in charge of the situation. He smiles at me. I have seen some lovely grins in my time—grizzlies, politicians, Mormon missionaries, and other predacious types, but I am telling you that this grin was absolutely ferocious.

"Move," he says, eloquently.

So, I move. I am out of the hero and brave-defender business for the moment. All hell is breaking loose behind us, and we walk like charmed men through the few yards of turf that separates this ungodly mess from the plain old earth, you know the one, the sort of place that you can plant flowers in.

Outside the ring of that ferocious violence there was

calm. If I hadn't had that bayonet three inches from my left eardrum I would have been downright bored.

The enormous nigger who had invited me along—he'd have made even Liver-Eating Jack seem downright puny. I mean, this man was so large he looked like he would eat a nice hippopotamus for dinner or some such.

"You will be treated well," he said, in the most insufferable boarding-school English I had ever heard. And then the sonofabitch said, "Your people are a nosegay of arseholes. Sergeant Major Simeon Kambula of the Queen's Own Natal Native Police, at your service. As you will be at Cetshwayo's, if he don't decide to have you skinned alive and crucified on an anthill. Or have a stake driven up your arsehole, or. . ." Now I recognized him. He'd brought the nigger troops across the river. Last I'd seen him, I'd given him my spare pistol, the ungrateful bastard.

I was so tired and so disgusted—my horse, my horse—that I told him to go fuck himself, and several other impossibilities, which just made him smile. He had a voice like a bass organ, those low notes you can feel but not hear.

"Ulundi," he said, "for we have need of you. There."

Zulus can run, by God. He kept me at a trot until we came to the Buffalo River, and we swum across, with his bayonet never more than a foot from my ear. We run up the bank, we run past the mess at Isandhlwana—there was paper everywhere, and I could see Chelmsford with his escort down there. But Sergeant Major Kambula saw me thinking of hollering for help and gave me that big grin again, so we went on and trotted over the green hills of Zululand without a murmur from me, and I began to pass out from the heat and the exertion.

Some Zulu warriors come up out of nowhere, cursed me in their own tongue, tossed me on a shield, and carried me. I was borne on to Ulundi about half conscious. I did not remember the night.

38

I remember waking up and seeing the most beautiful pair of eyes. They were large and so brown that they seemed black. She was holding a calabash of beer to my lips. I saw paintings of her in Egypt, once. She was so gentle and kind. I suppose I was foolish. I was also delirious.

The chanting Zulu warriors' had dropped me at some encampment, and an old man come out of the main hut—he stank of grease and blood—and beat me over the head with a small club, which didn't even hurt much. I suppose I just didn't want to wake up, for I slept when I should have been thinking of escape.

I woke up again and there was that beautiful face, and she gave me some more beer and a kind of curdled cheese, and some halves of a fruit like apricots. A couple of thugs came in and dragged me back outside.

There was a cluster of warriors standing there, and one grizzled old buzzard out in front of them, he had some white ostrich plumes on his head and a batch of worse-for-wear wretches sprawled on the ground in front of him. When the old fart stopped for breath the warriors rushed forward and stabbed the men and then picked up their limp bodies and hauled them up the hill. They were back in a little while. I was much more than somewhat tired, and all in all it didn't make as much of an impression as a lot of hangings I have attended, except perhaps my own. Well, that's another story, makes my neck itch.

What happened next was for my own benefit, I suppose. This time the two on the ground were one man and one woman, and after the geezer had berated them for a while the warriors pounced on them and pounded stakes up their asses. They began to scream, of course, a terrible bubbling sound, and then they were thrown on shields and carried over the hill, not far enough to be out of earshot, though they were out of sight. The screaming went on all day and for the first two hours of the night, and then the screaming got choked off, started again, and finally stopped, and then there was a chorus of insane laughter from the hyenas.

Kelly, I says, I think you had best mind your p's and q's because your best bet is that they brought you here for something. Do think hard when you find out what.

They motioned me back to the hut.

A couple of mean-looking warriors ducked into the hut at dawn and threw me out like so much offal, and then double-timed me through the village. It was dark, and we seemed to go on forever. Apparently I had been out on the edge, and this kraal was perhaps three miles across.

We come to a hut not much bigger than the others, but it was set away from the others, and there were guards ranged around it, and several more of what the Zulus call inDunas, what amounts to their brigadier generals. My escort service flung me in the door. It was smoky in there and there was the smell of a lot of humanity in too small a place, about like New York or Chicago.

There was a small fire in the center of the room, and I could see eyes with reflections from it to either side of me. Straight ahead, across the fire, there was a huge feller, black as the inside of your pocket. He was seated on a stool, legs spread some and hands on his knees. Alone of the men I had seen here he had on a leopard-skin cloak and kilt, and he was wearing the sort of crown you buy at the place they sell elephant hangings and theatrical gewgaws.

He motioned me to come forward and I slunk past the righthand row of black faces, only one or two of them hissed. There was a small white man seated on the ground next to the King or Chief or whatever he was. Longing for company, I set myself down there, too. What with the events of the last seventy-two hours any sort of company looked good.

A sort of rumble came from the bird on the stool.

"He says welcome. This is Cetshwayo," says the little white feller, in accented Dutch English, "and he has some questions to ask you."

"Fire away," says I. "Be of any service that I can."

"You'd better," says the little feller. "The King is not in a good humor."

Someday I hope to meet a king who's in a good humor. Met King Edward the VII once, and all he was was stupid, which didn't count.

I won't give you the back and forth, just the gist of what the King wanted to know. It was the same thing that Red Cloud wanted to know, and a lot of other chiefs I have talked to. What in the pluperfect name of all that is right and good are you bastards doing here? We didn't invite you. We scrupulously have observed the terms of the treaty. I could have said something to the effect that they was sitting on perfectly good land, they was black and those who wanted it was white, and if they was looking for justice or even common sense they'd be wiser to go get drunk or something else fun.

Cetshwayo launched into a two-hour harangue, and his amen chorus grunted happily from time to time. The little feller—his name was van Rijn—translated for me.

First off, Cetshwayo was bewildered by the fact that he had got an ultimatum from Governor Bulwer of the Cape Colony, saying in effect that the Zulus would turn over all of their cattle and disband their army and await eagerly any more absurd instructions. Cetshwayo was aware that there was something called the Cape Colony, which was fine by him, but he wanted to know how the English was different from the Boers. The Zulus had been fighting the Boers for fifty years and had agreed to a boundary over somewhere west and in order that there be no misunderstandings had made sure that the Boers placed the first stone on the beacon cairns which marked the border. Cetshwayo had met quite a few Englishmen, and thought that they had their uses, but preferred that immigration be limited to a few folks bearing useful items of trade.

I couldn't think of much to say to that.

The real reason that I had been brought to the royal kraal here at Ulundi finally came up.

"The King has a responsibility to his people," said van Rijn. "You invaded Zululand. The army had been eager to come to grips with the invader. It would be difficult to explain to the army that they were not to do that. The army went off, and attacked one of your armies, and wiped out most of it. In doing so, three thousand or so were killed outright, and many more so badly wounded that they will not live. The King feels that a few more victories like that and the Zulus will be no more. Whom does he negotiate with? You had three armies, and now you have two. Whom does the King send messengers to?"

Of course. The King gets messages from Bulwer, and
that ass Shepstone, and he hears rumors that there is
some general who he can parley with, but he don't know
the man's name or which of the three columns the general
is with. Or was he killed in the attack on the main camp at
Isandhlwana?

Thinking quickly in spots like these is why I am still
here to tell you about them, prevarication and outright
untruth being in my survival kit. On top.

"His name is Chelmsford," I said, "and he's with the
column over to the west of here."

There had been a muttering growing behind me, and
now a feller of about thirty-five sits halfway up and rum-
bles along for a bit. Cetshwayo listened for a while, and
nodded.

The feller sat down, and then another started in, and
Cetshwayo spoke to him pretty sharp and the hut got real
silent.

"The King's brother, Dabulamanzi," says van Rijn. "He
had you brought here and he thinks that you are lying. He
suggests dealing with you harshly."

"Tell the King that Chelmsford was with the column,
but he left that very morning, seeing that they had got
safely launched into Zululand," I says, not mentioning that
by leaving the camp in the command of that incompetent
Pulleine he done the Zulus' work for them, too. "Chelmsford
is on his way to the western column and that is where he
can be found."

Cetshwayo pondered for a while.

"You will guide my messengers," he said finally.

There was a fine uproar at this, with a lot of suggestions
being made about how to dispose of Luther and I am sure
general comments upon my character, all of which van
Rijn was kind enough not to translate.

Me and three Zulus left at first light. One of them was
the fierce old buzzard who had clubbed me when I first

arrived, and a couple of hard boys who were obviously going to chop me up the first time I made motions of escaping.

There was another escort, who would keep with us until we was in sight of the western column.

They give me a horse, one with a British army brand on it, and two of the warriors held a rein on each side, while another held the rein that they had around my neck. Nice British army saddle, too.

The Zulus trotted along, tireless—which was truly amazing since they had run down to wipe out the central column, and Dabulamanzi and friends had trotted a good deal farther to fight at Rorke's Drift, and then home again, carrying me. I wasn't sure that the horse could outrun them, even if I could wriggle out of the prudent extra precautions that they had taken.

We covered nearly fifty miles by nightfall. We slept for four hours, until the moon rose, and then the whole bunch went on.

Late the next day we come near on the place where the scouts for the western column would be.

I went on with my three companions. A patrol spotted us, and charged us, there being only four of us. I run out in front, screaming.

"I have messages for Chelmsford," I said. "Hold your fire."

They was part of the Irregulars. They circled us for a while, checked out the tracks of the group who had brought us, and then we walked at a slower pace onward. A couple of riders had gone on ahead. One returned with a spare mount for me.

"These messages are from King Cetshwayo," I says.

I was wholly exhausted. I rode on a speed for the camp.

I babbled something to a sentry when I come in, and then I fell off my horse. I was stuck in a hospital wagon for the night. I must not have made any sense. Someone asked me questions, but I don't know who.

When I got up in the morning the first thing that I saw was the three messengers, swaying in the morning breeze. They'd been hung from a gallows improvised from the raised tongues of two wagons.

39

Buller was angry. Buller generally was angry, but now he was really mad. Seems that after sending me in, the leader of the Irregulars—good old Browne, and one of the worst bastards ever spawned—had reported to say that they had rescued me in dire peril and that he had hung three spies. Fortunately for Browne, Buller was asleep, and an aide took the report. Browne also prudently took off while Buller was still asleep.

Buller did a lot of roaring and found out that Browne had been aided by some of the Boer conductors—they was the ones put up the wagon tongues and no doubt heaved on the ropes.

Buller finally got calm enough to think—at least as well as he ever did—and sent for me. I repeated what Cetshwayo had told me. Buller had it all copied down neat and sent it off to Evelyn Wood, the General Commanding, who, as soon as he had heard of Isandhlwana had turned on his heel and headed back for Kambula, which wasn't a town, just a small tavern some distance from Dundee. Buller was withdrawing the last of the wagons and some of the scouting parties who had been staying out for two or three days at a time. They was close to the crossing at Landman's Drift and there was signalers between where we was and the encampment who would light beacons if help was needed.

It took two days for us to crest the last rise and see the Buffalo—another slow track—but scouts reported no Zulus in the area.

Browne come in and Buller raged at him for a while and then sent him out, under guard, swearing that he'd court-martial him. Nothing ever came of it, of course, it never does. I figured that Cetshwayo would give up on trying to talk now, since his messengers couldn't get through, except to get hung.

I recovered pretty quick, and was sent on swift as I could ride to Chelmsford, who questioned me thoroughly for an hour and then dismissed me.

Then he sent for me again, and he looked pale and as angry as I have ever seen a man. Now he wanted to know about Rorke's Drift and my version of Isandhlwana. He was a shrewd and kind man, under a lot of strain, and when I finally pointed out that the only folks who could verify the truth of my story had been hung some days before, he sighed deeply and gave me a glass of port.

"I have to destroy their army and capture the King," he said wearily.

"You ever hear of General Crook?" says I.

He nodded.

"Well, he told me that fighting Indians was bad enough, but the worst thing that he found of it was that it was wrong. They were there first. It's their land. They seem to like how they live well enough."

Chelmsford shot me a sharp look.

"You Americans don't know how to think imperially."

"The hell we don't," I says. "We just don't have much of a navy, and besides that we haven't been at it long enough."

He looked at me again. He threw back his head and laughed.

"If every man in my forces who had enlisted under an assumed name was thrown out I would not have much of an army, Mr., uh, Adendorff. Both Buller and Harford say that you have given good service, and I have more pressing problems than finding out who you really are. You are to return to your unit and resume your scouting duties with young Harford."

I began to sputter—I could imagine what would happen to me if I got caught once again by the Zulus. "Your troops hung the messengers of the King who I was escorting in to parley."

"Since you are the only survivor of capture I doubt it would be much worse than the general run of luck," he says. He looked at me for a long time, again.

Finally he spoke, and spoiled my day something good. "Do you know a George Hanks, a correspondent for one of your American newspapers?"

"Never heard of him," I says.

"That will be all," he says.

"Yes, sir," I said, saluting smartly.

Chelmsford began to chuckle, and waved me away.

Well, suddenly Buller and Harford didn't seem to be such a bad idea—I was not eager for the British to hand me over to the Americans who would be investigating the matter of the disappearance of the Duke. (Jack did a good job, he was never found.) I would do a little skulking and spying and maybe contrive to be brave once or twice in front of an officer senior enough to recommend me for such, and then I would damn well leave Durban on the first boat and right during the celebrations of the victories over the Zulu nation. Wouldn't even hang around to collect the medals and the thanks.

So off I went, back up to Kambula.

I had ridden maybe five miles along the track when I began to get a prickling on the back of my neck. Someone was staring at me. My neck prickled for about ten minutes. I saw to my rifle and took the thong off the hammer of my revolver. I rode slowly around a curve in the torn-up road. There was a huge blue gum tree to my right. I looked real hard at it, waiting to see some movement on either side of the trunk.

Well, I should have been looking up. Someone landed with a thud on my horse right behind me and put their arms around my neck. I damn near pulled the horse over backwards.

It was little Marieke. She started laughing as soon as she got a little wind back.

"EEEEE Kelly," she shrieked. "If I was someone else you would be dead. Hah."

I was furious and more than a little embarrassed. This wench had made a fool out of me—fairly easy to do—and I ain't got the best of tempers. I started swatting at her but she'd just wriggle out of the way.

A little light-colored nigger with tight peppercorn hair come out from behind the tree. He had a long slender bow in his hand and some arrows in the other and all he wore was a sort of little apron of greasy leather. The little bastard was laughing like hell, too, but to be polite he at least had his hand over his mouth.

"Enough," I roared, throwing my leg over the back of the horse and sweeping little Marieke off. She slid over, twisted in the air, and landed on her hands and bounced to her feet.

"Listen, you little brat," I snarled, "this ain't funny."

She laughed some more at that. Well, I did have to grin.

"This is Baso," she said, gesturing to the little feller with the bow. She rattled off a long string of words in the strangest language I have ever heard—sounded like a field of locusts, all clicks and whirrs.

Baso laughed like hell at what she was saying.

So I dallied with Marieke for a couple of days. There wasn't anything about Marieke that you didn't see in the first five minutes, if you could see it, but like folks of that sort, her very lack of guile made her pretty opaque. I found it hard to believe that she had decided, for instance, that we would go to America and get married and live with the Indians. My opinion in the matter was of no interest and so as not to embarrass me, it was never brought up.

I went to a little crossroad sutler's store to get possibles and some tinned food the next day and saw a wanted poster with a bad drawing of her on it. Her father was no doubt popping out piles in throbbing dozens. He offered twenty-five pounds for her return. If he'd been there I'd have told the old bastard to save his money. He was already beat.

Baso was a Bushman. His arrows was poisoned and he could track anything. Anything at all. Marieke said the Bushmen can go to a place where an animal or man has crossed, go into a trance, and track where they went, even if they passed that way years before. Creepy little bastards. The Boers hunt them down and make house servants out of them. Usually they kill anyone over ten, but in Baso's case he had just wandered into the farm one day and indicated he wanted a job. Baso never frowned, never looked angry, never spoke sharp. Smiled all the time. He made me nervous. I was afraid it would rub off.

Marieke and I would lay in the shade by a small stream and she would run her finger over my chest and ask me questions about America and the Indians. She had figured out that I would be a good father. We were going to have two boys and two girls. I'd had enough brats for my life just growing up with so many. When I said so she just looked at me like I had remarked on what a good idea it was and how much I was looking forward to it.

"You go on home," I said, on the second day. "I have to get back to this here war."

"No," she said.

"Suit yourself," says I, "but I have to go now. They'll hang me otherwise."

"I wouldn't let them," she purred.

So I rode off shaking my head. I knew that a little blonde head and a dark, woolly one would be sticking up from time to time. I just hoped that they would watch their backs.

I reported to Buller, who sent me to Harford.

"Fine work," he said. "I'd heard you were dead."

"Found any good beetles?" I snarled.

"Aplenty," says he.

Both Chelmsford and Harford understood me, damn them.

"I believe we will be leaving in the morning to do a bit of scouting across the river," says Harford. "Wouldn't do to have the Zulus catch us napping. Just the two of us. By the way, how was Isandhlwana?"

"A perfect example of how them things go," I snarls.

"Most unfortunate," says he. "And Rorke's Drift?"

"Downright tragic," says I.

"We should see to your kit," says he.

We spent most of the rest of the night patching up some gear for me—what I most regretted was that now I would be much more lightly armed. I was able to get a revolver, but the rifle I was to use would have to be a Martini-Henry.

We took off in the dark the next evening, headed for a

place called Hlobane, a flat-topped mountain some forty miles in, where an allied tribe of the Zulus lived. It was a perfect defensive position, Harford told me, for there were only two ways up, nearly four hundred vertical feet, and the rest of the mountain was so sheer-sided that you might as well try to fly up, and carry your horse.

We skulked for a couple of weeks, saw no Zulus, and spied out this other tribe, who weren't up to much—sensible folks, having a nice place like that to wait and see just what was going to happen.

The Zulus was being scarce—after the mauling they'd got at Isandhlwana and Rorke's Drift, it made sense. Evelyn Wood had recruited some Bushmen and other trackers and these spies reported regularly. The Zulus aren't hunters, so they aren't good at that. Harford told me that they would, when the taste for wild meat hit them, surround a huge area and then close in. This amounted to European hunting, so far as I was concerned, and I couldn't imagine them closing in—this was Africa, mind you—on rhinoceroses, elephants, various big cats, and those black mambas.

We left on the twenty-seventh of March, in force, to assault Hlobane and provoke the Zulus. There had been a large detachment surrounded at Eshowe, in Zululand—the east column closest to the sea—even since Isandhlwana.

To add to my pleasure, all of the goddamn Uys brothers was riding with us. Harford was teaching me Zulu.

I wondered where the Uyses' blasted little sister was.

40

Hlobane. Certain portions of that glorious engagement were unique. Hopping from one boulder to another—the boulders being the size of houses, for instance—and the ridiculous bad luck. Actually it was like most military campaigns, it's a wonder any of them ever accomplish anything.

This was more on the order of a large raid—no tents, just mounted men with several days' rations and a lot of ammunition. We reached Hlobane Mountain about four in the afternoon and then split up, about half of us to go up one trail, and the other half to go up another, and catch whoever was up there between us.

Hlobane was a plateau—about five miles long and six hundred feet above the plain—with a smaller plateau stuck on at one end, about a hundred feet from the top of it to the river below. There was a sharp spur ran from the big mountain down to the smaller plateau, narrow enough so a man might lead a horse down it, provided he blindfolded the horse first and he himself had a very good reason for going.

Buller was leading the troop going up the trail to the high mountain, and the plan was to drive the natives off the top down to the spur and then either negotiate or charge, depending.

The Uyses held a prayer meeting before we began to ride up—the Boers are very religious. Piet Uys's explanations of this whole business was larded with a lot of quotes to the effect that the whites had dominion over the blacks. The whole Zulu war was simple to them, as simple as black and white. The whites would own all of the good land, the blacks would work it, and everybody would be happy. It seemed to me to be just a question of money, but then it usually is.

We started up, and dodged a few boulders which the natives up top tossed over just to keep things lively, and a couple of men were hit and several horses. Our fire drove the natives—they was called the abaQuabalitini or some such—off into hiding. We thought.

We got up top about an hour before sundown, and the place seemed pretty much deserted.

One of Buller's scouts had noticed that there was another trail down off the mountain which went off to the east—it couldn't be seen from below. He sent about eighty men down it, to flush out any natives there, and we moved west. I moved out to flank, got close to the edge of the sheer escarpment, looked over, and my heart went up in my throat. There was an easy ten thousand Zulus pounding toward us from the east, and I gaped for a moment. About a third of them broke off to cut off any retreat down the trail that the Border Horse had just gone down, while the rest loped toward the lower plateau. Wood's and Buller's plan had been a fine one, and now the Zulus were going to use it on us.

I raced to find Buller, and as I pounded up to him a lot

of fire erupted from cover on top of the mountain. The abaQuabalitini had seen the Zulus and made their decision. I would have done the same.

Buller swore and bellered orders and we forced our way down toward the razorback ridge which led to the lower plateau. Either we got down it before the Zulus below sealed it off, or we was going to join with the rest of them that made Glorious Last Stands.

A few of our men fell, and Buller insisted in stopping and picking up the bodies. The firing stopped—we had driven off the abaQuabalitini for the moment. We slung the dead across their horses and went on, and there was only one badly wounded man, who Buller held in front of him. He bled to death in minutes.

The trail was narrow as soon as it plunged down off the tabletop, and we were slowed terribly and strung out. Some of the men plunged for the narrow trail at the same time, and horses went down and the retreat was halted still further. The abaQuabalitini sensed our confusion, and began to come out of hiding and fire on us again. We lost perhaps half an hour, and when maybe one hundred of our hundred and fifty were still on the slow trail down, the Zulus plunged round the last spur of the mountain and raced to cut us off. The twenty men lowest on the trail made it to the plain and the safety of free flight (barring warthog holes or other unfortunate accidents to horses).

The Zulus were coming by the hundreds, and a nasty melee developed right at the base of the mountain, and then the ones cut off turned and spurred their horses uphill. Several hundred warriors went after them, while the others pursued the mounted men whose blown and sometimes injured horses were heading off toward Kambula.

Lucky me. I had been far enough back to draw future disembowlment over having my guts ripped open right now. When we got back up to the sloping saddle between the lower plateau and the huge upper one, there were a couple of hundred abaQuabalitini leaping down the trail to join in the fun.

I couldn't remember when I had been so happy. Off to our left there was a frightening jumble of boulders which tumbled down to the plain, and we made for that, spurring our foaming horses down. Some slipped and fell, throwing their riders into crevices.

My horse made four huge bounds, throwing sparks off the rocks from his iron shoes. We were about halfway down when he caught a leg in a vine—I heard the bone snap, even with all the racket around—and he pitched me forward. A scrubby little tree broke my fall, removing portions of my face for the favor. The boulders here was not so big, and I scrambled down to the plain and scurried off, more afraid of being crushed by a horse bouncing down from above than I was over the Zulus just then.

And here come Buller and such men as he had with good horses.

One of them swung me up behind him and turned around and we galloped on a zig-zag course through the thornbush, heading toward Kambula. The man put me down about six or seven miles away, well along the track, and I followed the trail, listening good for Zulus behind me. I was sure that a detachment would be sent down the trail toward Kambula after the folks who escaped from the mountain.

All of this was going on in a thunderstorm, too, for which I was grateful, as all the lightning and rain was distracting and I could use all the distractions luck could give me.

A few men on blown or limping horses caught up to me, and we went on at about the same pace toward safety. I must admit I was a little off to the side and mostly out of notice, being tired and out of sorts and not wishing company.

For once this got me into more trouble than not. I damn

near stepped on two Zulus who were hiding behind a
thornbush—they must have been scouts sent out some
time before and likely had no idea of what was going on a
few miles to the south and east of us. I didn't see them
until there was a sudden flash of lightning. They was
intent on watching the trail and the racket from the storm
covered over my own sounds.

I was suddenly angry. I still had my pistol, drew it, and
found the cylinder had fallen out—fine British goods,
that—and these two fellers was lying full length facing
away from me. I found a nice rock and bashed in one's
head, and when the other rolled away in surprise I jumped
him and used an old trick Washakie showed me—kicked
him in the throat. Man with a busted windpipe sort of
concentrates on it, you know. I finished him off with a
spear and went back to the trail.

At about first light Buller and such as he could save
came up and hallooed us. They was two to a horse, mostly,
and we was all ragged and wet, and as a military disaster
goes I thought it sort of second-rate. I'd been in lots
worse. Recently, even.

There was pretty good light in an hour or so. I looked
down at the ground, and at my left leg. My jaw dropped
open. I had a tremendous gash up and down my thigh,
and the blood had soaked my trousers—I'd been wondering
why they felt kind of lumpy, and why that boot squelched
different.

To this day I have no idea when I got speared—must
have been someone I didn't even see and I must have
been mounted—and until I commenced to wonder about
it, it didn't hurt, and then it hurt like hell and then I
began to limp

"You're wounded," I heard Buller growl behind me.
"Come on then, up behind me." He sort of plucked at me
and I swung up—Buller was one of the strongest men I
have ever known.

He was slashed and hacked, his uniform had been shredded, and he had, I found out later, sabered his way back through the Zulus time and time again to get someone out. One of those iron sorts. Head of oak, the British say.

A party come from Kambula late in the day with fresh horses. They had a surgeon with them. He give me a big slug of brandy and then sewed up my leg, me biting a twig damn near in two during the process. Hell, I thought, it will only hurt worse later. Then they slung me up on a horse, and we moved at a fast trot on to Kambula.

As soon as we were in the camp I pitched off the horse and landed with a thud in the mud.

41

There wasn't much to do for the next twenty-four hours but sleep. I had lost a lot of blood and rode or walked a long damn way. I was in a hospital tent with about twenty other wounded men. A couple of them had fever, and one was so delirious that they had tied him to his bed and put a rubber plug in his mouth to keep him from swallowing his tongue. The man in the bed next to me had a bad wound—it had gone gangrenous. The stink was awful.

When the medico bustled in—reeking of the medicinal brandy—he tried to look at my leg and I snarled at him and made a few gestures with my crutch. You know the type, you go in for hangnail and he'll end up killing you. So he blinked at me and moved on to the feller with the gangrenous leg, took off the dressing, tut-tutted, slopped some sort of disinfectant on it, and then put the same bandage back on.

This was too much. As soon as the addled sonofabitch

tottered off I looked over at the feller. He was feverish, but still alert.

"I can fix that wound for you," I says. "If you let that old bastard at it he'll kill you."

He didn't look a bit frightened, just raised his eyebrows. "Really?" says he.

"Got to get some maggots on that," says I. "They'll clean out that proud flesh in a hurry."

"Really?"

"My father was a doctor, not a quack like this old fool," says I.

"By Jove, do it, if you can."

What an upper-class Brit was doing in the tent with the rest of us scum was beyond me, but there he was.

He had a crutch next to his bed, which I borrowed, and using him and mine I stumped off—they'd left one boot on, mind you.

Finding maggots wasn't difficult—there was always a pile of something around an army encampment. I scanned the horizon for a tornado of flies, went to it, and found all I needed. I filled half a water glass with nice wriggly ones, stumped back, and poured them bit by bit on his wound.

There was a bluish-black hole in his lower leg; he'd likely scratched himself on a thorn or something and gone on sick call—a mistake—and I covered the wound liberally with maggots and tore off strips and a pad and covered it up.

"When these ones ain't eating so fast we'll scrape 'em off and get a fresh batch."

When the doctor came back we both growled and waved our crutches at him. He was even drunker than he had been earlier, and went out without a murmur, probably thinking that we was some sort of hallucination.

Late in the afternoon Buller stopped by to congratulate all us brave subjects of the Queen, etc., etc. Buller looked fit and rested and had on a new uniform. I figured he'd only ridden forty miles today and killed maybe twenty Zulus, just to get the blood up, don't you know.

He came up to where I was laying and says something to the effect that he appreciated-it-old-chap-is-there-anything-I-can-do?

"Yes," I says. "Can you get the two of us out of here before that drunken idiot kills us both?"

"Oh," says Buller. "Quite."

He went off, and I heard his bellering, and inside of fifteen minutes we was put up in a roomy tent by ourselves, with a nice bottle of brandy on the folding nightstand between the beds. I took a poke around and discovered that the tent was Buller's—he shared it with another officer.

The maggots did their work in about a day, and where there had been a big black hole with a white and green end to it, there was now just angry red flesh—but it was live.

"I feel much better," said the feller. "By the way, my name is Arthur Ansall. The Honorable Arthur Ansall."

"Adendorff," says I.

Arthur was pretty wore out, so he went to sleep, and I didn't see him again for a few years. By then he was Lord Beaker.

I hitched a ride on an outgoing cart, after telling Buller in a note that I was just going to Durban until my wound healed and would be back and hoped sincerely that he would have found new and interesting ways to get me killed by then. Left the forwarding address of my hotel.

The driver of the cart was a Boer, name of Pretorius, and I have never moved faster in anything else with wheels that didn't also ride on rails. The Boer picked up relays of horses across the country, and turned his reins over to another man at nightfall. So, I thinks, they are carrying dispatches or something.

Anyway, I come to Durban the following night, a bit bounced around and my leg sore, and I went to the Hotel Durban and rented a room and soaked in a lot of hot water for several hours.

I rested up for a couple of days and ate as well as Durban could offer—the fresh fish and the oysters was best—and didn't do much else. My wound was healing nicely and I have long found that staying in bed with something like that will make you weak and the wound heal very slowly. You got to get up and walk.

The fourth night there was a knock at my door and a young officer in the fanciest rig I had ever seen on a man was standing there. He dripped with gold braid over white, with all sorts of green piping, said he was Lieutenant Wilson—this with me blinking at him because the glare was so blinding—and would I do the Governor the honor of attending tea tomorrow. The Governor was most anxious to hear my accounts and I had been mentioned favorably in dispatches. (I figure it is a favorable mention if they don't say "Please hang or shoot immediately.")

"Of course," says I.

"You are Adendorff?"

"Yup."

"Hmmmmmm. I thought you'd be Dutch."

"Canadian," says I. At which point he got an expression like there was something nasty in the way of smell in the air and stumped off.

Tea the next day was one of the strangest experiences I had ever had. There was a few officers—mostly Navy—a lot of florid-looking civilians, and their ladies crammed into silk dresses with tulle wraps and reeking of some muskrat scent—and we all passed in a line, where we bowed and curtsied, depending. I thought of curtsying but thought it might just confirm the Lieutenant's suspicions about Canadians. He was standing by the Governor—Sir

Bartle Frere—and his wife, looking at me as though I might steal the Governor's gold buttons.

Frere was as bored as I was with all of this. He ho-hoed for a while, and made the rounds, and then made a nod in the direction of a double door guarded by our Lieutenant Wilson. We slipped in there. It was a conservatory, with a piano. We sat on the bench and Frere fiddled at a cabinet and brought up a couple of stiff drinks.

"How's the governing business?" says I.

"Beats the law all down," says Frere. "I have good reports from Buller and Chelmsford upon you, Mr. Adendorff. There is much talk about the disaster at Isandhlwana. Chelmsford was not in the camp—blameless, of course—and there are few accounts that make sense. I thought you might tell me what you saw."

I told him as well as I could, and bluntly that the whole and only reason that it happened was that Durnford had put his troops in the wrong places. I told him about what I saw of Rorke's Drift and of what I had seen of Cetshwayo. And then of Hlobane. That was a happy accident for the Zulus—they had come on us at the only good time for them. One half hour more or less and we would have just rode away. It couldn't be called a surprise attack. They just trotted over the hill and there we were on the damn mountain.

I suppose I talked for half an hour. Frere took no exception to anything I said, just nodded from time to time. I finished.

"I have a delicate matter I should like to discuss with you," he said when I was through. "Extremely delicate. There is a young woman who . . . ah . . . cared deeply for Durnford. And he for her. Poor Durnford married early, and there was a scandal, and a divorce, and the court awarded custody of their two sons to Durnford. What with this damned morality, there was nothing that they could do until Durnford's first wife died. Which she has not."

"Obstinate, ain't she?" says I.

Frere snorted. "I beg you when you speak with the young lady to spare her such levity, Mr. Adendorff. She is an intelligent young woman of great gifts. She would like to speak with you about Isandhlwana. It is something of an obsession with her."

"So I say he fought like a lion and was last seen rallying one sergeant and two men for a death-or-glory charge. Fine," says I.

"She is not stupid," says Frere. "She is obsessed with transferring the blame from poor Durnford to Chelmsford. It would be helpful to her if you could speak quite frankly, without the addition of your—succinct assessments."

"The blame would have to be shared by both Pulleine and Durnford," says I. "Chelmsford had left the camp with a sufficient force. It was those two idiots who threw away the time needed to prepare to meet the Zulus. That's all there is to it."

Frere shrugged and led me back into the reception hall.

There was a beautiful, slender, young woman near the door. She was dressed fashionably, so I liked her—my watered-silk waistcoat wasn't exactly the hit of the party. She had too-bright blue eyes—from crying, I expected—and she wore no jewelry or wraps.

"Mr. Adendorff, this is Miss Harriet Colenso," says Frere.

I bowed. Hell, I come from a good home.

We chatted, the three of us, about nothing much. Then Frere wearily went back to his pumphandle work, smiling grandly.

Miss Colenso asked me kindly—she had a deep voice for such a slender, small woman—how I liked Durban. There was no gushing or hysteria. She said her father, the Bishop of Natal, would like to meet me. Could I come to dinner tonight?

I accepted, and left gratefully.

42

All of the good horses in Durban had gone off to war. There was a kind of fever in South Africa which infested certain grazing areas and the imported stock took a few bites of grass, swayed, and fell over dead about nine-tenths of the time, so the local "salted" horses was selling for unbelievable prices. The cabby told me this as we lurched along behind the two sorriest lumps of dog meat I have ever seen.

I got to the Colensos' a bit late, hat in hand. Walking would have been quicker, but I wasn't sure where they lived. The house was a big old pile built some years before, and a lot out of plumb. There was a votive candle in the window. The black maid who answered the door motioned me in. I was willing to bet that I was the only dinner guest.

The family was seated in the parlor, singing hymns to the wheezing of a pump organ. Well, hell, what do you expect in a Bishop's home? The last strains of one of them songs died away and the bishop put down his hymnal and come to greet me. He waved away my apologies and shook my hand heartily. He was a tall, heavy man, with shrewd eyes behind bifocals, and the sort of lines that trouble and kindness put in the forehead.

I was introduced to his wife, named Frances, and a daughter, named Frances, too, and we chatted amiably about nothing much until the same black maid took us in to dinner.

The dinner was awful, as only the English can make food. I have eaten with Apaches, Plains tribes, and Eskimos, lived on jerky and what greens were around for weeks at a time, but this was a meal only the English could have done. Roast beef from a cow must have been about forty, some sort of mashed roots might have been potatoes when they was younger, and vegetables boiled so long they looked like them glassy noodles you get in Japan. We drank water with a dab of some wine in it. I chewed away and tried to swallow. All the Colensos had real strong jawlines.

That ordeal over, I was hauled off to the parlor again and given a cup of good tea, and then Harriet commenced into drilling me, with her family sort of standing by ready to pounce on anything she missed.

I performed rather well, describing the battle, and what I had seen of the beginning of the end, and remained noncommittal on who could possibly be to blame. When I was asked questions I didn't want to answer, I said I was only a sergeant of volunteers and hardly privy to staff conferences. Besides, I had been out on patrol, and when I had seen the huge imPi in the donga and ridden back to warn the camp everything seemed normal. (Durnford, of course, proceeded to make every available wrong decision. He was as big a genius as Custer at doing the wrong thing at the wrong time.)

Harriet kept at me, and I kept being noncommittal, and

she finally stormed off, I supposed to cry. There was an awkward silence, one of those that make you remember you have an appointment, and when I rose and stammered something the Bishop took the cue and he offered to drive me back to town himself. The coach was all made up, so I suspected the old geezer had known right along what was going to happen. We took off, and he didn't say anything until we got back to my hotel.

"Mr. Adendorff," he said, "I appreciate your kindness to my daughter. She is distraught." He shook my hand and wished me godspeed and drove off. There wasn't much more to say.

I had a couple of shots of grog in the hotel's bar.

Durban had several newspapers, and I idly looked at one. I finally saw an ad for an appearance at the Stage Theatre by, of all people, my friend the actress Gussie Walker, and I thought, I haven't seen anyone who knows me for months. Then I thought that that was why I was here. Then I thought that George Hanks was no doubt hanging around the mess tents up north and getting kicked around. So I called the same cabby with the same two pieces of dog-meat-at-your-service and found the theatre. I sent in a note by the guard at the stage door and in a few minutes Gussie herself came out and said she was delighted to see me, Mr. Adendorff—I'd said my own name, of course, in the note, and that I was traveling incognito, as it were. Gussie, when stage pickings are slim or she's tired of the life, does bunco games and picks the occasional pocket, and so I had no trouble there. Always stick to good honest business people, if you can.

She was staying at my hotel, and we just hadn't seen each other.

It took her an hour or so to scrape off the layer of paint she'd put on for the evening's murder of Shakespeare and scrape on another, which was her everyday wear, and we took the cab back to the hotel. The little bastard at the desk glanced up once and then went back to his dirty postcards—actresses and Americans will be that way you know. We had oysters and an incredibly good South African champagne and then Gussie sighed and took my hand and said what she always says when she sees me.

"It's so good to see you, Luther. I don't know why. I don't ever miss you until you're here. Why are you here? Being a hero? You have saved beautiful maidens from ravishing, out of the noble impulse to be first. You have dashed to warn the stagecoach of approaching savages, and made off with the strongbox while the poor fools are looking to their ammunition. You have carried messages hundreds of miles in below zero weather, sleeping under the snow, because that was safer than staying in the fort while the wind piles snow up the stockade walls for the Indians to climb up. You are a dear, Luther."

"Good to see you, too, Gussie," says I. "And what happened to that rich racehorse owner you was gonna marry?"

"Sleeping with the vice-president of his bank was a small price to pay for knowing he wasn't as rich as he said."

We liked and understood each other.

"What's the news from home?" says I.

"Ain't been there in a year," says Gussie. "I have been spouting Shakespeare to boobs in Australia, and anyway even Cape Town beats Sydney all to hell."

"Figure you can head back to the States pretty soon?"

"Another year. I am saving for my trousseau."

"Saratoga Springs?"

"Yesssssss," says Gussie dreamily, "where I'll meet some rich old fool with a lot of money and a bad heart. With good luck and my best efforts, he'll die on the wedding night."

After a while we crawled into bed and fucked like minks, and had the best old time.

"Luther," she says, "what are these black women like?"

"A nigger wench is like any other," says I. "I sort of like them because when they talk I don't know what they're saying."

She pinched my ear for that one. We went at it again.

Gussie slipped out sometime in the night. I saw her at breakfast in the morning. Just to confound everyone we ignored each other.

Later I learned that the English always do that.

43

I wasn't exactly boiling with eagerness to get back to the war, so I limped as convincingly as I could until Gussie set sail for an engagement in Rio de Janeiro, which place she assured me had a large population of Englishmen hungry for Shakespeare.

"Well," I says at the dockside, "I hope they don't like Shakespeare too much. One of 'em might...oh never mind...."

"Go to hell, Luther," said Gussie, flouncing up the gangplank.

I searched around for two more days and found two salted horses at an outrageous price. Didn't seem outrageous to me, what with the war on and how bad I might need 'em, and I got two nice new repeating Winchesters and a pair of Colt's finest and a thousand rounds of ammunition for 'em. That episode with the cylinder falling out my fine British piece had soured me on English firearms. I also bought one of them leaded snakewhips and a few luxuries.

So off I went toward the second act of my Zulu War, which I hoped would be nice and uneventful and dull. Hell I did. I was bored witless, in all the meanings of the word. I kept thinking about Marieke, which made me mad.

During my slow and painful recuperation there had been two more battles, one at Kambula, on the west, and one at Gingundhlovu on the eastern track closest to the sea. The Zulus had been defeated with heavy losses and now Chelmsford was grinding up the center track to Ulundi and the end of the war, we all hoped.

So off I went on a sunny morning, riding one good horse and leading another, birds singing their fool heads off, grass smelling all nice, warm, not a care in the world, heading north and west at an unhurried pace.

Now usually when I am feeling good it makes me very nervous. I was down on the Cimarron once feeling like I did now and all of a sudden Comanches was everywhere and my partner ended up being tortured to death. They stuck him full of pitchpine slivers and set him alight. Would have done the same to me the next day, only Quanah Parker was bored with the local competition and needed someone to play chess with. By carefully allowing myself to be beaten after hard and prolonged—especially prolonged—matches, I kept alive for a week. We had also spent a lot of time jawjacking, and one thing about old Quanah is he had a hell of a sense of humor. So he had me tied backwards on a horse and sent off, which I didn't mind one bit.

I had that good, full feeling this morning and I should have known better. But here I was one hell of a long ways from any Zulus, passing Boer farms and peaceful country, seeing stupid bunches of cattle, passing by the occasional postrider.

I come to ford a small river, went across, and struggled up the bank, which was muddy and slippery even with the corduroy underlay. Got remounted and headed for two close bunches of trees. Kayrist, I was even *whistling*. Terrible habit.

A loop of rope come out of the bushes and settled over me. Something spooked the horses, and there I was sitting on my ass in the dust, somewhat out of wind. I had the presence of mind to pull out my revolver.

A little figure in rough Boer clothes stepped out, and she was pointing one of those rifles the Boers use for shooting rhinos and elephants and such at me. The bore on the damn thing looked like an open wellhead.

"You bastard," said sweet Marieke. "You copper-bottomed redneck bastard. You son of a bitch. I am going to shoot you."

I wanted to laugh, but I felt it would be real impolite.

Marieke went on in that vein—she was a poor cusser, but then she wasn't but sixteen or so—all the while keeping the gun pointed at my head. Her Bushman chum was squatting in the shadows, grinning.

Marieke finally came over and gave me a few boots in the ribs, but she did loosen the rope and let me get up. I knocked the dust off with my hat while she went on with her limited vocabulary about what a disgrace I was to the human race, an opinion I heartily shared and would have raised my voice in the chorus but I somehow felt that it would not be the sort of thing she was looking for.

She walked around in front of me and looked up at me with her pretty face.

"I am going to marry you," she says, "and I am letting you know right now that I am never again going to let you out of my sight so that you can go sleep with whores." Then she slammed the butt of her elephant gun down on my left foot hard enough to have me hopping around and adding to the general din. When I stopped, the damn Bushman had fallen off the log and was holding his sides.

This wasn't the sort of audience approval that Marieke had been looking for, so she stalked over and kicked him, in a listless sort of way. He jumped up and ran off. A Bushman can disappear like smoke.

We caught my horses and went over to where she had hers tethered. But Bushman reappeared, still grinning like he'd never had such a good morning in all his life.

"I'm going with you," she says.

"I have to go back to the war," I says.

"I'm going there with you," she says.

"Look," I says, "you'll be noticed and sent right back to your family. Your father and brothers are up there."

She spurred up her horse for an answer.

We rode north and west, keeping away from the little towns and roadhouses. When we stopped that night and made camp, I made about one attempt to talk her out of it and got cracked across my shins for my pains. All right, thinks I, this is pissing into the wind.

"I don't have to go back right away," I says. "Why don't we just go off for a few days?"

"Of course we are going off for a few days," says Marieke.

44

Marieke and me spent the next day walking around in what I suppose was circles, holding hands, sometimes sitting on rocks—Christ, I even picked her some flowers—and generally acting like the moonstruck idiots that we was. I loved her. She was a little spitfire—had to be, with them brothers—and she acted old sometimes and sometimes like a very young girl. She was her own.

I was waiting for questions about Gussie, and they never came. Oh, she ranted on now and again about all of the whores in Durban and such, and it came to me all of a sudden that she probably hadn't even gone into the town.

"There ain't no whores in Durban that I know if," says I at one point, making it the purest seaport in all the world.

"All whores," she snapped. Well, she had a point.

"You never even been there," says I.

"No."

"Why?"

"I don't like cities," says she.

"Me neither," says I. Our love-talk was downright Shakespearean.

So it went. We slept under the stars rolled in our arms and we'd ride here and there and point and say look at that and spend a lot of time just sitting. I remember the time, and even now it causes me pain to do so, but I can't actually say what we did. It is lost in some sort of golden fog.

"I got to go," I said one morning.

She nodded.

I saddled up and rode away. I should have broken her leg.

Chelmsford had crossed the Buffalo River two days before I got there. He wouldn't get to Ulundi much before the first of July because he had chosen a longer, safer route over more open country. One more disaster and they'd promote him.

I finally found Buller, who was with what was now called the Flying Column, irregulars officered by Imperial officers. Very few of the fresh-faced young men who had ridden off to war last January looked anything like their old selves. They had seen too much.

Buller clapped me heartily around the shoulder and said that young Ansall had healed marvelously—he would limp for the rest of his days. The drunken surgeon had got a bad case of the DTs one night and wandered out of camp. A lion got him. This news cheered me up some.

"The leg has healed well," Buller said. "Good. Good." Not a word about the fact I had spent over a month in Durban, and he surely would have heard about Gussie.

"Well, well," said Buller, "well, well. Harford will be delighted to see you. We have need of good scouts. Look him up and be responsible to him."

I launched into a stream of profanity, one I learned from

a buffalo skinner who could burn the air for five minutes without repeating a phrase.

Buller stood there nodding his head and grinning, and when I was through he congratulated me on my performance and pointed out Harford heading this way. This sent me off again but Buller just walked on and Harford sauntered up. He smelled very strange.

I couldn't help wrinkling my nose at the smell. It was horribly pungent. And I have smelled some things . . . Never mind.

Harford looked at me, puzzled.

"You stink," I said, "in a proper, insufferable manner, of course."

"Oh, that," said Harford. He fingered the uniform he was wearing. It was a dark brown corduroy. "We were so ragged that we had to be issued new uniforms. The British being who they are, they bought these from a wog named Mr. Ghopal. We got them two weeks ago—the smell was much stronger, I assure you. There has been endless speculation on what Mr. Ghopal used for dyestuffs. The consensus is that it is a half-and-half mixture of hyena shit and buzzard vomit. . . ."

"I ain't scouting with you in that," says I. "We're close enough in size so you can just take some of my spares."

"What a nice idea," says Harford.

"Wearing that in the damn dark wouldn't be a lot of good to us. You, rather. Smell you for miles. Zulus *do* have noses. Maybe it would be better if you kept 'em come to think of it. . . ."

"Don't be unchristian, Kelly."

It took me a few moments.

"My name is James Adendorff," says I, "no matter what that little bastard George Hanks says."

" 'Fraid not," says Harford. "The three Uys boys who survived Hlobane came to see you as you lay—mildly concussed, I suppose, which is why I suspect you were telling the truth. Hans asked you some questions—he is the only one with much English, and you answered them. Including admitting that you are the famous Yellowstone Kelly. I happened to be there. Now, Kelly, neither I nor Buller nor Chelmsford gives a damn why you are here. We have a war to fight."

He stripped off the vile corduroys and took the clothes I gave him—I even said he could have one of the rifles after he stared at it, politely clearing his throat for maybe fifteen minutes. Maybe I was still in shock.

That done, we stowed my extra gear in one of the commissary wagons and went out to look to the north and west—there were scattered parties of Zulus striking in groups of from two to ten, armed with the Martini-Henrys and sometimes even mounted. There would be only one more pitched battle with the Zulu army, and that at the gates of Ulundi, and I suppose both the Zulus and ourselves knew it.

We rode off, unconcerned, until we could drop down into a donga and sort of cut our way out of the line of sight for a few miles, and then creep up a hill with good cover and take a look.

I suppose we rode for four hours like that, slowly and as quiet as we could. Then we decided that we would go up a little donga and tie the horses, and creep up to the hilltop and take a look. One of us take the horses, and hold them quiet, and the other take his shielded binoculars and carefully look.

The donga wasn't very deep, maybe ten feet, but it had steep walls.

The problem with this sort of thing is that it may occur to someone else. So I come round a corner and here is this gigantic Zulu, creeping quietly. We stare at each other for about half a minute.

The Zulu is carrying both a Martini-Henry and a spear, and while he's figuring out which one he wants to use I blow his brains out with my Winchester. He has five friends behind him who take exception to this.

For a few seconds the donga roars with fire. Three more Zulus drop—Harford moves up beside me, and then he drops his rifle and drops to the ground on his hands and knees.

The other two Zulus are about eight feet from us, spears up and shields forward. I have no time to go to Harford. I knock one Zulu down with the rifle and desperately grab my pistol and the Zulu stabs at me twice before I can knock him over and finish him off. I jam shells into the rifle and my pistol and look around for any more Zulus. I can't hear very well. I hear a voice behind me.

"Kelly," shouts Harford happily. "Look at this, entirely new to science."

He was holding up a beetle about four inches long, bright emerald green.

"It's a *Findibulus Harfordi*," says Harford.

I walked over to the bastard, cracked him on the forehead with my revolver, and spent the next two minutes in Zululand hopping up and down on his damn bug.

Then I went and got the horses.

45

Chelmsford ground on toward Ulundi, and we of the Flying Column went off to Chelmsford's left, presenting a threat, offering a smaller possibility of battle. The Zulus had had it, and they knew it, but the war wouldn't be over until Ulundi had been burned and the King had been captured. They would fight there.

Harford and I kept going out, sometimes right close to Ulundi itself. We worked well together and after I stomped on his goddamn beetle, he at least knew how not to provoke me. I found two more and stomped them, too.

The Zulu army wasn't massed at Ulundi—they were off to their home kraals, as much as a hundred miles away, tending their wounds. We had their scouts to contend with—I taught Harford a few things about night killing and tracking, and he taught me a lot more about Africa and how to avoid trouble.

The last week in May we come back for one of our rare evenings in camp, when for the sake of our comrades we would chew—seemed like for hours—on a stringy slaughter beef and eat lots of bread. One of General Wood's peculiarities was that he demanded fresh bread for his troops, and there were two mobile bakery wagons, and even one fit out as a hen house. It had a milk cow tethered to the back of it.

One evening Buller summoned me and Harford to his tent. Buller was awfully jovial, which in commanding officers means that they are about to hand you a wildcat, a red-hot knitting needle, and a pat of butter, and ask you to stuff the butter up the wildcat's ass with the needle, if you please. Or I'll hang you. Which is what Buller did.

"What in Christ's name is he doing *here*?" I snarled. "No. No, god dammit. NO, NO, NO."

"Can't be helped," said Buller. "You two are the best we have, and he would be safest with you."

This put a new light on things. If we were to keep Napoleon the Fourth alive and in good health we would, therefore, keep ourselves alive and in good health. As much as I hate Frogs, this put a somewhat greater value on the health of Frogs than I'm inclined to give, as a usual case.

"Sergeant Aden . . . Kelly," Buller said, waving the brandy at us, "may I remind you that you are addressing a superior officer."

"Yes, sir," I said, watching my glass as it filled. "Fuck you, sir."

Buller roared with laughter at that. Harford joined in.

"I suppose," said Harford, "we are, I gather, to let the little fool think that he is actually at war without letting him get anywhere near it."

"Quite," said Buller.

"Can't we take him down to Durban and keep him drunk for a month or two or however long it takes to get this fool war over with?" I says.

"His mother would hate you for it, and she *is* a Queen,"

said Buller. "He is an earnest young chap. Just can't afford to let anything happen to him. If he stays near to camp the young fool will chase every Zulu scout he spots and he don't listen to orders very well. Born to the purple, you know."

"He'll damn well listen to me or he'll be wearing his ass for a hat," says I. "I don't like Frogs to begin with and the Head Frog starts off lowest of all."

We went back and forth for a while, and finally it was agreed that it would be smarter to have young Napoleon do something useful. With an escort, of course. Like making maps.

We had come close to Chelmsford, very close now—we had been drifting northeast and would be up to him in a couple of days. The Flying Column would join the procession and on we would go to the final act.

That evening, late, we was introduced to the future emperor of France, if they'd have him, which weren't likely. He turned out to be a nice feller, even for a Frog. I had expected some insufferable little bastard—more like an Englishman—but Napoleon was a bright, self-effacing young subaltern who wished only to do his job well. He was eager, I could tell that, but honestly wished to be no trouble. I should have broken his leg, too.

Buller sent us out the next day, with an escort for Napoleon of a sergeant and four troopers, and Harford and me had left in the night and scouted the area that they were going to map. We did this for several days.

The Flying Column had grown to about fifteen hundred men by now—guards from Natal had been released, and scattered units that had been raiding into Zululand, stealing cattle and burning small outlying kraals, came in as we closed with the main body.

I had wore my boots about out and needed to touch up my tack. I was sitting there crosslegged, sewing away, when a shadow fell across my work. I looked up and there was Napoleon IV. He was a slender boy of twenty or so, with a cheerful face, and he squatted down on his haunches and watched me for a moment.

"I understand you are an Indian scout in America's Wild West," he said, with the faintest French accent. "I have read about you, I think. I would very much like to come and see your West and hunt your buffalo."

"Well," says I, "don't believe that pack of lies you read, and if you come and I'm there look me up and we'll go hunt something. The buffalo will likely be gone by then."

"Pardon?"

"The Plains Indians depend on the buffalo for everything," I said, "so it was the thought that if they destroyed the buffalo they would destroy the Plains tribes. Millions are being killed, the hides taken, the rest left to rot. The tribes are broken. This is called statecraft in some circles, I believe."

"That's terrible," he said.

"Ain't no different from what we are doing right now," says I. "We'll destroy the Zulu army and take all their cattle and land and make beggars out of 'em."

"But these are savages," said Napoleon.

"Horseshit," I said. "They're a different color, and they're in the way. They don't have good guns and we do. That's history. How would you feel if the Zulus invaded France, and their weapons were better than yours and they just took it?"

"I would fight to the death," he said.

"That's just what they'll do," says I.

We went on to other things. He asked me about what I was doing—being a Prince Imperial you never get to do *anything* for yourself, not even wipe your own ass, I suppose. Napoleon was a splendid horseman, and I saw him do a demonstration of work with what turned out to be his great-uncle's sword that still makes my head shake. He rode flat out at an orderly, who threw two potatoes in the air, and he sliced them both from horseback, one on each side, so fast I didn't really see the blade.

Anyway, we spent a pleasant afternoon, him asking questions about tracking, and the Plains tribes, and what guns I used and why, and why I had a knife in my boot (it's called a slip, long and thin and double-edged. You slip it into a man's heart from the back, striking up) and how the Indians trained their horses—I told him that they sometimes break colts by riding them in the water, which makes it less dangerous for both the horse and rider. He said he thought it lacked courage.

He invited me to have dinner with him and his colleagues in the Officers' Mess, and so I went. The officers were a bit put off by having a mere volunteer foisted off on them, but no one was out-and-out rude and Buller was so jovial to me they finally warmed. We ate the same thing everyone else did, but the officers had a lot of claret and brandy, and after the mess was cleaned away we sat on camp stools and talked.

Everyone but Buller and me was eager to impress Napoleon—the British are that way about royalty. But there was one feller there, a Lieutenant Carey, who was downright groveling. He followed Louis around, offering him seegars, and once when I was standing near, talking to Buller, I heard Carey say something that damn near made my jaw drop off.

"Here," said Carey, holding a crumpled daguerreotype, "are my dear wife and daughters. Are they not lovely? I shed tears each time I think of them (he commenced to snuffle); they are such perfect examples of sweet Jesus's creations."

He went on in that vein for some time, with Napoleon being kind to him. I had to leave, but before I went I stopped by Buller and asked for a word.

"Certainly, Kelly," said Buller. "We'll step outside."

We stood under the stars—we was up high enough so that the night was cold.

"I have scouted here for nearly five months now," I says, "and though Harford and I ain't turning up a damn thing I have this feeling. It's a feeling that I have learned to trust, one that I can't really explain. They are around, we just haven't found them. Just make sure Louis has a strong escort. And have whoever is running the damn thing stay the hell away from that tambookie grass. A whole damn imPi could be in one of them stands and you could be ten feet away and not know it. The grass rustles in the smallest breeze and puts out a hell of a clatter."

"I will see to it," says Buller. "Carey will receive his instructions. . . ."

"Carey?" says I. "That godwalloping bastard?"

"His turn," said Buller.

The officers had been taking turns squiring Napoleon around. Never know when a little sucking up to royalty will stand you in good stead.

"Send Groves or. . ."

"It's settled," said Buller. "I'll talk to Carey myself."

Buller strode back into the tent, and I looked up Harford.

We slipped out and commenced to ride in the direction that tomorrow would be taken by the Prince Imperial and his escort.

46

Harford and I slipped along in the dark, sniffing the air for woodsmoke, looking for a tiny point of light, checking at the places where trails cross for any sign. We found some, though not a lot. We found a good place to hide in while the dawn rose—the dew steams off and makes a fog for about an hour—and I held the horses while Harford slithered up an acacia tree to glass the countryside. He was up there longer than he usually was, and when he come down he looked puzzled.

"It doesn't seem that unusual," he said, "but about five miles ahead I saw a flight of ducks taking off. Anything could have startled them, I suppose."

We didn't know exactly where the Prince's party was headed; they would map for a bit, look for campsites for the supply train, and whether they went left or right was purely a matter of whim. I kept telling myself that Lieutenant Carey knew what he was doing, and then I would answer myself: the hell he does.

Some ten miles out, which was as far as the wagons could hope to go, I saw some crushed grass in a little hidden meadow, up ahead of us. Harford saw me stiffen, we saw to our guns. I dropped the reins of my horse on the ground and went back to him and put my face close to him and whispered that I thought it best we not just ride through it, but come on it sort of sideways-like. And quiet.

Harford held the horses, and I went forward to look, sliding through the acacia and come-hither thorn. That sort of bush is full of little pepper-ticks, but they ain't as lethal as assegais or the 480 grain lead bullets from Martini-Henrys. It took me a couple of hours to convince myself that there was nothing there now, though I was damn sure that there had been.

The tracks was of maybe a dozen Zulus, four or five hours old. It was easy two in the afternoon by now, maybe later, and the days were getting shorter as we got toward the twenty-first of June, which is the shortest day of the year down here.

"There were some here," I said, "and I don't think we can handle a dozen."

We wondered a bit. Then we decided to get up high and devil damn the thought of Zulus seeing us, we could outride them or hold them off with the Winchesters. We would try to spot the Prince's party and tell them to get the hell back to the main group.

That decided, we rode ridges, only plunging down into the dongas at bare places to get up top the next one.

I saw them finally, about five o'clock. They was maybe five miles away, and they dipped out of sight as soon as I laid eyes on them. But at least now we knew which direction they was in. I rode flat out, with Harford behind me, cursing Carey for not having headed back an hour ago. It would be damn dark in an hour and there was high cloud moving in from the Indian Ocean, so there would be no light from the stars.

"Damn them," Harford snarled, "oh, damn, damn, damn."

We rode as hard as we could, but I knew already we were too late. That is where the Zulus were headed, and the Prince was in the lead, not Carey, as it should have been.

To go five miles across a flat and level plain is one thing, to go that far in this broken country took longer. It was more than an hour until we came to the place I had last seen them. We looked down the track and saw a disheveled trooper riding hell for leather toward us. The man had no rifle. He would have run right over the top of us if I hadn't yelled at him to stop. He had near to blown his horse and he was shaking so bad that it was a minute or two until he found his voice.

"Are there others?" I yelled. The man calmed down and said he thought that three others of the party had got away. That left four unaccounted for.

"Get back to the camp and tell them," I said.

The man rode off as hard as he had ridden up. And then here came our Lieutenant Carey.

"I suppose Buller would hang me if I just killed him," I said to Harford. "Will you look at that sonofabitch. Not for him to check for his troopers."

Carey stopped and then rode back—he was a mile away, so it wasn't my remark that did it, and pretty soon he come on with two troopers in tow.

If you are wondering why we didn't go down there, it's simple. Whatever had happened was over.

Carey and his two troopers came pounding up and reined in, and Carey was crying.

"We must pray... I am ruined... the Prince is killed... oh, woe is me, woe is me." He really said "woe is me." I almost shot him for that—it was one of Custer's favorite expressions.

"Get hold of yourself, man," snapped Harford. "You must report to General Wood."

We pounded back across the veldt, startling antelope which had put up for the night out of their beds. My horse was the fleetest, and I was used to riding hard in this sort of country, so they followed strung out behind. We cut a line straight across as near as we could, but it was damn dark before we pulled up at the camp.

Both Buller and Evelyn Wood were pacing about, Buller with a huge unlit cheroot in his clenched teeth. The sight of Carey made the veins in his temples throb.

Wood was a lumpy little man, nearsighted and always blinking, but tough as nails. One of those deceptively soft little fellows who it is unwise to ignore. Carey dismounted and walked off with them to Wood's tent. They went inside, and a lamp flared up. I swung down and led my horse to the picket and off-saddled and rubbed him down and grained and watered him and checked his hooves. He would need shoes soon.

Harford was next to me.

"There will be unholy hell to pay for this one," he said. "I am sure that Chelmsford will have someone's ballocks."

"Ought to be," I said, rubbing my horse with a handful of dry grass. "Letting that arsehole Carey lead the damn thing. I'll bet he was trying to butter up the Prince and made him an honorary Colonel for a day, you lead the patrol, sir, we're right behind you. I knew he was a wrong 'un."

Buller found me shortly, his forehead and cheeks glowing even in the dark.

"What the hell happened," he said. "They. . ."

"What happened was that arselicker Carey let the Prince be the leader for the day is what happened," I said, "and the boy decided he would stay out late so he wouldn't look like a fraidy-cat."

"A what?"

"Cowardly," I said, "that he must indeed be a parfit, gentil knight, if you want."

"Can you find the place in the dark?"

Now I lost my temper.

"Yes," I said, "and we can go out there with five hundred men and it won't mean spit. He's dead. All going out with the troopers now means is that some of them will get killed by the Zulus or thrown from their horses."

"You insubordinate bastard."

"Yes, sir."

Buller took a deep breath, and I'm damned if he didn't apologize to me.

Nobody slept much that night. Wood sent for me eventually—I think he was vaguely aware that I was in his command.

He was quite courteous, but his soft questions got everything out of me that I knew, including that last glimpse I had of the little troop as it went over the hill and down into the donga, with the Prince in the lead.

Wood got a sad look on his face—he looked like a basset hound that has lost a favorite bone—and he lit a mangy old pipe after giving me a glass of brandy.

"He thought he was at war, but he was only a boy playing at war," said Wood. "Well, perhaps the course of European history changed this afternoon."

"Ain't there more of them?"

He nodded. "A sorry lot," said Wood. "They have no political chance. If you will excuse yourself, Sergeant, I must write my report to Chelmsford. You will be present for the court of inquiry."

I got a couple of hours' sleep and got ready before the others—Buller started shouting orders a good hour after I got up and maybe an hour before the dawn we rode off, a thousand strong. There was a Frog correspondent name of Deleage in camp who begged to go, but right now the English didn't need any further juicy details leaked out. Like what the Zulus do to their dead enemies, for instance, or live ones if they capture them.

We clanked across the veldt, the mist broke, and about nine in the morning we come to the spot where Harford and I had waited for the survivors.

Buller was beside me, Harford right behind.

"I'd suggest you let the two of us go ahead for a hundred yards or so," I said. "And then we can wave you to the sides when it is time to fan out."

Harford and I went on ahead and then we heard the troop start up behind us. We went three miles, actually, with the tracks of Carey and his troopers coming straight at us, and then I saw one set of hoofprints come in from the side, and I got off to walk around and squint at the ground. Harford rode on ahead and then he dismounted. I waved to Buller and he began to send out parties to the side.

Perhaps a half mile on there was a deserted kraal—hadn't been deserted too damn long, there were still live coals in the ashes of the fire and some mealies—they're a kind of corn—that hadn't been picked long. I could see by the tracks what had happened. They had come here, a bit past the kraal, dismounted, and sat down on a couple of convenient logs to do a little sketching. The logs was about ten feet from a huge stand of tambookie grass—eight feet high and bunched at the base, a man can walk through it easy. The warriors had come up, maybe fired a shot, and in the confusion the troops scattered, horses rearing.

I heard a whinny.

I swung up and rode toward the noise—it was the Prince's horse, a gray gelding name of Percy and he was real skittish. The saddle was under his belly. I got down and caught Percy, and fixed the saddle on his back and tied the stirrups together over the seat. The saddlehorn was torn plumb across right to left as you are facing forward on it, so there it was.

The attack came, Percy shied, the Prince got a grip on the horn but the horse was moving too fast for him to swing up. He went a ways like that, and then the saddlehorn tore—it had no iron core like ours do—and the horse was gone and the Prince was alone. I walked along, Harford beside me. We stopped and looked at each other once and then shrugged and went on. Found a silver spur, all twisted out of shape, and then the Prince's terrier pinned to the ground with an assegai, and another spur, and then a blue sock with an embroidered "N" on it.

The Prince was a little farther along, lying on his back, naked. The Zulus hadn't ripped him open. He'd been stabbed once through the left eye into the brain. His left arm was hacked and chopped where he'd warded off blows. I knelt and looked at his right hand. The fingers was clenched and they was clenched around a big clump of Zulu hair. Well, he'd done all right by himself, as unnecessary as it had been.

Harford hallooed and Buller come in and that ass Carey, who threw himself on the ground and wept. The other three troopers had been found; they'd pretty much been torn to bits. A burial detail went off to tend to the common folk. Napoleon was wrapped in the canvas that was used for wagon covers and slung across a horse, and so we went back.

The court of inquiry was held that afternoon. I gave 'em what I knew, which wasn't much, and they couldn't very well put down what I thought.

Harford and I went out again that night. We looked for Zulus high and low and didn't find a trace.

47

The Prince Imperial's carcass was sent back down the line to the thanks of a grateful nation—they was a lot more upset and grieving about poor Napoleon than they were about the fifteen hundred line soldiers who had also fallen to the Zulus. Us line soldiers went on toward Ulundi and the end of the war, and it was a damned sour business.

We were smack in the middle of the rainy season. Strung out on the march our column stretched for seven miles and most of them miles was mud and mud and mud. The teamsters and conductors had the worst of it—it sometimes took forty oxen to drag a wagon up the rutted side of a donga. Everyone was wet all of the time, except maybe me. I had a rain slicker. Those of the troops who had early stages of TB were falling away, coughing their lungs out on the hills of Zululand.

Harford and I were out most nights, but now as vedettes, drifting in the dark and picking off the occasional Zulu scout. They weren't very good at the job—hell, they

was farmers and cattle herders—and the only reason that
Harford and I did it was that staring at each other in the
camp was worse. It was miserable, wet, and seemed
endless. The troops had it better, at least they could have
fistfights, and the sergeants had their hands full keeping
the men in line. The British army didn't exactly recruit its
privates on the playing fields of Eton, mind you, and a lot
of the dockside scum and common drunks was somewhere
in the Empire, in uniform, making it safe and profitable
for decent folk.

Ulundi was barely twenty miles away now—three days'
hard travel for the column. The Zulus didn't even harry
the line much—they didn't know how to clean the Martini-
Henrys, and after fifty rounds or so the pieces were so
fouled it was even money that they would blow up if you
touched off a round, not to mention that the piece kicked
like a Missouri mule when the bore was spotless, and
things went downhill as the powder residues and such
built up.

Mostly, I think, they didn't want to. There would be one
last battle for the honor of the Zulu nation, and thousands
of them would die, and most of what they had known
would pass away, and this gave them a sadness I have seen
too many times in the Indians. The new world was worth-
less, and the godwallopers are bad enough on a good day.
No doubt there were several dozen following the army like
crows follow a plow, ready to pounce as soon as the Zulus
were down and give them a good dose of Jesus.

The next night Buller come to us and asked us if we
would mind awfully taking a wide circle around Ulundi
and taking a look at possible avenues of escape that the
King might take after the battle went against him. We said
hell yes, we mind.

"In that case it is an order," he said, his moustache
twitching up and down happily. I have never known
anyone who actually thrived on bad food, endless rain,

mud, and being in the saddle twenty hours a day except Buller. I hated him.

Harford and I headed well west for the entire night—with the rain the Zulus probably weren't much out in it, but we were damn careful. We had a dark lantern with us, and could study the ground on the trails.

There was old, rain-washed sign, of men and cattle, but they had long gone. We passed a few small kraals, but they seemed deserted.

We laid up the whole day in a donga under a cutbank, eating cold food—a fire would have plumed badly in this wet air—and cleaned ourselves and our horses as best we could. The rain let up and the sun came out and we poached miserably for the afternoon. Nothing moved in the donga except a warthog, which came by looking a lot like a Chicago alderman on voting day, smelled us, snorted and backed down his burrow. He'd stick his head out every once in a while to see if we were still there, and even a snort from a horse would make him back down. It made the time pass, watching him.

The going was much better that night. I was thankful that we weren't on the Powder River—I have been as paralyzed by gumbo as ever I was by snow, and the Powder River is the worst place in all the world when it rains.

The ground here was rock and sand—we had climbed maybe a thousand feet. There was no sign of anything like Zulus. We took a chance and rode at a canter, and made a loop of thirty miles that night, coming to a long scarp that stuck out over the plane. The fires of Ulundi were a glow far off on our right, and from where we were, we could see twenty miles across the plain straight out and about that to the north. We holed up good and cut fodder for the horses and grained them, and I lay down to glass for an hour on the faraway while Harford kept his neck swiveling and his eyeballs on the up close.

Nothing much happened in the morning, except a lone Zulu trotted down the trail far out on to the plain, coming down from the north. He was unarmed, and I assumed he was carrying an urgent message.

"If Chelmsford suddenly had to face the Zulus and the Shangane Nation he might find it sticky," Harford said.

I asked who the hell the Shanganes was.

"About fifty years ago there was a battle royal for the crown of Zululand," said Harford, "and Shaka won and Shoshangane lost. The battle was indecisive, and Shoshangane took his people and his army—it was a considerable number, about forty thousand—and went on up north. There isn't any real possibility of the Shanganes coming, but the thought is amusing."

Harford had a strange sense of humor.

I was doing the up close, rifle at the ready and nostrils twitching, when I heard Harford gasp. He was peering off to the south and the east, and whatever it was I couldn't make out. It was too far away, though I could see some movement. Harford followed whatever it was for a long time—perhaps an hour.

"It's the King," said Harford, handing me the binoculars. "With a dozen retainers and a dozen wives bringing up the rear."

I lay full length on the rocky ledge and watched. Through the glasses I could make out Cetshwayo—he was taller than the others and broader, and he had on some sort of damask cloak, red on gold. I looked closer. It was a tablecloth. A couple of youngsters walked beside him, holding an umbrella. The sun wasn't hot enough yet for the Royal brow to need shade.

"We must get back," Harford hissed, "with this."

"Be a simple matter to sneak down there and ambush him," I says. "I'm good to five hundred yards with my piece."

Harford sighed. "Kelly," he said, "this comes from, no

doubt, your various faults as an American. Her Majesty's forces do not wish to kill Cetshwayo. He is much more valuable alive. We wish to extend the hand of friendship after our little tiff. Now would you please pull your oafish carcass away from that pitiful sight and ride, or I shall do it alone?"

He meant ride, too. We didn't skulk and we didn't hole up. We rode straight as we could, steering perhaps five miles west of Ulundi, and only once did we see any Zulus. There were three of them, mounted on horses, and they gave chase, but not having had much practice they all fell off the first two miles or so. Saddles might have helped.

We come on to the column just at dusk, and it was only perhaps five miles from the royal kraal at Ulundi. There was maybe twelve thousand warriors around the kraal, all of the regiments that had been at all of the battles, and they was all sitting on the ground in companies and ranks. The battle would commence just as soon as the haze lifted in the morning, and the Zulus and the British and the one American knew it.

Harford was admitted at once to Chelmsford's tent, while I held the horses and thought about how far away and long ago it seemed that I had tottered down the gangplank into Durban.

Harford wasn't five minutes with Chelmsford—this was the last battle and he must have had a lot on his mind.

The whole column was laid out now as a huge square, maybe half a mile on a side, and the men were digging trenches and piling up breastworks, leaving channels near the corners for the cavalry to exit through. Each of the four corners had a Gatling gun at it—you ask me the damn doctor that invented it should have struck to lancing boils and otherwise being useful. The gun can fire three hundred rounds a minute in trials but it always jams in battle.

We slept on the ground in the center of the square, with the casuals and grooms and conductors—Boers, who stayed up all night drinking gin and reading from the Bible. I never have found anything funny in the Bible, but they was laughing like hell. It was cold out and I couldn't sleep anyway, so I wandered off and found a conductor who had a small liquor business on the side and bought a bottle of brandy and two huge black cheroots. I went back to Harford and we sat up all night drinking brandy and smoking. The stock inside the square was restless—the wagons was about three miles behind, circled around the oxen—the horses stamped and whickered and men laughed and joked.

We waited for the morning here, and they waited over there.

48

There was a lot of Victoria Crosses awarded for Ulundi—I guess the British public was getting impatient for heroes or something—but as a battle it was pretty damned one-sided. Some of the crosses was awarded for a stupid sally made by Buller and a few troopers early on, when the ground was slick, and four men were killed and a fifth captured alive. He was handed over to the women in the kraal and his screams went on for hours.

His last bellers were apparently the signal, for the entire Zulu army rose at once and began to trot toward us, the horns suddenly racing out to the sides. They was yelling and coming on. The right horn went into a stand of tambookie grass a thousand yards away and the Gatling ripped a sighting burst into them and many warriors went down, knocked ten feet by the force of the bullets. The bullets are an inch in diameter and weigh one-sixth of a pound, so a man hit with that is through.

Chelmsford held his fire until they was four hundred

yards away, and then the sides of the square rippled with flame and smoke and hundred of warriors went down at once. They kept coming, and volleys rang out, and they fell, and they kept coming, and not one ever got within fifty yards of us, except a ten-year-old kid who overshot the troop he was following. A soldier reached over the breastwork, grabbed the little bugger, hauled him in, cuffed him into peacefulness, and sat on him for the rest of the fight.

It wasn't long. The warriors went down like grass before a sudden wind, until suddenly they could take no more.

They retreated, and then they ran, and Chelmsford gave the order and the Lancers poured from the gaps in the corners. The troopers rode down the Zulus. A lance would dip. A Zulu would fall. The lance was pulled free with a sideways flick of the wrist, swept upright, down, and then the trooper would ride down another.

Some Zulus began to raise their shields over their heads and stop, but the troopers speared them anyway.

"That's the Zulu sign of surrender, Kelly," said Harford. "I don't think that anyone has seen that for fifty years." His voice was very soft and more than a little sad.

There wasn't much left of the Zulu army. They lay in heaps out in front, the wind ruffling some of the ostrich feathers they wore; a few gutshot ones were screaming. Here and there a wounded Zulu would struggle to his knees, many rifles would fire, the body would roll away.

The troopers came thundering back.

Flames began to lick at the thornbush zareba around the kraal, the fired thatch of the huts began to smoke.

The Zulu war was over.

49

It only remained to capture the King. Chelmsford had been replaced, apparently, and had a couple of days more gone by before the Zulus gave battle, Chelmsford would have been retired in disgrace and never would have lived Isandhlwana down. He left.

Harford and me were ordered to find out where Cetshwayo was hiding. We knew only that he had been headed to the north, and that he had very few retainers.

The Zulus were completely broken. The few survivors had gone home, and most had taken their womenfolk and cattle to the high Drakensberg Range, to little mountain valleys. Since the Zulus made only total war, killing all men over twelve and taking the women and cattle, they expected the same.

Buller wanted Harford and me to take a troop with us, which we protested against. We was both sure that the King was in hiding because he was certain that he would be killed, and that once we impressed upon him the fact that the English would at most place him under house arrest for a while, he would come in. For one thing, all of the satellite tribes that had lived in terror of the Zulus would be pretty bold now and many of them had ample reasons for wanting to kill Cetshwayo "in any number of interesting ways," Harford added. Buller jerked on his moustache for a while and then nodded. "If he's got too many men you can get help—there will be fifty parties combing the area," he said. "Just find him, that will do."

Harford and me rode due north, skirting the burned kraal of Ulundi. The blackened ring was about three miles across. When some excited junior officers entered into the Royal hut and probed the floor of the hut with assegai blades, looking for hidden treasure, they had hit a metal strongbox buried about six inches deep. They dug it up, all in a lather, and opened it to find some three dozen boot-blacking brushes, mostly the worse for wear.

Harford had questioned captured Zulus as to the King's whereabouts, and they loyally refused to tell him anything, even when we tried the old trick of taking one of them over the hill and firing a rifle over the bound and gagged native. We returned scowling and looking as fierce as we could. One of the women giggled and I couldn't help smiling.

Then Harford had tried a different tack. Zulu family relationships are unbelievably complicated—they have forty words for cousins, and because they are polygamous, things get more than a little confused. But by piecing together Cetshwayo's tangled relations Harford was able to find out that Cetshwayo had a fifteenth underassistant left-handed shirttail relation who lived high up in the Drakensberg, in a small canyon that had a narrow mouth and then opened up into a wide meadow, a place easy to defend and easy to keep the cattle in. The directions were pretty specific, so we rode toward it, planning to stop and move by night when we got close.

The weather had come off better—the rains had ceased being a constant drizzle, and we just got an hour or so in the late afternoon.

Africa was a beautiful country—a lateral one, the trees seemed to be constructed of piled lines of branches that ran with the yellow and red and ochre of the land. We saw a few lions asleep in the shade of a grove of acacias, and once a rhino, with a little white bird sitting on top of him.

Harford found lots of beetles. I found the critters interesting when they wasn't collected in the middle of a pitched battle against fearful odds, me being the fearful and they being the odds. Harford finally told me that the damn beetle wasn't particularly rare that he'd been crowing over while the Zulus was trying to kill us, but the opportunity for a joke was too good to pass up. I resolved that Harford was gonna get one real good before our association ended.

When we came nigh on to the place that Harford's best guess was that the King was hiding in, we switched over to night work and began to work our way up the ridges. It was so simple to find. We crept to the edge of a steep hill in the early dawn and looked on down and saw a little valley maybe a mile by three, with a small kraal—a four-hut one—near a little stream. The herdboys was moving about a hundred head of cattle out to pasture, the women were making breakfast, a smoke haze rose from the cookfire. Not much of a place for a King, but then he hadn't much of a kingdom left.

Nothing to do but wait. If he was there he'd have to come out to piss, and when he did we'd know, and that would be that. The mist burned off. A huge eagle flapped through the valley and then floated up on the breeze blowing up the hills.

Mid-morning I saw a woman take a calabash and a wooden plate of food into a hut and then she came back out. I kept watch while Harford slept—he'd never seen

Cetshwayo, as I had. Nothing happened for another hour. Then a man emerged from the hut the woman had taken the food to and stood up. It was Dabulamanzi. Cetshwayo was right behind him. Cetshwayo stood up with Dabulamanzi's help and he hobbled painfully off, holding his feet wide, like a man who's been kicked in the balls hard.

Cetshwayo took fifteen minutes to get to where he could take a leak. He flung the damask cloth off and pissed for a long time—it hurt him so much to move that he must have been clenching his teeth against the pain in his bladder until he couldn't stand that anymore. He slumped down on an old log when he was through and put his head in his hands, and Dabulamanzi sat beside him with his hand on Cetshwayo's shoulder.

I nudged Harford awake and pointed and gave him the glasses. I whispered that the King was hurt. There was no sign of the guards. An old man came out of another hut and walked down toward a little stream and splashed water on himself.

"I think we can just slither down there and catch him," I says. "I don't think he has any guards. Except Dabulamanzi. We tell 'em that the King won't be harmed nor anyone else—and some of those troops looking for him will harm him damn well, especially the Boers—they have sixty years of hate."

"Dark would be better," says Harford.

"They can't see who is with us in the dark," I said, "so we'll end up shooting Dabulamanzi for sure."

"I doubt you could hit him," says a familiar voice behind me. "You leave a trail like an ox dragging a log."

Marieke, of course, with her chum of a Bushman, still grinning.

Harford and me contested as to who could look dumber.

"What..." I managed to croak out, "in the hell..."

Marieke laughed, low and soft, stuck her tongue out at me, and then laid down her gun and stuck her hands by her ears and waggled her fingers at me. Bushman grinned and contributed farting noises.

I ain't never been that dumbfounded.

". . . are you doing here?" I finally stammered, lame as a one-footed mule.

Marieke bounced down and capered around us and she was laughing so hard that she had tears flowing down her cheeks.

"Great scout," she says, "I have followed you ever since you left. You two oafs. I didn't want to hurt your pride. I have often been ten feet from you."

"They do say the Bushmen are better than any," Harford offered.

"Go eat some bugs," I snarls at him.

"I thought of slipping down in the night and cutting Cetshwayo's throat," says Marieke, "but I didn't. Aren't I good?"

Harford was making the choking noises upper-class Englishmen emit to signal that they are having an attack of mirth.

"You could have been killed!" I says. I was scared for her.

"No," says Marieke. "You would have been, but my Bushman and I killed them first. Perhaps you don't know what you are doing here so well."

"I say," said Harford, "we still have to see about Cetshwayo."

"We go down on foot," I says.

"Want me to lead you?" says Marieke. "I wouldn't want you to fall and hurt yourself."

"You'll have to stay up here," says Harford, looking at Marieke. "Cetshwayo would rather die than surrender to a party which included a woman."

"I'll stay," says Marieke. "The three of you can keep your little secret."

"I still think that we should ride," says Harford.

"Not on your damn life," says I.

"Call if you need help," says Marieke.

"I still think we should ride," says Harford.

"No," I says. "Let's go."

Harford gave way, and we tied our horses good and slipped down the mountain, keeping to the brush and stopping to look every once in a while. Cetshwayo waddled back to his hut and went inside, and Dabulamanzi sat crosslegged in the shade by the door.

We slipped into the kraal through a gate in the back and the first inkling that Dabulamanzi had that something was wrong was when I hissed at him from about five feet away, with my rifle pointed at his head.

Harford babbled a steady stream of Zulu at him and Dabulamanzi answered with a number of angry questions, and finally they quieted down. Dabulamanzi stood up, looking at me thoughtfully for a long time. I gave him a seegar. He went over to the fire and got a glowing brand and brought it back and we smoked out in the sun. Harford crawled through the low door of the hut and commenced to speak to Cetshwayo. I could hear his deep bass rumbling, and Harford's baritone reply.

Harford come out in about fifteen minutes.

"The King can't walk," he said. "He's so fat the insides of his thighs are rubbed raw from his flight. We'll have to find a cart."

Carts being a scarce commodity in this end of Africa, I wondered how we were going to do that.

"Why don't you go up and get the horses and we'll see," said Harford. "We have some salve in the packs, don't we?"

I climbed back up. Marieke and the Bushman were sitting on a rock, grinning. I got our horses and brought them back down and Harford and Dabulamanzi and Cetshwayo were by this time out in front of the hut. Cetshwayo was sitting on a big carved stool, his raw legs spread and his hands on his knees. He looked at me when I come up, and rumbled a question at Harford.

"He asked why should he trust a man who had his messengers hung," said Harford.

"They was hung by a troop of scouts who had no business doing it, and when I wasn't there," I says. "Tell him the man responsible was hung, too." It was a lie, but under the circumstances I thought it was a good idea.

The cart was a real problem. I finally said to Harford that we ought to rig a travois and at least get the King down to the plain. There was likely to be several hundred men down there and we could figure out something then.

I cut some poles and we took some cowhides from the hut and rigged a sling that would hold Cetshwayo and after a considerable amount of argument got him to try it, after Harford spoke to him sharp and told him it was either that or walk. Dabulamanzi watched us go. He wasn't wanted for anything and it was safer here for him than it was most places.

I led my horse with Cetshwayo behind. The trail was good, mostly sand, and the one rocky place we come to jounced him around a little, but he was used to it by then.

Harford spelled me every hour, leading my horse while I rode, and about five in the afternoon we come out on to the rolling hills below the Drakensberg and seen a troop of men on the horizon. I waved to them and they begun to ride over.

They was Imperial troops, led by a captain name of Knox Leet. I mean both those words was his last name.

Harford told him about the capture of the King and how bad off the King was in the way of walking and that the King sure as hell couldn't straddle a horse, not that he would anyway, never having done it. So they hung a litter between two horses and lifted the King onto that. Off they went bearing their prize—and be damned to them, I said.

"Cheer up, Kelly," said Harford. "They are true sons of

Empire. They are good and honest men. They won't claim that they talked Cetshwayo into surrendering, modesty will forbid it. They won't mention us. Gentlemen respect the modesty of others. Christ, I'm tired of the whole mess."

Marieke popped out of the bushes as soon as the last of the troopers cleared the far rise.

"I'll be on my way," says Harford, sweeping off his hat. "And my compliments to the young lady." He rode off west.

"Where's your nigger sidekick?" I snarls. "Never mind. I can *hear* him grinning back in the bushes."

Marieke had learned real quick that the best way to aggravate me was just to smile sweetly. She'd save her breath for appropriate moments when a real cutting insult would best bring on a fit of the apoplexy in me, an affliction which my family always had. Piss us off enough we just drop dead. I figured I'd be lucky to see thirty, which was a bit over a year away.

"When we get married," she says, "I want to go to America."

"If we get married," I says. "I'll think about it."

"I'll tell my brothers that you have fornicated me."

This did give me pause. With any luck, all her damn brothers was dead—her father had died at Hlobane.

"And if they can't manage your death, I'll tell my cousins."

"How many cousins you got?" I says.

"Enough," says she.

"How many is enough?"

"One lame rabbit farmer," says she.

Our conversations were always more or less like that. In her young heart she was as much a black Irish as I, even though she was Dutch.

We made our way south, keeping to the trails and avoiding the roads. When we passed by Ulundi the wind brought a horrible stink from the corpses. The sky was full of kites and a funny stork-like bird that acted like a vulture. It had two long feathers sticking out of the sides of its head straight back.

"Secretary bird," says Marieke. The damn thing did sort of look like a clerk in a stingy banking house.

One night when we lay looking up at the stars, I asked her if she wouldn't be sad to leave Africa. She said no. I couldn't understand it. All of the time that I had been here, the way the land lay and the things that grew on it and the animals that walked on it had seemed so strange to me. I didn't fit and there wasn't any way I ever would.

By and by we come to the Uys home farm. Marieke rode on down. It was evening, and she hadn't been inside but a few minutes when a fearful bellering and caterwauling erupted. Her two brothers and her mother and Marieke come spilling out onto the porch and then into the dusty yard, all hollering at once. Marieke cracked one brother so hard in the knee with the butt of a pistol I had given her that he sort of fell out of the discussion and leaned on this and that around the porch, clutching his kneecap and whistling through his nose. The three who could walk went back inside and there commenced the sounds of a lot of breaking crockery.

I waited a decent interval until the noise reached a good, steady roar, and rode hell for leather toward Durban. Well, that's the sort of bird that I am.

50

The clerk at the hotel smiled pleasantly at me and told me that there were no rooms available. I told him that I would take an unavailable one then and to please get the manager. The manager came and found one for me—a cramped little thing in the attic—and I sent the bellhop out with some money to get me some new duds.

I had my first good meal in weeks, and I sauntered around for a while after dark. The shops was all decked out in bunting and there was Union Jacks fluttering from every porch and the sounds of gay parties came spilling out into the streets. They was celebrating the great victory of Ulundi, of course.

The next day I spent getting drunk with Harford.

I asked him what the King had said in the hut.

"He asked me to shoot him," Harford said, "since he thought the English would decapitate him—it is the custom to do that to deposed Zulu rulers, and he could see no reason that the English would not treat him so. Then he wanted to know the fate of Dabulamanzi, and then he wanted to know why the war began in the first place."

"Could you tell him?"

"I told him it was no different from the rise of the Zulus—as a nation they are only about fifty years old. They were founded by a man named Shaka, who I gather was as ferocious a creature as ever walked the earth. He was the one who invented the regiments and the Zulu method of attack. He was something of a horror—once developed a mild interest in embryology and cut open three hundred pregnant women by way of research. Alive, that is."

We swapped war stories for a while, and this and that, but the truth of the matter was that we really didn't like each other much and we made an early evening of it.

Cetshwayo was brought in three days later, riding in a mule cart, with a new damask tablecloth around his shoulders. He stood for a moment as he passed the cheering crowds and looked puzzled.

They was cheering him, too. I'll never understand the damn English. They put him on board a steamer and the boat sailed away. I was down at the dock with the rest of the gapers.

Gussie had spoke well of Australia, sort of. I thought that I might see that next, on my way home.

51

I booked passage to Perth on the P & O Line—still had some ten thousand in gold plus my pay, which was laughable, but on the other hand they didn't hang me for desertion. The gold strikes there was long past, which I liked, gold camps being somewhat worse in the matter of general health than pitched battles, and I figured that I would want to get my land legs halfway home. This was half-witted of me, but that is for another time. Ned Kelly, and all of that. . . .

My passage out was tomorrow, so I had one more night in Durban. Gussie was long gone and I wished I was, too. I skulked a lot, but Marieke never showed. I had just washed up and was going out for a stroll—the rain was coming down in sheets, but I was itchy, like I get in rooms.

I stopped to leave my key at the desk—the ten thousand in gold was in the safe and my bags were already on board the *Fancher*. I wandered down toward the docks, and then away. There were long lines of sweating coolies coaling the ship up, and all manner of ruckus going on. This time there wouldn't be a damn floating stockyard under me, and, of course, this time I could be a little more particular about how I got where I was going. Had a nice new passport, too, courtesy of Her Majesty, mine having been nobly lost at Isandhlwana. I had asked Chelmsford for a recommendation of character. He bit his seegar in half and choked for a while, but he did it. Decent fellow. They'd never send him out to war again, but I don't think it bothered him.

I was restless, and not all that much taken with Africa. It was not like home, if I had one or would recognize it if I should see it. I had seen another piece of history, and it was very much like others that I had known. Sad.

Someone tugged at my sleeve, and I looked down to my left and there was a small nigger smiling up at me while hauling on my cuff like he was trying to see whether or not my eyes would shut and open to his tugs.

"Baas wan you," he said, gesturing toward a carriage a little behind us.

"Baas who?" I says, and wished I had a pistol. The British are very strict about going fixed on board ship, so my guns were in my trunks.

"Ha, Adendorff, hey there," said John Dunn, leaning half out of the door. "A word with you, sir, a word."

"A word about what?" I says, suspicious-like, since I hadn't laid eyes on him for months and here he was following me in the street. There was more than just a word being wanted here.

"Get in, man, get in," said Dunn, throwing the door open. The coachman pulled the horses up and looked straight ahead—being paid not to see anything, no doubt.

I backed away two paces.

"Whatever it is you want ain't for you, Dunn," I says. "Now spit it out and maybe I'll join you. Maybe not."

"Oh, nothing foul, Adendorff, nothing foul. Word of honor"—he actually made it have three syllables.

Dunn leaned out and looked up and down the street. "Miss Colenso wanted you to come."

"Well, I'll just wander on over to their log pile and knock on the door then," says I, "since it is on the way back to my hotel. I'll go there now."

"No!" Dunn hissed. "She's not there. For god's sake, man, please come. No harm was meant or is." He had been drinking a lot of brandy and the gusts from his talking hit me like bay rum from a barbershop door.

I shrugged and got in. There couldn't be anybody in Zululand who could possibly want to do me any violence, and I was fresh out of secret maps to lost mines or where the damn elephants go to lay their tusks on the pile that's just waiting for some lucky fool out there somewhere in ten million square miles of jungle.

Dunn whistled up the carriage as soon as I was in and we went through the last of town and out a bit into the country, and then turned off at a kraal next to a building that they store blasting powder in, away from everything except the poor niggers, who wouldn't be missed.

Dunn led me to a hut and motioned me inside. A stench hit me the moment that I went in, and I knew that there was someone in there who had a bad wound, one that had gone gangrenous; it smelled like syrup on rotten fish. Dunn scrambled through behind me and I blinked for a moment. There was one small oil lamp, and I could see the tiny, tight face of Harriet Colenso in the feeble light. She was putting a cloth on someone's head.

She whispered something to the form on the pallet. A low bass growl answered. Dabulamanzi. I'd know that voice anywhere.

Harriet slid past me and went on out into the evening. Dabulamanzi motioned me closer. His face was sunk, and his black eyes glittered feverishly in their yellow whites. The stink was coming from him.

Dunn come up, too. Dabulamanzi rumbled at him in Zulu.

"He says to ask you if you liked this war," said Dunn.

"No, not a lot," I says, still wondering why I was here.

"Good," says Dabulamanzi. "We had a shaman who said that the ruin of Zululand would begin with a single missionary. Unfortunately, he was an epileptic and a cattle thief and not a Zulu, so we didn't listen. But that does not matter now. My brother is in chains and I am soon dead and Zululand can ask for the return of our bones."

"They ain't going to kill Cetshwayo."

"True, but with him gone another King cannot be elected until the return of his bones, so for the People of the Sky—Zulus—it would have been better had he died in Zululand."

He began to shudder, from pain, I thought, but caught himself.

"I remember that you shot at me from far off, and I thought it a gift, that you would be so afraid of me that you would not wait until I got closer," said Dabulamanzi, "and so I have brought you a gift, too. I will give it to you when you go."

I waited. Dabulamanzi blinked up into the darkness, though whether that in the hut or one of his own I couldn't tell.

"Now the Boers will pour in and they will take our pastures and our cattle and we shall be their slaves. Here, look at this." He threw back the light blanket over his leg. It had been cut off, but not soon enough. Black gangrene, and it was in his blood, and if he hadn't been the color of obsidian I'd have seen the poison in his skin.

"One of your Martini-Henrys," said Dabulamanzi. "I was never wounded in any battles. A son of mine dropped one when it was loaded and you see what it left. The missionary woman wants to write a true history of the war."

"Meaning she sets down everybody's lies and lets the reader take choice," I says. Dabulamanzi laughed. He was still a long ways from dead.

"Dunn tells me that you went through our land and we never knew it, and that you were at Hlobane and Ulundi. You know, some of your shots came pretty close. So you remember what happened here. That is all. And as for your gift, it is here."

He motioned to a large calabash. I picked it up and hefted it. Not too heavy.

"Now go."

Outside, by the carriage, I took the top of the gourd off. It was Dik Uys's head. His face had been painted with cedar oil, but I could still make out the features.

"Curious," says Dunn. He'd seen so much that I suppose that amounted to a scream of horror.

I put the lid back on.

"When we get to a good spot let's toss this in the bushes," I says. "I need a drink."

"I have a bottle in the carriage," says Dunn.

"Good," I says, pitching the gourd into a tangle of thorns.

I was sure lookin' forward to Australia. Cheerful place, so I'd heard. This part of Africa was not going to do well.

The next day I watched Africa slide away until it was gone. I thought of Marieke for a long time. It hurt some, but she'd be all right, and so would I.

A sailor on lookout was playing a harmonica. I didn't know the tune, but it was a sad one, and therefore Irish. When the sun sank into the sea, the reedy music stopped, and after a while, even the gulls quit squalling.

Epilogue

Ollie's place wasn't too peaceful to practice the writing trade in, so I come up here to a little place I have on Lake George and spent the summer and fall and winter and spring and the summer again scribbling away.

This is how I remember it, anyway, but I'm fifty and those two years was over twenty years ago. When I go down to the drugstore for a seegar and shaving soap, I forget one thing or the other and have to go back, or maybe I just want to walk.

I cut this book off as I was leaving Durban—I could have gone on, as I really did, to China and Australia and Europe and Arabia and Alaska and South America. But about midway through the damn thing I went down to the bookstore and bought a book—not too fat and not too skinny—and I counted the pages about what I figure I've got. So I quit here. I'm tired of it. I got calluses on the first two fingers of my right hand.

The Indians is all dead now, or in jail, even if the jail is a big patch of ground, and they've been there a long time.

The Zulu and the Shanganes are fighting either each other or once in a while the British, but they are small tribes. As wars, they don't amount to much. Hell, they're barely good riots.

The Boers are kicking hell out of the Brits now.

Well, good luck to them all. This new century stinks of blood. I got a nose, and I don't like the wind.

Some one of them Boston ladies what wears blue stockings and commonsensical shoes run me down about July—she's one of them women throws herself in front of horses to get the vote. Well, fine, says I to her, why don't you take the damn vote for a while and us men will just look on. You couldn't possibly do worse than we have. She blinked. Then she got real frosty and said I shouldn't take such an important subject so lightly. I told her I was serious.

"Mr. Kelly," she says, deciding that changing the subject was her best bet—which it was—she meant well and warn't too bright, you know the kind, got one idea and looking for throats to jam it down—"you were involved in the brutal and unjust destruction of the American Indian. Why did you do it? Did you forget the words of our Lord and Savior?"

"While I was single-handedly slaughtering all them damn Indians—and I killed them all, Mrs. Pettigrew," I says, "the Army just carried the bodies away and held my coat—I never once forgot this—that it was wrong. The kind of wrong happens when one big bunch of mean folks needs land for farms and homes. So they kill the weaker fools that was already there. And at least all the Indians I killed died clean and quick, and didn't perish of misery and boredom listening to the kind of pinch-faced god-wallopers descended on them later. I was a killer, but I warn't cruel."

Mrs. Pettigrew got a look says there is this bad smell in the room. She had been escorted to my digs by a godwalloper looked like he lived on snails and twigs. He began to make little choking sounds. This encouraged me greatly. Maybe he'd die of the conniptions right there on my porch.

A bird hopped up on the feeder I keep filled with seeds out near the little stone birdbath I brung back from China.

"That bird out there is a starling, Mrs. Pettigrew," I says. "Now that starling was brought here by some ass who wanted all of the birds mentioned in Shakespeare to be found in America. Them starlings is doing pretty well. But you never see a bluebird around here any more."

"I don't understand what you mean," she says.

"I mean that if we hadn't broken the tribes, we'd be in deep trouble. See, our country would right now be a worse place if we hadn't rushed to fill it up. If we hadn't got the Russians out of North America, we'd have to fight them. So we had to take the land and fill it up with farmers. They don't move around much. Actually, they ain't no fun at all, but there you have it."

"I still don't understand."

"Can't have two roosters on one perch, Mrs. Pettigrew. Two nations on the same patch. I had a teacher when I was to school, a lady name of Soames, who taught me Greek and Latin and history. She used to say that nations have interests, period, and those interests will lead them to cruel places. She had lost her husband at Shiloh. We didn't fight the Civil War to free the slaves, we fought the Civil War to keep the British and the Russians and the French out of our spot. I was just along for the fun."

"You enjoyed killing Indians?"

"No, ma'am," I said, "I didn't. That's why I was so good at it."

"Our noble Civil War?"

"Was a bloody incompetent business fought by amateurs. War always is. And I can't explain it to some fool like you who thinks them stupid paintings of glorious charges or last stands is a right way of seeing it. It isn't."

"You shock me, Mr. Kelly."

"Go to hell, ma'am. Take your damn bookend with you."

The godwalloper arose to give me a good lecture on proper manners and I arose to see if maybe I could knock his pointed little head into the middle of Lake George. Well, I am a killer, damn it, and he saw whatever it was that my eyes said and he run like a striped-ass ape off toward their carriage.

"Noble feller," I snorts. "I hope he didn't leave his smelling salts."

"You, sir, are a beast," said Mrs. Pettigrew.

"Couldn't agree with you more, Mrs. Pettigrew. Why don't you go talk to Pawnee Bill Lillie? He's Temperance and Born-Again Christian and he never fought an Indian in his life but he'll tell you that he did and how bad he feels about it now. He's been suffering for years for things he didn't do. I'm sure you've heard him speak, and been greatly moved."

Mrs. Pettigrew was flouncing down the steps. I recognized the flounce. Time she got down to the train station, she'd be cussing herself (in modulated tones) for not having said a lot of things back, but right now she couldn't think straight. Well, she meant well, damn her.

But she had bothered me, though I hated to admit it. I thought of Joseph and White Bird and Yellow Wolf and the Nez Perces. They should have been left alone. They was farmers and horsebreeders and good people. But that don't seem to matter much. I have seen whole tribes destroyed by whiskey and common measles. I chased them down, and I didn't like it much. It wasn't like I was there to save anything or make anything better. Hell, I liked the excitement and I liked the country, and I got to be a scout because I knew more about it than anyone else available. When I began, I was eighteen, same age as most of the boys in the Gettysburg Cemetery, if you go and look.

I pleaded with Red Hand and I pleaded with a lot of others to demand U.S. citizenship and just go to court like every other American. They wouldn't listen, and I can't blame them. When your introduction to the white man is goldminers and trappers, it don't give you real confidence in what's coming along behind. The Indians' life was dead but not stiff yet the moment Columbus stepped off the boat. Same thing happened to the Zulus. And the bluebirds.

I began humming a song, one I heard a lot in Africa and later in Australia. It says all that there is to say about any of it in one little verse.

> *Whatever happens we have got*
> *The Maxim gun and they have not.*

Then I decided to go and get me a *real good* attack of gout.

The next day, the mailman came with another letter from Miles. It said, "Africa soonest."

Again? Damn him.

TERRY C. JOHNSTON

Winner of the prestigious Western Writer's award, Terry C. Johnston brings you his award-winning saga of mountain men Josiah Paddock and Titus Bass who strive together to meet the challenges of the western wilderness in the 1830's.

☐ 25572 **CARRY THE WIND**–Vol. I $4.95

☐ 26224 **BORDERLORDS**–Vol. II $4.95

☐ 28139 **ONE-EYED DREAM**–Vol. III $4.95

The final volume in the trilogy begun with *Carry the Wind* and *Borderlords*, ONE-EYED DREAM is a rich, textured tale of an 1830's trapper and his protegé, told at the height of the American fur trade.

Following a harrowing pursuit by vengeful Arapaho warriors, mountain man Titus "Scratch" Bass and his apprentice Josiah Paddock must travel south to old Taos. But their journey is cut short when they learn they must return to St. Louis…and old enemies.

Look for these books wherever Bantam books are sold, or use this handy coupon for ordering: